Nearra nodded, not ⟨…⟩ the pages. "I think this may have been written by a wizard Anselm knew. There's talk of the author being asked to make a map showing where to find the cursed wizards—our map!" She shook her head and closed her eyes. "I'm going to have to read this further later. I'm sure it'll help us find the mine."

"Sounds like a fascinating text," a voice whispered from the shadows. "Does it talk about the part of the tale where you *stole my beauty*?"

THE NEW ADVENTURES

TRINISTYR TRILOGY

Volume One

WIZARD'S CURSE

BY CHRISTINA WOODS

Volume Two

WIZARD'S BETRAYAL

BY JEFF SAMPSON

Volume Three

WIZARD'S RETURN

BY DAN WILLIS

(May 2006)

THE NEW ADVENTURES

TRINISTYR TRILOGY
VOLUME TWO

WIZARD'S BETRAYAL

JEFF SAMPSON

COVER & INTERIOR ART
Vinod Rams

MIRROR STONE

Trinistyr Trilogy

WIZARD'S BETRAYAL

©2006 Wizards of the Coast, Inc.

Cover art by Vinod Rams
Cartography by Dennis Kauth
First Printing: January 2006
Library of Congress Catalog Card Number: 2005928112

9 8 7 6 5 4 3 2 1

ISBN-10: 0-7869-3993-1
ISBN-13: 978-0-7869-3993-0
620-95475740-001-EN

U.S., CANADA,
ASIA, PACIFIC, & LATIN AMERICA
Wizards of the Coast, Inc.
P.O. Box 707
Renton, WA 98057-0707
+1-800-324-6496

EUROPEAN HEADQUARTERS
Hasbro UK Ltd
Caswell Way
Newport, Gwent NP9 0YH
GREAT BRITAIN
Save this address for your records.

Visit our web site at www.mirrorstonebooks.com

FOR DONNIE AND MARIETTE,
FOR THE THREATS OF NO CAKE.

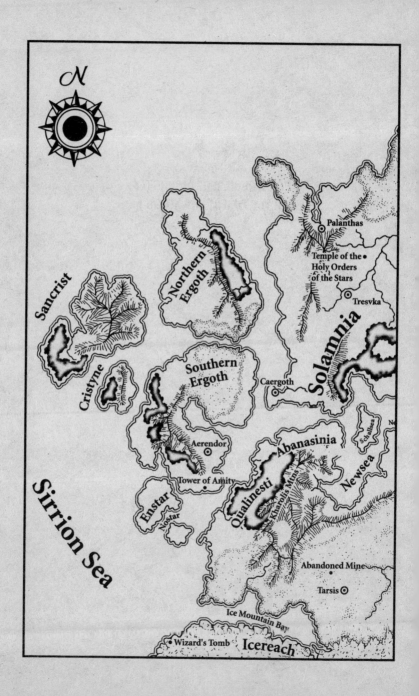

TABLE OF CONTENTS

PROLOGUE. 1

1. REFLECTIONS 12

2. KENDER TRICKS 23

3. STOLEN BEAUTY 35

4. CLERIC'S VENGEANCE 48

5. CORNERED AND CAPTURED 58

6. CLIPPED WINGS 72

7. BEASTS 84

8. MINE 96

9. DEPRIVATION 105

10. A DEADLY BARGAIN 114

11. TOUCH 124

12. THE FINAL PATH. 134

13. MADNESS 143

14. QUICKENED 153

15. A FAREWELL AT DAWN. 164

16. DUST TO DUST. 174

17. UNSPOKEN TRUTHS 183

18. THE UNDERTOWER 193

19. DESCENT. 204

20. MIRKEN 214

21. A NEW POWER 224

22. CURSED. 233

PROLOGUE

356 YEARS AGO . . .

The Istarian soldier lay on the icy cavern floor. Blood streamed from a gaping wound, flooding down his side before mixing with icy slush that had melted from the heat of his body. Water and blood flowed together as a crimson river.

The woman, a cleric and betrayer, stood above the soldier's corpse. She held her hands high as she received the rush of dark power sent down by her god. An evil smile creased her features.

Anselm watched her from where he sat against a pedestal of rock and ice that jutted from the cavern's floor. His body was numb, more from all he had seen and endured than from the cold. He watched as the blood drained from the soldier's face, the dead man's features twisted into a silent scream.

"This is the last one," the woman spat as she stepped over the lifeless body and strolled toward Anselm. Though she appeared forty or fifty years old, she wore the white robes of a cleric of Paladine tight against her body in a vain effort to seem half her age. She tossed her hair—the color of yellow flame—over her shoulder. "Did you hear me?" she demanded. "Do not sit there and stare, Anselm. I know you are not that broken."

Anselm tilted his head back and met the woman's hate-filled gaze. "I heard you, Kirilin," he whispered. Cold air rushed to fill his lungs, freezing him to his core. Trembling, he lifted his hand and gestured toward the cavern's entrance. "He is almost here."

Kirilin smiled and turned away. "Good. You know what you have to do. Comply this time and your children will live. Try and stop me and my god, and they will die." She glanced at Anselm over her shoulder. "Just like your wife."

Anselm couldn't help but shudder and close his eyes. But closing his eyes only brought back memories of his torture, of heated bars branding his flesh and sharp knives drawing blood, of potions injected into his body, and dark spells inflicting him with plague.

It brought back memories of the moment Kirilin broke him, once and for all: hearing his wife's screams as she was murdered as he watched, helpless to do anything to stop her agony.

It had been a long, terrible journey to that point. The god-granted vision he and his cleric wife had been shown had at first seemed like a miracle, divine intervention to keep a great catastrophe from befalling Krynn.

The Kingpriest of Istar, they had been told in the vision, was plagued with madness. His actions while consumed by this madness would bring a great fiery mountain from the sky that would kill many and usher in an age of godlessness and despair.

But they and three other wizards could stop it. Deep in the icy caverns of the frozen lands to the south was a sacred pedestal. Upon this pedestal was an artifact that would heal the Kingpriest of his madness and keep Krynn from its ruin.

The artifact they were shown was a small platinum statue in the shape of a regal dragon with sky blue eyes. The gods Paladine and Mishakal had forged it themselves.

It was called the Trinistyr.

Anselm looked up at the pedestal high above him. Stoic, the Trinistyr sat where it had for centuries. Daylight streamed in from the cavern's entrance and glinted from the Trinistyr's flawless surface, sending silver light shimmering along the waves of ice on the ceiling high above.

The Trinistyr was to have been Anselm's weapon against the forces that would lead Krynn to ruin. But that was before Kirilin had posed as a fellow cleric of Paladine alongside Anselm's wife and captured them, before he had been forced to inflict an eternity of pain and suffering on his companions.

Now, only he and one other wizard remained.

"Anselm!" The voice echoed through the cavern, along with thudding footsteps and a screech of boot on ice as someone nearly slipped on the slick path.

Kirilin crouched in front of Anselm. "Do not fail me," she hissed. "Do not try to stop me. Even if I somehow fall, your children will die. I have seen to it. Understand?"

The wizard nodded. Smirking, Kirilin stood and retreated to the shadows. As she passed, the air above the body of the Istarian soldier shimmered. His figure melted into the frozen ground and disappeared.

"Anselm!" A man burst into the cavern, darting between frozen stalagmites and stalactites that had formed together into towering white pillars. Overgrown brown hair was plastered in serpentine forms across his sweaty forehead, and he wore a cloak of furs over his dingy white robes. In his arms he carried something long, skinny, and wrapped in brown fabric.

"Are you here?" the wizard called, his dark eyes frantically scanning the cavern. "I was chased through the snow, but I have lost my pursuers. I have the staff!"

Trembling, Anselm parted his chapped lips. "Rudd," he wheezed. "Rudd, I am here."

The wizard's eyes widened at the sight of Anselm lying against the ice pedestal, body broken and bruised. Immediately he ran to Anselm's side and dropped to his knees.

"Are you all right?" Rudd gripped Anselm's shoulder. "What happened? Where is your wife? Where are Flomana and Tudyk? The Day of Gratitude is tomorrow!"

Anselm shook his head, sending unwashed white-blond hair tumbling over his shoulders. "They are . . . on their way. We were besieged, as you were. I led our attackers away, but we are safe now." He glanced at the long package clutched in Rudd's hands. "You have the staff?"

Nodding eagerly, Rudd tore at the string tied around the package. Brown cloth fell to the ground in a pile. Now that it was freed from its covering, Anselm saw the staff for the first time.

It was long, two arms' lengths high, and meticulously carved from the wood of an ancient vallenwood tree. Etched on its upper half were images of flames that flared into the shape of a dragon claw as they reached the top of the staff. The wooden claw gripped a sparkling crystal orb.

The staff was dormant, as were the other weapons they were to have recovered. But now that the staff was close to the Trinistyr, Anselm could sense it begin to pulse with power—power that would have protected him, as the other weapons would have, while they made their final strike to heal the Kingpriest.

"Help me stand," Anselm said, his voice raw. Rudd nodded and gripped the older wizard's arm to haul him to his feet. Damp from his sweat, Anselm's robes clung to the icy pillar behind him.

Reaching out a withering hand, Anselm caressed the carvings on the staff. Jolts of energy leaped between his fingertips and the arcing carvings of flame. Pale blue and orange light flickered deep within the orb.

"Magnificent," he whispered. "Truly magnificent."

"I would hope so," Rudd said, "for all the trials I endured to rescue it. But we have it now, and the other weapons. We can follow Paladine's vision."

Sensing his body shake with emotion, Anselm lowered his arm. The hem of his long sleeve fell to hide his trembling hand. "Yes," he said.

He cast a sidelong glance into the shadows. Kirilin stood there, shrouded in darkness almost as black as her soul. Her eyes watched with intense passion as the scene played out before her, and a lurch of revulsion roiled through Anselm's body.

Clenching his eyes closed, Anselm reached his hand out again and gripped Rudd's shoulder. "I am sorry, my friend. Truly I am. But my family must be saved."

"Anselm?" Rudd's brow furrowed as he gave Anselm a questioning look.

Speaking words of crackling power, Anselm lifted his free hand and gestured toward Rudd. With a flick of his wrist, the young wizard was lifted from the ground and flew backward. He crashed into one of the ice pillars with a loud snap. A crack snaked up along the pillar's milky white surface as Rudd slid to the ground.

"What are you doing!" Rudd roared, his confusion giving way to surprised anger. His staff still clenched in his hands, he stumbled to his feet and tried to leap toward Anselm.

Again Anselm motioned with his hands. Ice crystallized around Rudd's boots, frozen shackles binding him between the towering pillars.

Rage contorted Rudd's features as his cheeks and neck flushed red. "What have you done to Flomana and Tudyk?" he shouted. "To your *wife*?"

Anselm parted his lips to speak, to try and defend himself, but no words came. Instead, with one more glance at Kirilin, he began casting his spell.

Rudd's staff flared with bright orange light. Black smoke curled between the wizard's fingers as the heat of the weapon seared his hand. Screaming in pain, he tried to shake the staff from his grasp, but it would not fall free.

Then the staff burst into flame.

"*Api dalam*," Anselm muttered. "*Mu keawetannir metat indir api.*" Waves of power coursed through him, from the pit of his stomach to his outstretched hands, dark, consuming power that made him want to fall to his knees and retch. This was the magic of the dark mages. This spell was a curse no white-robed wizard should ever have cast.

Rudd's screams turned into mournful wails as flames climbed up his arm. An awful scent of cooking flesh filled the air.

"Yes, do it!" Kirilin's voice was a whisper, but it echoed in Anselm's ears.

"Betrayer," Rudd whispered. Unable to move, he closed his eyes and let his head fall.

Anselm spoke the final words of his spell, and the air between the pillars erupted into flame. Gasping for air, he fell back against the ice pedestal.

Before him, Rudd was a shadow in the pulsing river of fire. But, despite the agony the wizard was certainly feeling, he had stopped screaming. He did not move.

Anselm watched, his heart pounding. Rudd was so still, so silent. Perhaps, unlike the others, he had died. Perhaps he would not suffer for eternity. Perhaps . . .

The flames parted like a curtain and Rudd's head snapped up. His skin was blackened, his hair had burnt away. His eyelids opened, revealing hollow shells.

"No," Anselm whispered.

"Betrayer," Rudd's lips cracked at the corners as he spoke the word again.

His voice sounded different—stronger.

"I am sorry, Rudd." Anselm let out the sob that had been contained in his chest. "I never wanted this."

Rudd pointed a withered finger at Anselm. "You were sent on a divine mission," the young wizard intoned. "But now it has been confirmed. The people of Krynn have lost the path."

Clenching his fists, Anselm forced himself to stand straight. "I had to save my family!" Unbidden tears fell down his cheeks. "Do you not understand? I was her husband and I failed her! I will not fail my children!"

"But you *have* failed your children," Rudd growled. Harsh shadows danced in his sunken cheeks as magic fire licked the sides of his face. "For saving your children, you have doomed thousands. For being narrow in your focus, you have cursed this world. You shall be punished."

"No," Anselm whispered. His energy sapped, he fell to his knees and closed his eyes. His white-blond hair fell forward, a shroud covering his face. "No."

Raising the staff and his other hand, Rudd looked toward the heavens. Foreign words of power burst from his lips, words that Anselm had never before heard.

Above Anselm's head, the Trinistyr rattled on its perch. The air felt heavy, as though a thunderstorm were approaching. Then the sacred dragon statue erupted into silver light.

Howls echoed through the massive chamber as the light swirled into a tornado. The magic of the Trinistyr roared through the air and headed straight toward Anselm's heart.

Anselm let out a cry as the first tendril of power pierced his back. Then more magic came, flowing from the Trinistyr and through his body. Anselm's head snapped back and his arms fell to his sides as the power lanced through his limbs.

After worming throughout him, the magic finally surged forward and tore through his chest. Silver light swirled back into the Trinistyr, and the howling faded away.

Anselm collapsed to the ground, gasping for air. Something was missing. Something that had been a part of him his entire life had been stolen.

"What did you do?" he murmured. Looking up, he met Rudd's empty gaze. "What have you done!"

"You have been cursed," the young wizard said, his voice still much too strong. "The Trinistyr has been sapped of its power, for the people of Krynn had their chance to heal the Kingpriest and failed. And for your betrayal, Anselm, your magic has been taken away. Not just from your body alone, but from your children and their children—your entire bloodline. For as long as you have descendants in this world, not one will be able to use magic. They will be born as peasants and will live without the power they were to have been blessed with. This is your punishment."

"No!" Anselm howled. He tried to climb to his feet, tried to run to Rudd to plead his case and beg for mercy. As he did, he slipped and fell. His knees met the ice with a loud crack.

Closing his empty eye sockets, Rudd let his head fall. As it did, charred skin fell away to reveal an unmarred face. White robes reappeared. Hair flowed long and brown once again.

He was reformed.

But then the torture began anew. His new flesh crackled. Robes flaked into ash. The young wizard screamed in agony as the flames consumed him once more, as they would for all eternity.

Anselm covered his face with his palms and wept.

Steady footsteps clicked behind him. Through his fingers, Anselm watched as Kirilin walked to stand before the wall of flame. She raised a key-shaped jewel and mumbled prayers.

Rudd's screams disappeared. Looking up, Anselm saw that ice had formed in front of the flames, a makeshift tomb to hold the doomed wizard at bay for all eternity. Kirilin continued to pray, her back still to him.

To his left, Anselm saw the Istarian soldier's body, now no longer hidden by magic. It shuddered as a spectral form rose from its back, gaunt and pale. The spirit of the soldier seemed to sever in two as it walked forward, as though it were nothing more than a piece of parchment that had been torn in half. Both halves pulsed with blue light and then reformed into two guards. They were halves of a whole, now unable to work as one to fight the dark cleric who had raised them from the dead.

The ghostly soldiers took their posts on either side of the icy tomb, just as they had when Anselm had betrayed Flomana and Tudyk. They stared forward, resigned to their fates as guardians of this wizard's tomb.

Her work done, Kirilin lowered her hands and turned around.

The dark cleric's skin glowed, young and fresh. Robes streamed from her slender shoulders to flow around revitalized curves. She was a picture of youth, no older than twenty-five years, a seductress ready to corrupt every innocent she could find, stealing their souls for her dark god.

She laughed with delight and looked down at her unmarred hands. "Look at me! That wizard's life-force is mine, just like the others. Just as my god promised. I shall never age. I shall never die!"

Anselm could watch no longer. Head down, he crawled backward until his feet hit the pedestal. Then he leaned back and hugged his knees to his chest.

He felt weak, drained. For all his effort to save his children, now that it was done, all he wanted to do was let himself die and float off into the Gray.

Kirilin was before him in an instant, her features creased into a cruel expression. "You did well," she said, her voice velvety and alluring. "My god's will has been done, and I shall keep my end of the bargain. Your children will be set free, and you three can flee to whatever dark corner of Krynn that you like."

"We are not free," Anselm whispered. He looked over Kirilin's white robes as she sneered down at him. "We have kept up this charade long enough. You aren't a true cleric of Istar. If you were, you'd want Paladine's Trinistyr. Instead, you allowed Rudd to curse it!"

Closing his eyes, Anselm leaned his head back against the ice pedestal. "Now it is worthless," he went on, his voice once again a hoarse whisper. "And it will be impossible to break the curse since magic has been stolen from me and my family."

With an exasperated sigh, Kirilin put her hands on her hips. "I'm surprised it took you so long to work it out. Yes, I serve a dark god. I am a cleric of Hiddukel. My job is to steal souls, not heal them. Besides, curses can be broken."

As though hearing someone, the cleric tilted her head. After a moment, she tilted her head back and smirked. "My lord has told me that the curse on your family is simple. A magic-using descendant of yours must relive the tortures you have inflicted and restore the Trinistyr." With a false gasp, she put her slender fingers to her lips. "Oh, but I have forgotten already. None of your descendants can have magic. I suppose you are right—it *is* impossible to break this curse."

With another dark laugh, Kirilin turned and walked out of the cavern, her robes an ivory wave behind her.

For a long time, Anselm sat against the pillar, rocking back and forth. He was without hope, without a future.

Then he looked up and saw the Trinistyr. No power emanated from the once glorious dragon statue. Its color was flat and black, and it seemed empty and dead a shell.

Groaning with the effort, Anselm pulled himself up the high

pillar and gingerly picked up the Trinistyr, then slid back to the floor. The figure was small and light, deceptively so. Certainly no one would know of its true power. Certainly he could keep it hidden from those who may want to destroy it, lest it ever be restored.

Looking through the milky white sheet of ice that entombed poor Rudd as he writhed in flames, Anselm made a decision. He had been punished for his betrayal, as was only just. But even if he were now powerless to stop evil, he could make up for his weakness of conviction.

He would seek out a white-robed wizard to make a magic map that would show where his cursed companions lay. He would keep the Trinistyr and pass it from his children to their children and on and on, a sacred heirloom. And he would not let the tale of their family's curse ever die.

But first, he would find the children he had sacrificed so much to save, and embrace them.

With one last mournful look at Rudd, Anselm forced himself to walk out of the cavern and begin the treacherous journey over the frozen lands and back to his family.

CHAPTER

1   REFLECTIONS

J aneesa? Tylari? Are you there?"

      Jirah clutched her little mirror as she gazed into her own reflected blue eyes. The glass and its gilded silver frame shimmered in the light from her candle.

Shadows swayed back and forth in the small room's corners, like deadly wraiths watching and waiting to strike. A chill wind crept through the inn's thin-paned windows and slipped beneath her nightclothes.

Jirah shivered.

"Janeesa?" she whispered, trying to ignore the uneasy feeling creeping up her back. "We're in Tarsis, I need—" With a gasp, she stopped speaking.

In the mirror, her reflection had begun to change—to *decay*. Flesh peeled from her fingers to reveal stark-white bone. Her cheeks sunk deep into her face as her skin paled, then turned a sickly green. Locks of black hair fell from her scalp until all that remained were a few stiff, brittle strands.

Jirah threw her arm toward the pack lying open beside her. She scrambled to grab anything to protect herself—a dagger, a hair-brush, a book. She tried to look away from the deadly reflection, but her gaze was locked onto its glassy eyes.

The corpse-like image of herself parted lips pulled tight against rotten teeth and began to laugh—a deep, male laugh.

As Jirah watched, the decaying image faded away. Instead she saw her true self. Sweat beaded at her temples, and her skin was pale, but she was most certainly not an undead creature from the Abyss.

"No fetch today," a male voice said from the mirror. "But I scared you, didn't I?"

Jirah gulped for air. Her free hand was clenched so tight that her fingernails cut into her palm. "Th-that wasn't funny," she said.

"I really believe it was." The disembodied voice sounded half mocking, half serious. Jirah found herself trembling even more.

The room was dark, small, and cramped, and she sat cross-legged on a pallet in the corner. Her half-melted candle sat beside her, the only light in the cloud-covered night. Beyond the wooden wall to the south, she could hear the grumble of someone's muffled snores.

Jirah and her companions—her sister Nearra, would-be-leader Davyn, cocky elf Icefire, and the kender-dog comedic duo of Keene and Pip—had ended up in the once-great city of Tarsis on their quest to break a curse that had long plagued Jirah's family.

Tarsis was cold and bleak, even though Krynn was nearing the end of summer. The trek north to the city over the frozen tundra of the Plains of Dust had been trying, though thankfully dull in comparison to the trials they had faced in Icereach. Jirah's lips still felt blistered from the icy winds.

Icefire had used his wiles to get them inside the gates and find them rooms in one of the few inns that had been completely rebuilt in the few years since Tarsis had been attacked during the War of the Lance. An uneasy feeling had tugged at Jirah from the moment they'd arrived. She could almost swear she could smell a lingering, ashy scent of burnt timber from the siege upon the city.

"How is your sister?" A new voice came from the mirror, female and commanding. Jirah's reflected lips moved, miming the words, and it was almost as though she were speaking to a twin.

"She is well, Janeesa," Jirah whispered. Jirah looked around the room, studying the ghostlike shadows for movement, expecting to see someone spying. No one was there.

"Is she enjoying my staff?" Tylari's voice was clearly annoyed. Jirah's eyes in her reflection, controlled by Janeesa, glanced sternly at something to her right.

"You will have the staff," Jirah said. "I promise."

"The curse was supposed to have been broken, and the Trinistyr and staff were to have been ours." Tylari's voice lost none of its edge, and Jirah swallowed nervously.

Jirah and her companions had recovered a staff empowered with fire magic from deep in the caverns of the frozen continent of Icereach, after Nearra had relived the suffering of a wizard who had been entombed there. Doing so was supposed to have broken a curse of non-magic that had been placed upon their family centuries ago when their ancestor Anselm had betrayed his fellow wizards. Reliving the suffering was also supposed to have restored the godly power of an ancient artifact known as the Trinistyr, a small black statue shaped like a dragon that was currently in Nearra's possession.

Or so Jirah had been led to believe by Janeesa and Tylari, who called themselves the Messengers. She was working with the two elf mages in secret, helping them to restore the Trinistyr, though for what reason they needed the dragon statue she didn't know. They in turn were providing her with the means to break her family's curse so that she and her father could become wizards, though sometimes the price that the Messengers demanded for their help seemed much too high.

But Jirah and her companions had found that freeing the wizard Rudd in Icereach was only the first step. There were still two other cursed wizards entombed in hidden areas somewhere on Krynn. Even worse was that a centuries-old cleric named Kirilin was following them with the intent to kill them. She had been granted the life-forces of the cursed wizards by her dark god, and if the curse on Jirah's family were broken, Kirilin would die.

Kirilin had aged dramatically after Nearra freed Rudd. But Kirilin did not die, as they had believed would happen before they knew about the remaining wizards. Faced with her death, Kirilin was undoubtedly hunting them down even as they rested in the seemingly safe inn. Until the souls of the remaining wizards were freed, the curse of non-magic on Jirah's family would live on, Kirilin would be alive to hunt them down, and the Trinistyr would remain a powerless black statue.

Janeesa and Tylari didn't seem too concerned by Kirilin, but they were none too pleased that the Trinistyr had not been restored.

"None of us knew this would happen," Jirah stammered. "We didn't know that there were more wizards and that Kirilin would not die. I think Nearra should probably keep the staff until we free the other two wizards, just in case we need it to protect ourselves from the cleric or to give the Trinistyr back its power. That's what you want, right? I promise we'll do it, and you'll get what you want. I promise."

The voices from the mirror fell silent. Jirah was much too aware of the creaking of the wood around her, of the mournful sound of the wind rushing past the window. She bit at her fingernails nervously.

Her reflected lips parted. "You have been making many promises," Janeesa's voice said, "and quite a few excuses." She let out an exasperated sigh. "Jirah, what did I say I about biting your nails?"

Quickly, Jirah lowered her hand. "Sorry."

"Vile habit, Jirah, and not at all becoming of a future wizard. The quality of a mage's hands is important." Jirah's reflection shook its head, sending short black hair bobbing back and forth. "Tell me, what are your plans?"

Jirah let out a breath she didn't know she had been holding. "The map you gave me showed us the location of the second wizard's tomb. It's an ancient mine somewhere to the west of Tarsis. But the map is wrong."

"Wrong?"

"I mean," Jirah hastened to add, "that it's of Krynn before the Cataclysm. We're supposed to look in some sort of library here in Tarsis, to try and research a better path to the mine before Kirilin catches up with us. Icefire knows someone at the library, and he says she can get us in."

"The Library of Khrystann." Tylari's voice was a harsh whisper, his tone knowing. "Icefire and I had made plans to go there. That half-breed left me behind!"

From what Jirah had gathered, Icefire had once been the third member of the Messengers. He was currently helping the Messengers as well by guiding Nearra on her quest, but only because he owed them some debt. He had parted with the brother and sister many years ago to pursue other dreams.

"Tylari, hush." In the mirror image, Jirah's reflected lips curled into a smile that somehow seemed completely insincere. "The plans sound fine, Jirah. Go to the library and research the path. But be as quick about it as possible. Time is running short."

Jirah fidgeted with the bedsheet beneath her. "Janeesa, the library sounds vast. I don't know if we can be quick. There's so much to look through and—"

"Are you planning to stall further, girl?" Tylari snapped.

"N-no! No, I—"

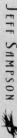

"You'd better not be backing out on us again," Tylari's voice seethed. "It's too late to change your mind now. You wouldn't want me to send the fetch to visit your good friend Keene, would you?"

Before, after they'd freed the wizard Rudd, Jirah had wanted to give up. Janeesa had asked Jirah to make Davyn fight Icefire and for her to kill Nearra once the curse was broken. The guilt of what she was doing had started to become too much, and so she had stood frozen, waiting for the undead beast that was the fetch to drag her into the Abyss and end all the lies. But Janeesa had made it quite clear that doing so would lead to the death of Keene, the kender who was probably her only true friend.

"I know, Tylari," Jirah whispered. "Please, don't send the fetch. I'll do my best. I promise."

"Your 'best' is hardly good enough," Tylari hissed.

Janeesa let out another sigh. "I'm sure I have some magical item here in the shop that can help find the right book. I'll look for it. Contact us as soon as you reach the library, understand?"

"Yes, Janeesa." Jirah swallowed. "I understand."

Janeesa did not speak further. Jirah continued to stare into the mirror, hands trembling. But soon she realized her features in the mirror were mimicking her true self, not those of Janeesa. The Messengers were gone.

Still shaking, she lowered the mirror and took in a deep breath. *This is for my family,* she told herself. *I'm doing all this so Father and I can have magic as we were meant to.*

What about Nearra? she thought back. *Am I to do this even if it means that my friends and my sister have to get hurt in the process? After all that we've endured together?*

Jirah opened her pack and placed the mirror inside a padded pocket. For a moment, she stopped and stared at the silver and glass mirror, frozen in her thoughts.

It was never supposed to be like this. She hadn't meant to go this far. But she was lying to everyone around her while secretly working with the Messengers. She had even tried to kill an innocent elf girl because they had told her to. Was it really worth all this?

It's too late to change your mind now. Tylari's words echoed through her head.

"Too late," Jirah whispered. Tears beaded in the corners of her eyes. "It's too late."

"That girl." Janeesa turned from the antique mirror hanging from the wall of her shop, her hands balled into fists. "Humans," she muttered.

"What was it you said once, Sister?" Tylari asked. "'Have a little faith'?"

Janeesa flung her golden hair over her shoulder and shot Tylari a stern look. He sat stooped on the staircase leading to the upper story, his arms crossed over his knees. Long bangs shrouded his eyes in shadow, though she could still see his mocking stare.

Janeesa let out an exasperated sigh and unclenched her hands. "You were right," she said. "She's not trustworthy. But we're too close to give up on her now."

Red robes flowed around her as she swept by Tylari. Rounding a set of enchanted armor she had on display, she strode out into the main area of her shop. "And I think I know the exact item that will get us closer."

After their banishment from Silvanesti elf society for daring to choose wizardly robes other than white, Janeesa and Tylari had traveled to the port city of Caergoth. There, they bought a shop from an aging wizard and made their home in the upper story. The money used to purchase the shop had been inherited from their father, and he was the exact reason Janeesa had created the plan to purchase the shop in the first place.

Janeesa peered through the magically impenetrable glass that sat above the tables displaying her most precious wares. The mystical items flashed orange in the light from the brick fireplace near the mirror. Beyond them, shelves were piled high with decaying spell books and bottles of spell components. Magical scepters and enchanted swords hung on the stone walls.

Dimly lit and filled with antiques, the shop had the air of a museum. The shutters were always drawn, whether it was night or not, to keep the space closed off and private. The musty scent of old books and the aroma of herbs filled the air. Janeesa had designed the atmosphere to purposefully draw a certain clientele—the kind of people who would be willing to trade rare and unusual artifacts.

For years she had been on a search to find a cure for her father, a great white-robed Silvanesti mage. She loved her father and had admired his abilities for most of her life. She had planned to become a powerful wizard just like him.

Then the madness had settled over him—the madness that drove her mother away. This madness caused the other elf mages to cast spells on him that were meant to heal her father but had instead destroyed his mind forever.

Running her fingers lightly along the glass case, Janeesa studied her items carefully: a pendant that cured boils, a gem set in an amulet that could be used in healing potions, a map of mazes beneath the wastelands of Khur.

A map. That was what she needed, some sort of map of the library. It had been a map that had helped her before, in fact. Though she had kept it secret from Jirah until the time was right, the magic map that showed the location of the cursed wizards had arrived at her shop on a sleepy morning over two years ago. A letter had been with it, its ancient paper brittle. The words had been scrawled haphazardly, betraying an author who was rushed. It was in a long-dead language that she translated after a few days work.

The letter told of an artifact that could heal madness, one whose magic was bound by an ancient curse. Not one day later, a man and his daughter had entered her shop with that very artifact.

It had to be fate. She was destined to help end the curse on the Trinistyr. She was meant to heal her father of his madness and reap vengeance on the elf mages who had destroyed him and, in so doing, had destroyed her family.

Looking up, Janeesa saw Tylari. He sat unmoving in the same position on the stairs where she had left him. The metallic silver and red threads sewn through his black robes glinted in the firelight. He continued to watch her with those same dark eyes.

Janeesa turned away and let out a sigh. With Tylari, it had started slowly—brief manic fits. But now, the fits lasted longer. He mumbled incoherently about becoming a god. Paranoid thoughts consumed him to a point where Janeesa wasn't sure he could control himself from using his magic haphazardly. It seemed what had plagued and destroyed her father was now attacking Tylari, and he didn't even realize it.

"I need the Trinistyr restored," she muttered.

Hiding in the corner of one of her display cases was a tarnished shallow bowl. Engraved around its outer lip were looping designs showing circles within pointed ovals—eyes.

"Here we are." Muttering a spell, Janeesa waved her hand over the glass case. There was a quick flash of blue light, and the glass seemed to ripple as though transformed to water. She reached through the glass and picked up the bowl. As her hand and the artifact pulled free of the cabinet, the glass flashed once more and turned solid.

"This should do," Janeesa said as she strode back toward Tylari. "A bowl of a seer. I recall that the woman who sold it to me said it had only one use left. I think finding the texts that will help restore the Trinistyr is worthy for its last use, don't you?"

Tylari did not move. "If you say so, Sister. I just want the staff."

"I do say so." She approached the shelves and began picking up and studying the bottles of spell components one by one. She read the labels as she did so, setting them to the side when they proved not to be what she was looking for. "We're finally going to get the Trinistyr restored, and then we can heal Father." In a whisper, she added, "And you."

Tylari's head shot up. His expression was blank, though his eyes still bore into hers. Reaching up a trembling hand, he grabbed the banister and started to stand.

"What did you say?"

Startled, Janeesa furrowed her eyebrows and met her younger brother's gaze. "I said that I would use the Trinistyr on you too."

Tylari's lips spread into a snarl. He shook with rage. "You would use that thing on me? You would destroy me?"

"What?" Setting down the bottle she'd been clutching, Janeesa turned to face her brother. "Of course not. The Trinistyr is meant to—"

"Take away my power!" Tylari's eyes darted back and forth. "I knew it. You're with the human girl. You're trying to destroy me too. You don't want me to be a god."

Janeesa sighed and let her arms fall to her side. "Tylari," she said. He took a step toward her, and his hand shot forward. His lips twisted as he formed magical phrases.

Holding her hands high to show she meant no harm, she took another step. "Tylari," she said again. "Listen to yourself. We are but elves. Yes, we have access to the moons' power and we are mages, but you are not a god."

Tylari stopped intoning the words of his spell and let his hand drop. "But I can feel it," he whispered. "I know what I am meant to be. I know . . . " His voice trailed off as his face fell into a look of confusion.

Janeesa reached his side. She placed a gentle hand on his shoulder and guided him to sit back down on the steps. She crouched before him.

"It's all right, Tylari," she said. "We're going to help you and Father. I do not intend to take any of your power. In fact, were you to be a god, I would do everything I could to help you ascend. Now calm yourself. We can't afford to lose control, not now."

"Help me . . . " Tylari repeated her words, contemplating them. His eyes searched the air as though it might contain the answers that would explain this all to him.

"That's right." Satisfied, Janeesa stood. "Don't worry. I'll take care of everything. It's late anyway. Perhaps you should retire to bed?"

"Yes," Tylari whispered. "I should rest."

With another reassuring pat on his shoulder, Janeesa turned and walked past the enchanted armor to continue her search through the spell components.

She watched his reflection in one of the glass cases as she pretended to dig through the shelves. For a moment, Tylari continued to sit on the stairs, lost in his thoughts.

Again his head shot up. He glared at Janeesa, the dark gleam not leaving his eyes.

"Good bye, Janeesa," Tylari said. Then he stood and walked slowly up the stairs, into the darkness of the rooms above.

CHAPTER

2   KENDER TRICKS

Who were you talking to last night?"

Jirah dropped her spoon with a start. It plopped into her bowl of cooked oats, splattering bits of the steaming mush onto her shirt.

Keene sat across from her, his head tilted like a curious puppy. Jirah took a breath.

"No one, Keene," she said. "Maybe I was talking in my sleep?"

The kender shrugged. "It sure sounded like you were having a conversation. I found the most interesting knob on the door to your room and couldn't help but overhear. Are you sure no one was there?"

Jirah swallowed, then picked up her spoon and swirled it in her oats. "Pretty sure."

"You weren't talking to Janeesa through your mirror again, were you? You always act strange after you do that, and—"

Jirah quickly shoved a large spoonful of the hot oats in her mouth. Though it burned her tongue, she did not swallow or spit it out. Opening her eyes wide, she gestured toward her full cheeks to show she couldn't speak.

But Keene had lost interest anyway. He'd spotted a silver fork on 23 another table in the common room and went to investigate.

Jirah and Keene were the only two at breakfast; the others had awoken much earlier and had already eaten. Jirah hadn't awoken until midmorning. Sleep had been elusive until near daylight, when exhaustion finally claimed her for a couple hours.

Dim gray light from the windows lining the east wall cast long shadows across the common room. Squat, round tables were set haphazardly through the room like wooden toadstools. Mugs and bowls were piled in heaps atop the tables, and chairs sat askew as though shoved aside in haste. A slender serving girl with curly black hair hustled between the tables, gathering dishes.

Aside from Keene, the only other customer in the common room was an old man. He sat with his head on the bar near the stairs that led to the upper floors. He snored in loud bursts and mumbled to himself. A few glowing embers were all that was left of the fire that had once roared in the fireplace beside him.

A heavyset barkeep, who looked to Jirah like a dull gray boulder wearing an apron, wiped the bar's counter with a dirty rag. With each crescendo of the old man's snores, the barkeep shot him a dirty look.

Jirah swallowed her meal and quickly downed the rest of the water in her mug. As she did so, she watched Keene study the remnants of what must have been a busy breakfast earlier that morning. The long auburn hair of his topknot swished as he darted under the tables and climbed on the chairs.

"You!" The serving girl's eyes grew wide as she spotted Keene examining the tables. "Hey, stop that!" Lifting up the hem of her dress, she ran toward Keene.

Looking up at the girl innocently, Keene stopped midreach toward something in the center of one of the tables near the stairs He stood precariously on the edge of a wobbly chair, almost on tiptoe, as he leaned his small body forward to grab his find.

"Is something wrong?" He blinked his blue eyes twice in a show of sincere innocence. Kender tended to be so infatuated with the things around themselves that they often shoved any item they found into one of their many pockets without even realizing it. Most people considered it stealing, but the more time Jirah spent around Keene, the more she realized it was just that he had so much curiosity he didn't even realize he was hoarding items to study later. He was too distracted with the next find to study it right then, of course.

Stopping before him, the girl put her hands on her hips and tapped her foot. Her black curls bobbed as she shook her head. "You were trying to snatch my steel. I saw it."

"Was I?" Keene's eyes turned from the girl and followed his arm to see where his hand was reaching. "Hmm, it appears I *found* your steel, actually. It was almost lost between all these dishes. Good thing I was here."

The girl rolled her green eyes. "Yes, good thing it was that and not a typical kender trick. Now get down before you fall."

"Me? Fall?" Keene leaned back and stood up straight. "Why, have you not heard of the acrobatic prowess of Keene the Amazing? Watch as I stand on one foot on this teetering Chair of Doom and yet do not fall!" With a great flourish, Keene stretched his arms out wide to steady himself. Slowly, he pushed himself to stand on his tiptoes. Then, trembling only slightly as he sought to maintain his balance, he lifted his right booted foot and stuck it out into the air.

The serving girl stared. Keene beamed as though he'd just walked a tightrope across a raging volcano. Jirah tried to stifle her laughter.

"Arf!" Canine nails clicked against the wooden steps, and Jirah, Keene, and the serving girl all turned to see a small dog with curly white hair running down the stairs as fast as its little legs could take it. It skidded to a stop just beneath the chair where Keene still balanced on one foot.

"Hello, Pip," Keene said with a cheery grin. He wavered slightly but managed to still keep straight. "Good to see you could join us!"

The dog blinked his large eyes as he studied Keene's balancing act. Then, with a quick wag of his plumed tail, Pip leaped forward and started walking on his front legs.

"Oh, how adorable!" the serving girl cried. She clapped her hands together in delight.

"Why, you mangy mutt!" Keene said. The chair wobbled beneath him as he started to shake in an exaggerated show of anger. "Trying to show me up! Well, I'll—Whoa!" With a great crash, the chair tipped over and Keene rolled across the floor.

"Oh, Pip! Now look what you made me do!" Keene stood and brushed off his fur vest and his blue trousers. "You ruined the show I was giving to the pretty— What was your name?"

The serving girl blinked. "Avina."

"Avina! What a tremendously beautiful name." He beamed, then turned to glare at Pip.

"Now, Pip, we need to find some way to apologize to Avina and— Pip? Where'd you go?"

"Oy! Give that back, ya beast!" Turning all the way around in her chair, Jirah caught sight of a flash of white fur racing across the bar. The barkeep shook his massive fist.

The old man who was asleep at the bar sat up, his eyes blinking rapidly. "Eh?" he said. His wrinkled features crinkled with confusion.

Pip reached the end of the bar and leaped forward. He barreled into Keene's chest and the kender fell onto his back, right at Avina's feet.

"Oof! Why, you little monster, I should have sold you as a meal to some draconians a long time ago!"

Pip stood on Keene's chest, his tail wagging. He held the barman's dirty rag in his mouth and tilted his head curiously.

"Why, old friend, what's this?" Keene exclaimed. "A rag! How perfect! We have a gift for Avina after all!" With a yip of excitement, Pip jumped down to the floor, and Keene bounded to his feet. Smiling, he presented the rag to Avina.

The serving girl watched the entire scene with her mouth wide open, apparently not sure what exactly was playing out before her. She scanned the rag up and down, blinked twice, then shook her head. "Er, well, thank you," she said. "But I have one just like it." She gestured to her waist, where a similar dirty rag hung from a sash she'd tied around her middle.

"Ah, but this isn't a rag," Keene said with a wink. "This is a bouquet befitting only the most lovely of serving girls I've met in all of my travels." With a twist of his wrist, the rag seemed to disappear and a bouquet of white-petaled flowers appeared in its place.

"Oh my!" Avina said. She reached forward and gently picked them from Keene's hands. "That's amazing! I didn't know kender could do magic."

"We can't," Keene said with a low bow. "But I never reveal the secrets of my act."

The serving girl took a deep sniff of the flowers, then turned to the barkeep. "Did you see that?" she asked. "Oh, Bezzil, you should smell these. They're wonderful."

The barkeep slouched onto the bar. "I'd rather have my rag."

"Don't worry, good sir. I'm sure we can find you a new one." Jirah glanced at the stairs to find Icefire leaning against the banister. The tall elf flashed a grin most girls found alluring. Indeed, the serving girl's face changed into the typical swooning expression Jirah had seen time and time again while traveling with Icefire, and she rolled her eyes.

"Eh, well I hope so," the barkeep grumbled. He crossed the beefy slabs that were his arms and frowned. "I got a counter that needs washin'."

Icefire raised one of his perfectly arched eyebrows and nodded. "Consider it done." He started down the stairs, his movements elegant and graceful. Were it not for his height and the taut muscle covering his bare forearms, he'd seem a pure elf through and through. But despite the harmonious mixture of features that led to his striking elven beauty, he was not pure. Much to the horror of his Silvanesti family, a long-dormant human bloodline was quite apparent in Icefire's exotic appearance.

The serving girl didn't seem to mind.

"Are these friends of yours, sir?" Smiling like an idiot, she curtsied slightly.

Icefire rounded a table and came to stand in front of Avina. He cocked his head slightly, then ran his hand through his waves of black hair. Again he flashed his grin. "That they are. I trust you liked the show? Keene and Pip are two of the finest comedians on Krynn."

Avina blushed and looked down from his intense blue eyes. "Oh, I did."

Jirah groaned and shook her head in disgust.

Icefire reached out a slender finger and lifted her chin. "I'm glad. I myself am a singer. We travel together, Keene, Pip, and I. Perhaps you might tell the inn's owner of the sample performance you saw? We've often earned our stay in inns between my voice and Keene's comedy."

"I can see why," the girl said. She took a nervous breath and clenched her bouquet tight. "I will, sir. I'll go talk to her right away."

Icefire nodded approvingly. "Perhaps you might first reward your entertainers with a kiss?"

Keene popped up at Icefire's side, his lips puckered. Beside him, Pip stood on his hind legs and cocked his furry head.

Avina giggled. "Of course." Leaning down, she bowed right past Keene and let Pip lick her lips. With a laugh, she leaned back and wiped her mouth with the back of her hand. "Thank you, Keene the Amazing," she said as she patted his head. "The flowers are lovely." With a quick curtsy, she turned and flounced toward the kitchens.

"I have absolutely no idea what's going on," the old man from the bar said.

The barkeep shrugged. "All I know is I lost my rag."

"Keene, run outside and see if Davyn is on his way back," Icefire said.

"But Icefire, I didn't get my kiss!"

"Maybe you'll find it outside. Now go."

Keene let out a sigh that was much too loud to be real, then turned his head to meet Jirah's eye. He winked. "Aye, Captain Icefire!" He turned and scrambled around the bar toward the main door, Pip at his heels.

The kender and the serving girl gone, Icefire turned and met Jirah's gaze. His look held none of the charm he'd put on so thickly for Avina. Jirah swallowed.

"Jirah," Icefire said. He approached the table where she sat and stood above her. He crossed his arms and looked down his nose at her. "You slept in. Late night?"

Jirah looked away and lowered her voice. "Janeesa needed to talk to me. And I didn't really sleep well after that."

"She does tend to unsettle a person, doesn't she?" Icefire sighed, then fell into the chair next to Jirah. "What does my old friend have you doing now?" he whispered.

Jirah picked up her spoon and fiddled with it inside her empty bowl. She gave a half-hearted shrug. "I just told her what we were doing today. She's going to help us find information in the library."

Icefire snorted. "I bet she is. She ask about my magic?"

"No," Jirah muttered. "She didn't ask about you or your magic at all."

Icefire raised an eyebrow, but said nothing.

Jirah wondered for a moment what would happen if she told Icefire about Janeesa's plans for Nearra, about how long ago the elf mage had made Jirah promise that she would kill Nearra once the Trinistyr was restored. Jirah had asked why, but Janeesa told her only that it was key to the breaking of Jirah's family's curse. Jirah had immediately agreed, but back then the notion of death was vague to her, something distant and far away. Everyone died, right?

Hearing footsteps from the landing, Jirah looked up to find Nearra descending the stairs. Long blond hair framed pale, delicate features that seemed lost in thought. Her gaze seemed unfocused. She wore her traveling dress and carried her pack on her shoulders, the long crystal-capped staff they'd recently recovered strapped to the bag's side.

"Nearra, are you ready?" Icefire put one arm over the back of his chair and tilted around to meet Nearra's gaze. As soon as she saw him, she smiled one of her perfect smiles. Icefire's grin went from cocky to goofy, if only for a moment.

Jirah felt a quick flare of jealousy and remembered her life before their father took her on the quest to break their curse. She remembered comparing her face to Nearra's, how it seemed so similar at first, but when you looked closely you could see that next to Nearra, Jirah's nose was a little crooked and her smile a little lopsided. Jirah's flat black hair never seemed to hang right, while Nearra's hair was always glossy and perfect, even when she'd just woken up. The neighbor boy would always become all clumsy around Nearra, and he never even remembered Jirah's name.

Nearra was special. People met her and could just tell. She was kind, loyal, hardworking, lovely, and had a singing voice that had won contests. In short, people thought Nearra was perfect, but that Jirah would never be anything if she wasn't a wizard.

Only now, Jirah wasn't so sure what to think. Now, as she watched Nearra approach, she saw sadness in her face. She saw the long scar on her arm, a remnant of an old battle. Her sister wasn't the goddess Jirah had always imagined Nearra to be. She was just . . . Nearra.

Icefire stood respectfully as Nearra approached. Again their eyes met, again they smiled. "I'm all ready," Nearra said. "I'm bringing my pack—and the Trinistyr."

"Good plan," Icefire said. "We can't be too careful, not when we don't know where Kirilin is."

Nodding, Nearra turned to greet Jirah. Immediately her features fell into concern.

"Are you all right?" she asked. She leaned down and put her hand on Jirah's shoulder. "You look bothered. Did something happen?"

Jirah swallowed and shook her head. "No, I'm fine. I didn't sleep much is all. I'll be all right."

Nearra's eyes scanned her own. She knew Jirah was lying, and Jirah knew she knew it. Jirah had done nothing but lie for the past half a year, and she wondered if she even remembered how to be honest anymore.

Unable to find the truth in her eyes, Nearra nodded and stood. "All right. But let me know if you need to rest, all right?"

Jirah rolled her eyes. "It's just a little sleep deprivation. If anyone should be concerned about her health, it's you. You look half dead." Immediately she felt a pang of guilt. She hadn't meant to say it, but by now the deceit had become habit.

"Is Davyn back yet?" Nearra asked Icefire.

The elf shook his head. "No. He went to go trade for some new gear past the old seawall."

"At the white-winged ships you told us about?"

Icefire nodded. "The one and the same. He figured he could get a better deal since the people there are much too poor to risk haggling much. I sent Keene to find—"

"Hey!" a voice cried from outside. "As long as you're holding me up here, perhaps swing me a little. I always wondered what it'd feel like to be a pendulum."

Icefire let out a quick snort of laughter and shook his head. They heard the sound of the main doors slam, then clunking footsteps, as an imposing Solamnic Knight in full plate armor rounded the bar. His black mustache quivered with annoyance beneath the nosepiece of his helm. Dangling by his topknot from the knight's outstretched fist was Keene.

"Hello," Keene said.

The Solamnic Knight grunted. He reached his free hand up and yanked off his helmet. "This belong to you?" he demanded in a gruff voice as he shook Keene.

"Ah, yes," Icefire said with a slight bow. "That would be my good friend Keene Waverider. If you don't mind, might you put him down?"

The knight let out another grunt and let Keene go. The kender landed on his feet, then spun around and bowed with a flourish. "Thank you for the ride!" he said. "Although I do think I could have walked in just fine."

The knight rolled his eyes as Keene sauntered to Icefire's side. Setting his helmet down, he leaned forward onto a table. Matted, gray-flecked hair fell into his eyes. "Look," he said. "This city has had enough trouble. It is my duty to keep it safe from any and all harm—including kender."

"I understand, sir," Icefire said. "We will—"

The knight held up his hand. Jirah gulped at the look in his eye. He wasn't playing around.

"Do *not*," he said, "cause problems while you are here in Tarsis. I do not need your smooth talking. I do not need your assurances. There is no choice here. Keep your kender in check and keep quiet, and everyone will get along fine. Got it?"

Nearra took a step forward and bobbed her head in a small bow. "Sir, thank you for returning Keene to us. It was very kind of you. We will do our best to make sure no one is troubled by our stay."

"Your accent." The knight's eyes met Nearra's own. "You are from Solamnia?"

Nearra nodded. "Yes, sir, I am."

The knight's expression softened, if only slightly, and Jirah's hands clenched the table so tight that her fingernails bit into the wood. Why was everyone so infatuated with Nearra?

"Hmph." The knight leaned back. "Tarsis has had its fair share of trouble with outsiders. This is your first warning. If I hear one mutter of any sort of problems with you, it's out the gates."

He met each of their eyes with a pointed stare. Then, with a respectful nod at the bartender, he turned and left.

Icefire and Nearra both raised their eyebrows.

"Keene, what did you do?" Nearra asked.

"Well, I was looking for Davyn, like Icefire asked me to," he said. "Then I saw this bright red *thing* flutter over my head and I thought, 'Well, unless that's a bird, that shouldn't be up there, seeing as how it's fluttering several stories up.' That's how I ended up in the tree. Then . . . "

Icefire and Nearra seemed enraptured with Keene's tale, but Jirah's fingers still hadn't unclenched. She looked at the side of Nearra's face and saw her perfect jawline, saw her eyes open wide with interest, saw her brilliant smile as Keene made her laugh. Watching the two boys around Nearra at that moment, Jirah couldn't help but feel as though she was outside a wall, unnoticed as she watched through a window. As always.

The main door slammed, and Jirah looked up. The others didn't notice, but Davyn stood by the bar. He wore a thick cloak over the green-dyed leather armor he always wore, and he carried packages of new supplies. Unruly sandy-brown hair fell into his eyes as he watched them talk.

To Jirah, the look in his eyes seemed very much like hatred.

Davyn slammed the packages on the bar to get their attention. Icefire, Nearra, and Keene turned to look up at him. Nearra's eyes quickly flitted away.

"Do you really think now's the time to tell stories?" Davyn asked. His look lost none of its edge. "We need to get on to the library before Kirilin catches up with us."

Icefire flashed a smile. "We were just waiting for you, my friend."

Davyn grunted. "Well I'm back."

Jirah noticed Nearra's face fall. She parted her lips as though to speak, but seemed to think better of it and said nothing.

"Ooh, are those new supplies?" Keene asked. He skittered to Davyn's side, Pip at his heels. Poking at one of the packages, he tilted his head. "I was in need of a new cloak. My old one was starting to fall apart."

Icefire leaped forward with a grin. "Well, sounds like we're prepared. What say we get these packages put away and set out? We have a library to explore."

Jirah watched as Nearra's face lit up once again at the elf's high spirits. She shook her head with amusement, sending golden hair dancing down her back, and walked to stand at Icefire's side. "Sounds like a plan," she said. "It's time we get back to breaking the curse and getting rid of Kirilin, once and for all."

JEFF SAMPSON

CHAPTER

3   STOLEN BEAUTY

Tarsis the Beautiful had once been the vast and rich Lordcity of Abanasinia. It had been a seaport city, and its grand white-winged ships would sail into the docks on the western edge of the city, their holds and decks overflowing with all sorts of fantastic fabrics, spices, and spell components. The markets had been packed solid with merchants and buyers. The spires of a towering palace had thrust toward the sky at the city's center, a testament to the city's wealth. Libraries had flourished because visitors from all over the world came to experience the unique blend of flavors that was Tarsis, bringing with them books from all corners of Krynn.

But that was before the Cataclysm: Before the gods sent down the fiery mountain that stole the sea from around Tarsis, beaching the white-winged ships. Before the lands surrounding the city froze into eternally cold and desolate plains. Before the Solamnic Knights had abandoned Tarsis to tend to matters in their own country.

Davyn studied the buildings around him as he walked the streets of Tarsis, remembering tales that his adoptive father, Maddoc, had told him of its history. He saw relatively new scorch marks that marred a brick building and imagined the terror Tarsians must have felt when the Blue Dragonarmy descended upon the city during the War of the Lance.

He remembered these stories and studied these remnants of war because he knew exactly where his thoughts would wander otherwise—to Nearra and Icefire.

Davyn walked ahead of everyone. He pulled his cloak tight to protect himself from the bitter, icy winds that flowed between the drab brick buildings. Elsewhere on Krynn it was nearing the end of summer, but it felt as though Tarsis and the Plains of Dust were caught in an eternal winter.

All around him, what few people were out that morning shopped in the markets. Awnings fluttered in the chilling breeze as bored merchants waited for someone to purchase their wares. A fat woman with a beak-like nose examined a wooden table covered with pots, as the eager saleswoman tried to convince her to buy the largest one. A heavily clothed child sucked on his thumb at the fat woman's side and stared at Davyn as he passed.

As Davyn walked through the nearly empty market and tried to ignore the companions behind him, he noticed the Solamnic Knights. Some stood alone, and some stood in small clusters at almost every corner. Gray light from the overcast sky glinted off chest plates engraved with ornate images of crowns or roses. It wasn't that long ago that the Tarsians—disgruntled at the Solamnic Knights for abandoning the city after the Cataclysm—would have killed a knight before letting one guard their streets. After the recent war, though, the city allowed the knights to return to help keep order as the city attempted reconstruction.

Keene's cheerful voice droned endlessly behind Davyn as the kender talked with Jirah. The petite, dark-haired girl seemed to like the little sailor, which surprised Davyn. Ever since he had met Jirah, she seemed to change almost daily. He'd never really considered her dishonest, but it had soon become clear that her behavior was unpredictable. One moment the girl seemed sweet and innocent, the next she was making snide remarks. Hearing her laugh with Keene as Pip raced to match their stride, Davyn wondered if he'd even met the real Jirah yet.

Though he tried very hard to let his thoughts be consumed by the city around him, Davyn heard Nearra and Icefire as well. Nearra giggled and, uncontrollably, his jaw clenched.

"Really," Icefire continued as Davyn listened in, "you should have been there. Tu was so shocked that she drew her scimitar. Bem jumped when he saw that, and . . ."

Davyn let out an annoyed sigh. Hunching forward, he turned his gaze to the street before him. The drab buildings became a blur in the corners of his eyes.

Icefire shouldn't be an issue anymore, Davyn thought. He and Icefire had fought side by side. Icefire had more than proven his dedication to Nearra's quest and to teaching her how to handle her new magical abilities, even though it meant leaving his beloved ship behind. His aid meant that breaking the curse would go easier.

Only that was it, wasn't it? *Icefire* was helping her. Icefire, who bossed everyone around simply because he'd borrowed enough steel from some friend to buy a boat and now fancied himself a captain. Icefire, who, with a grin and a song, could make any simpering serving wench fall in love. Icefire, whose eyes flashed with an unsettling darkness every time he used magic or even touched a magic item.

Davyn kicked a stone out of his path and reveled in the sharp crack it made as it clattered against a brick wall. This elf had come into their lives out of nowhere and seemed to easily take his place.

It wasn't all Icefire's fault. When Davyn looked at Nearra now, all he often saw was the evil sorceress who had once controlled Nearra's every move. All he could think about was how he had failed to keep Nearra from becoming a slave in her own body, how she'd killed his blood-brother, Elidor.

No, he reminded himself. Nearra hadn't killed anyone. It had been Asvoria. *Asvoria.*

He could never be in love with Nearra, not now. Not with his guilt and the memories of recent events so fresh that he couldn't look at her without seeing the sorceress's face. She knew it as much as he did.

He still cared deeply for her, and he still felt compelled to help her and her family, even though doing so was keeping him from his aunt and cousins, whom he had only discovered existed a few months ago. They were Arktos people and lived in a valley in Icereach. Davyn had never known a real family before and thought he never would, after learning that Maddoc wasn't his real father and that both his parents were dead. He longed to return to Icereach, but he had a duty to complete this quest first.

But as much as he wanted to support Nearra, it also meant supporting Icefire. And the thought of helping the cocky elf was something Davyn could hardly stand.

Nearra laughed again, and Davyn ground his teeth in annoyance. He quickened his pace.

Forging a course north, they left the market and wound through alleys littered with refuse and infested with rats, rounding corner after corner until, finally, they reached their destination—the ruins of the old city.

After the Cataclysm, all life in Tarsis had moved south and west, where it resided still. But the northern sector of Tarsis had once been the hub of the city, prominent with mansions and schools. Davyn stopped as he reached the unofficial border between new city and old, and he took in the sight of the destruction.

The old city hadn't been rebuilt, not in the time since the Cataclysm, and certainly not since the recent war. The giant slabs of white stone that had once been the building blocks of vast homes had toppled onto one another in useless heaps. Thorny brown weeds thrust through the broken roads and clustered in the shade beneath the rubble, where they grew to overtake the stone and make it part of the untamed wild once more. All that still stood were half-broken walls that did little to stop the constant frosty winds that swept through the dead portion of Tarsis.

"We're here," Icefire said as he came to Davyn's side. Black hair wisped across the elf's high cheekbones as a faraway look crossed his face. "I never thought I'd get to see it. The Library of Khrystann."

Auburn hair laced with wild feathers flashed by Davyn's right. With his hoopak staff planted firmly between the rubble and fingering the shortsword at his side, Keene looked around eagerly. "The library? Where? I remember you talking about it, Captain, and it seemed so very interesting. Thousands of stories for hundreds of years, all in one place! Now, I was never much of a reader myself—books always seemed to take too long to get to the good stuff—but Bem told me once about these barbarians that made book covers out of human flesh, and I wondered, what would that feel like? I thought like leather, only maybe softer. Then I wondered—"

Snapping out of his thoughts, Icefire turned to look past Davyn. "I can't imagine there are many books made out of humans in there, but there's bound to be something interesting. My master once told me of ancient spells and . . . " He shook his head. "Never mind."

With a gentle hand on Jirah's shoulder, Nearra guided her sister forward to join the others. Pip trotted at their feet, his tongue lolling out as he looked up at Jirah eagerly.

Nearra took a deep breath. "We're finally here. Now we can

find the mine." She squeezed Jirah's shoulder and grinned. "We're getting closer. We'll have magic sooner than you know, just like you wanted."

Seemingly uncomfortable, Jirah shrugged out of Nearra's grip. "I don't see any library either. Where's that woman you talked about, Icefire? The 'es' something?"

"Aesthetic," a voice said from behind Davyn.

Spinning around, Davyn saw a short young woman dressed in muted tan robes approaching them from one of the darkened alleys. There was something distinctly mousy about the way she looked, with her brown hair pulled back and her pert nose quivering. A pair of round spectacles sat in front of wide brown eyes.

Arms held behind her back, the woman lifted her chin high. "Icefire," she said. "You're late."

Icefire flashed a grin and stepped forward to greet her. "Kayla, it's been too long. How's your mother?"

Kayla nodded curtly, though her expression didn't change. "We've been well, ever since you and your shipmates helped us out during the war. I am glad that you have finally taken me up on my offer to repay you, though I had hoped my favor would not have been something like sneaking you into the library."

Icefire shrugged. "You did say you'd do *anything* . . . "

The Aesthetic sighed and shook her head. A faint smile creased her lips. "That I did, Captain Icefire. That I did." Her wide eyes, magnified through her glasses, flitted between the companions, sizing them up. Her look lingered on Nearra, and her lips tightened.

"Hi, Kayla!" Keene said, bounding forward. "Remember me?"

"Of course." She didn't seem too pleased by the notion.

"Remember when that dragon whooshed by, and me and Bem, we—"

"Well, mustn't waste time," Kayla interrupted. She walked away from the group, speaking over her shoulder. "The library is empty at the moment. Our leader, Lillian Hallmark, she's of the opinion we should see the daylight every now and again lest we all turn into mole people, so most everyone is out today. I don't know when they'll be back, so we should hurry."

Icefire tilted his head. "No time to catch up further, then?"

Kayla gave Icefire a cool look. "There's always later. You can buy me a drink. Come on."

Her robes flowing behind her, Kayla strode purposefully on. Davyn was the first to follow, stepping over a granite slab that blocked the path.

"She seems . . . nice," Davyn heard Nearra whisper as the others trailed behind him.

Icefire chuckled. "Kayla can take herself much too seriously sometimes. But she's a good friend. She's risking a lot doing this for me."

They fell silent as they continued following Kayla around crumbling benches and collapsed arches bearing glorious carvings. The only sounds in the desolate surroundings were the continuous whooshing of the wind, the shuffling of their boots, and the clicking of Pip's claws against the stone.

They seemed to be heading toward a low building, the only unmarred spot in a field of destruction. The walls were recently mended, and weeds and debris had been cleared from its entryways. Though it seemed much too small to be the vast library Icefire had told them tales of, the sight of the two imposing Solamnic Knights guarding its doors erased any doubt Davyn might have had that this was their destination.

As the companions neared, the two knights stiffened and drew their weapons. Their broadswords glinted in the hazy gray light, sharp and deadly.

Kayla raised her hand as they approached. "Stand down."

The larger knight, whose bushy red mustache curled down past his chin, loomed forward. "At whose command?"

Kayla rolled her large eyes. "Mine, you dolt." She shoved past him, muttering, "Solamnics."

The knights sheathed their swords and stepped aside, though both looked disgruntled. Davyn started forward to follow the Aesthetic inside, then saw Icefire step aside to let Nearra and Jirah enter first. Grunting, he stopped to do the same.

The companions walked beneath the archway and into a plain room lit only by a single lamp. Tomes were piled high on a corner table, behind which an aging dwarf with a shiny, hairless head stood on a stool. Engrossed in his reading, he didn't seem to notice the visitors.

A breeze wafted up from a dark void ahead of them, bringing with it a smell of mold and must. Kayla stood at the open doorway, trying to spark a flint to light a small lamp, but the breeze kept blowing out any spark she managed to create.

"Blast it," she muttered as she tried again.

Icefire strode to her side. "May I?" With her nod of approval, he took the flint. In a moment, the lamp blazed with light.

"Thank you." Kayla smiled up at him before hardening her expression to regard the others. "Now, if you'll follow me."

"Weapons," the dwarf grunted. Not bothering to look up from his book, he kicked at a trunk next to his desk. The lid snapped open.

Kayla let out an impatient sigh. "Right, the weapons. We aren't supposed to have any instruments of destruction down below, especially not magical artifacts like that staff." She gestured toward the staff strapped to Nearra's pack.

"Of course," Icefire replied. He quickly removed his sword to lay it in the trunk. Raising an eyebrow, he nodded toward the ornate sword strapped to Davyn's waist

"Yes, of course," Davyn muttered. He, Jirah, and Keene quickly removed their swords and lay them with Icefire's, the kender placing his tall hoopak in as well. After a moment's hesitation, Nearra added her staff and pack to the pile in the trunk as well. With that done, the dwarf kicked the lid closed.

"Be quick, Kayla," the dwarf grunted, still not looking up. He flipped the page of his book. "I'm not going to take the blame if Lillian comes back and finds these people here."

"Don't worry your shiny little head," Kayla said. Gesturing toward the windy void, she turned to lead the way.

As the lamp's light permeated the darkness, they found that the void was in fact a narrow spiraling staircase that descended deep beneath the ground, off of which several locked doors led. Ahead of Davyn, Nearra clung to Icefire's side. Jirah walked behind them as Keene zipped back and forth between the stone walls, studying every crevice. Pip trotted at Davyn's side.

"The library is built mostly underground," Kayla explained as they descended lower. The sound of their boots echoed around them as shadows danced in the lamplight. "That's how so many volumes survived the Cataclysm and the recent war. In addition to protecting the library, we have been rewriting the manuscripts. Many are so old they crumble at the slightest touch. There is a reading room full of finished rewritings, which I will show you, but anything that hasn't been worked on yet, well, you'll need to ask me to read it for you. Stay out of restricted areas." She turned to regard Keene, who still bounced around them. "Especially you, Keene."

"Aww." Keene's face fell, but only for a moment. He caught sight of something green and slimy growing in a crack along the wall and went to examine it.

Hazy yellow light shone below, and soon the companions entered the main reading room. Icefire gasped, and Davyn had to agree with the sentiment. The vast room seemed endless, for the light from Kayla's lamp and from the few larger lamps set on the tables in the center of the room did little to chase away the shadows. Wooden bookshelves towered from dusty stone floor to cavernous ceiling, lined with thousands of books. Rickety ladders leaned against some shelves. Davyn saw a thick rope partitioning an area beyond the first few shelves and tables. No lamps were lit beyond the rope, and Davyn could only imagine how much farther back the stacks went.

Kayla led them to the closest table and gestured for them to sit. "Do you know what you are looking for?" Her voice echoed through the rafters high above.

"Yes," Nearra said as she sat in one of the creaking wooden chairs and smoothed her dress. "We need books on locations within the Plains of Dust, and about a wizard named Anselm who lived before the Cataclysm."

"Hmm, well," Kayla said as she rubbed her chin with her free hand and studied the stacks around them. "We have several volumes on the Plains. I'm not sure about this Anselm person, though. I didn't rewrite anything mentioning his name, but that doesn't mean we don't have any texts on him. I will—"

Thuds echoed down the stairs and all heads turned to look up into the darkness.

"Kayla!" the dwarf's voice echoed down the stairs. "We have some . . . visitors. Get up here!"

"It's always something," she muttered. She turned to face the companions. "Begin looking here. I will only be a few moments. Just don't go past the rope; those books cannot be touched."

A dog's bark echoed and they heard the piping tone of Keene's unmistakable voice. Only then did Davyn realize that the little kender had disappeared into the stacks.

"Keep Keene in check, Icefire," Kayla warned the elf with a stern glance. "You destroy anything and, well, the punishment won't be pleasant. Trust me." With that, she turned to scurry up the stairs.

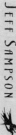

"Keene!" Icefire called. "Don't go past that rope!"

"Aw, but Icefire, I'm sure if there's a book made out of human skin it'd be in the forbidden area!" Keene's voice echoed, but from where, Davyn couldn't tell.

"Keene . . . " Icefire warned.

Keene didn't answer, and Icefire shook his head.

Nearra let out a quick breath. "Well," she said. "Where should we begin?"

Davyn turned to look up at the shelves surrounding them, his eyes first scanning past Jirah, who leaned against one of the shelves and looked at herself in her silver mirror. These books all seemed freshly bound, their leather covers dyed in greens or reds, in some color code they would never figure out. Icefire's little plan was starting to seem impossible.

Icefire himself seemed enraptured in a volume with an emblem of a dark circle overtaking a silver crescent on its spine. He approached the book and traced his finger over the shimmering symbol.

"Is that it?" Davyn asked, startling the tall elf from his thoughts. "Is that a book that'll help?"

Icefire shook his head. "I don't know."

With a sigh, Jirah stood. She glanced at her gilded mirror, then walked directly to a stack opposite Davyn and Icefire. From her chair, Nearra turned to watch her curiously.

Jirah ran a slender finger along the spines of the books on a shelf right above her head. "Look at the symbols on these books," she said. "They look like icicles, maybe? At least, they're about some-place cold. Maybe they could be about Icereach and maybe Anselm might be mentioned?"

With no other place to begin, they all converged on the shelf. One by one they pulled out volumes, scanning the text to see if there was anything of use. Nearra bit her lip as she scanned one particular book, then turned away from the others to study it further. She dropped the book heavily on the table, causing the lamp at the table's center to shake violently, as she sat down once more.

"Oh," she whispered as she scanned the scrawling text. "This is it." With a glint in her eyes, she looked up at her sister. "How did you know to start there?"

Jirah shrugged, then looked away. "Lucky guess."

Nearra clutched the book in her arms and stood. Davyn walked to stand behind her and look over her shoulder. As he did, he saw a shadow dart behind the front row of bookshelves. Keene.

"What does it say?" Icefire asked. He came to stand beside Jirah and looked over the table.

"It's all about Anselm," she said softly, her eyes flitting back and forth as she read. "It tells all about the curse. It says that Anselm and his wife were charged with finding three mystical weapons hidden on Krynn. They were supposed to bring them to the cave in what we now know as Icereach on the Day of Gratitude, which is supposed to be some sort of holy day. Then something would happen—I'm not too clear on this—and the weapons and the Trinistyr would be able to work together to help heal the Kingpriest of Istar."

"A holy day?" Icefire asked. He rubbed his chin thoughtfully. "That's the first we've heard of this."

Nearra nodded, not tearing her eyes away as she flipped through the pages. "I think this may have been written by a wizard Anselm knew. There's talk of the author being asked to make a map showing where to find the cursed wizards—our map! It also talks about how Kirilin posed as a cleric of Paladine to trick her way into Anselm's trust. How she . . . how she tortured him until he agreed to . . . to . . . " She shook her head and closed her eyes. "I'm going to have to read this further later. I'm sure it'll help us find the mine."

JEFF SAMPSON

"Sounds like a fascinating text," a voice whispered from the shadows. "Does it talk about the part of the tale where you *stole my beauty?*"

Davyn took in a breath and instinctively grabbed for the sword that wasn't at his side. He knew that hissing voice.

It was Kirilin. She had found them.

CHAPTER

4   Cleric's Vengeance

Kirilin stood between the stacks, shrouded in shadow. She clenched her hands, and her chest heaved.

Nearra dropped the book in surprise and stumbled backward into Davyn.

"Kirilin," Icefire said, spinning to face her.

"Yes," the dark cleric hissed. "Did you think you had seen the last of me?"

Kirilin stepped forward into the light, and Nearra gasped. The woman they had confronted before had been glamorous. Her features had seemed carved from marble, her body lithe, and her movements seductive.

Now, red robes covered a hunched body, and gray streaked what were once waves of molten blond hair. Her cheeks had sunk into her face, and blue veins spiderwebbed beneath the translucent flesh of her hands. Her thin, painted lips pulled tight into a sneer.

"You shouldn't be here, Kirilin," Icefire said. He grabbed Jirah from where she stood frozen and shoved her to stand beside Nearra. Nearra instinctively pulled her sister close.

"Oh, but I am," Kirilin said. "Do you see what your little friend has done to me by freeing the wizard in Icereach, Icefire? Do you see?!" Trembling, she lifted her hands and studied them in the dim lamplight. "My beauty . . . my life. Stolen!"

"As you stole it yourself!" Nearra shouted.

Kirilin pointed a gnarled finger at Nearra. "Don't you dare speak to me, *girl*. You do not know the powers you are messing with. You should have been dead back in the ice caves, and I will see to it that you do not leave this library alive."

Nearra trembled with rage, for Anselm and for her family. This woman was the cause of everything! Around her the stacks seemed to close in.

"You will not lay a finger on her," Davyn growled. He'd held Nearra from the moment they'd fallen against each other, and now he let her go to stand at Icefire's side. Jirah trembled, and Nearra pulled her in closer.

"You're right." Hatred flared in the cleric's green eyes. "I won't."

"No," Icefire said, realizing something Nearra didn't understand. His hand shot up to grab his earring as he fumbled with a pouch on his belt, probably to pull out some spell component.

It was too late. Kirilin was already casting her spell. As she mumbled prayers in a low voice, one hand clutched a silver medallion of faith that dangled from her neck.

The dark cleric raised her free hand toward the darkness above, and immediately, an oppressive weight seemed to press down on Nearra's chest. Her mouth opening and closing like a beached fish, she let go of Jirah and fell to her knees. Jirah fell as well, her fingers clawing at her throat as she gasped for air.

Davyn and Icefire fell under the crushing force too. Davyn shuddered, his hand spasming at his side as Icefire continued his attempt to cast a spell.

Pain seared Nearra's eyes. Her vision clouded, and her lungs ached to breathe.

"Hey, Kirilin," a tiny voice shouted from high above. "Is that your face, or are you wearing the head of a dead pig?"

Nearra could barely see Keene standing on top of one of the towering bookshelves. He held a stack of heavy books out in the air, right above Kirilin's head.

Without lowering her arm, the dark cleric stopped praying, tilted her head back, and scowled. "You stupid kender—"

Keene dropped the books.

The leather-bound tomes tumbled through the air like multi-colored bricks. Kirilin shrieked and raised her arms to shield herself, but it was too late. The books thudded against her skull with satisfying cracks, and the cleric slumped to the floor. Centuries-old dust swirled around her from the force of her fall.

"Ha *ha*!" Keene crowed from above. "Come on, Pip. Let's get closer." He disappeared back into the shadows.

The crushing force was lifted from the companions as Kirilin collapsed. Nearra gasped for air and clutched at her chest. "Jirah," she panted, reaching out to find her sister to see if she was all right. "Jirah . . . are you . . . "

"Yes." Hacking, Jirah grabbed Nearra's flailing hand.

Not wasting a minute, Davyn leaped to his feet. Gripping one of the wooden chairs in both hands, he stormed toward Kirilin, who arched her back as she tried to push herself up. Davyn brought the chair down, slamming it against her exposed back. Wood splintered and flew through the air as the aging cleric let out a shriek of agony and collapsed to the floor.

"Cleric . . . " Davyn wheezed as he tossed aside the remnants of the chair. "You . . . will not . . . hurt . . . Nearra."

"No," Icefire said, stumbling to his feet as he brushed himself off. "But they might."

Blinking, Nearra grabbed the edge of the table to pull herself up. That was when she saw them.

"Draconians," she gasped.

The baaz draconians—the same as they had faced in Icereach—stood the height of men, their limbs heavily muscled. Serpentine nostrils and razor-sharp teeth blended with human eyes to give them a grotesque half-dragon, half-man appearance. Leather and metal armor protected bodies covered in glinting bronze scales. Pairs of arcing wings jutted from their shoulders, and thick tails lashed out from the base of their backs. They descended the stairs in two rows, the edges of their swords and maces shining menacingly in the dim light.

"How did they get in here?" Davyn asked. "How could they have gotten into the city?"

"It is the will of Hiddukel!" Kirilin spat from where she lay on the floor.

"Davyn, grab her," Icefire commanded with a pointed finger. "Do not let her pray."

"What—"

Icefire didn't wait to hear what Davyn said. He raced past the table where Nearra stood, grabbing the lamp from its center as he did so. With a grunt, he threw the lamp at the nearest approaching draconian. Glass shattered against its metal breastplate, and flaming oil splashed into its eyes. The beast let out a guttural bellow and batted at its snout, backing into one of its companions as it did so.

"Nearra!" Icefire shouted, the word a command, not a warning. In one swift move the elf pulled a leather pouch off his belt and tossed it to her. She caught it and immediately recognized the feel of a small metal bar through the leather.

Nearra searched her mind for the spell Icefire had taught her for which an iron bar was used. Magic was still new to her. A twist of fate had given her some of Asvoria's power. The power was enough to cast spells despite her family curse—but only if she could remember the correct incantations, hand movements, and spell components.

Ah ha, she thought. Paralyze.

Icefire bounded up the stairs. One of the draconians leaped toward him, and the elf rolled away. Sharp talons slammed against the step where he'd stood only moments before.

Reaching inside the pouch, Nearra found the cool metal of the bar. Pointing it at the nearest draconian, she closed her eyes and imagined the beast as cold and as stiff as the bar she held.

"Mayat capik!"

Power stirred within Nearra's chest. She opened her eyes and saw the draconian freeze.

"Good job, Nearra!" Icefire called back, as though he wasn't weaving through three draconians at once. Flipping over one of the terrifying creature's outstretched arms, he landed in a roll across the dusty steps to the frozen draconian. On his feet without a stumble, he yanked the mace from its claws.

"Thank you, good sir," he said. Then he brought the weapon down in a killing blow.

Immediately the beast's skin began to harden. Leather and metal turned to stone as the draconian became a statue-like image of its former self. Icefire pulled the mace free just in time to keep it from being stuck in the stone, where it would have stayed until the beast crumbled into dust.

"We need our weapons!" Davyn shouted. He crouched at Kirilin's side, his strong hands clenching her wrists behind her back. The woman struggled, but she could not break free from his grip.

The fight had been long enough for the two draconians taken out by the lamp to get back to their feet and swarm toward Icefire. Their jaws opened in jagged, predatorial grins as they bared their claws, ready to tear Icefire's heart from his chest. Icefire backed down the stairs, holding the mace in both hands and meeting his opponents' gazes with just as much ferocity.

"You will never get past them," Kirilin hissed. "You will be slaughtered."

"Shut your mouth," Davyn said. He slammed her headfirst against the stone, knocking her unconscious, then got up and ran to Nearra's side. "Enough of this. Grab the table."

"Shouldn't we tie her up?" Jirah asked, her voice high-pitched. "We need to tie her up!"

"We don't have any rope, Jirah," Davyn shouted. "Grab the table!"

Nearra didn't hesitate. With Jirah at their side, Nearra and Davyn leaped behind the table. A single fat, round leg like the trunk of a tree supported the table at its center. Davyn hefted it onto his shoulder as they flipped the heavy wooden table onto its side.

"When I say," Davyn commanded, "push!"

Nearra and Jirah gripped the top edges of the table and tried to support their makeshift battering ram. Ahead of them, Icefire stumbled backward off the bottom step. The draconians closed in.

"Now!"

With Davyn bearing the table's weight, he, Nearra, and Jirah raced forward. The table wobbled, and they seemed to be going much too slow, but the sound of their scuffling feet across the floor was enough to grab Icefire's attention. Whirling around, he raced to get behind the table.

"Now why didn't I think of that?" he said with a grin as he helped Davyn support the table's giant leg. Davyn ignored him, his face contorted with the strain of holding the table's weight. He yelled a war cry, and Nearra could hear the pain in his call.

"Oh gods," Jirah said as they rapidly grew near the wall of draconians blocking the stairs. "Oh gods, oh gods!"

"Shove!" Davyn yelled.

The draconians roared and brought their weapons down as the

heavy table slammed into their leather and metal breastplates. An axe chopped into the table's edge, right near Nearra's head. Splintered wood flew past her face.

"Shove hard!" Davyn bellowed, and the companions pushed with all their might. The draconians fell back against the stairs as Davyn let out one more war cry and threw the heavy table on top of them. Jirah and Nearra leaped over the fallen draconians, with Davyn and Icefire right behind.

"Hey, wait for us!" a voice cried.

Icefire turned his head as he ran up the stairs, his black locks a tangled mess. "Keene!" he cried. "Grab the book!"

In the glow of the library, Keene grinned and saluted. "Aye, Captain!" Hefting up the brown tome from where it had fallen, he raced up the stairs with Pip at his side. They leaped over the draconians, even as the terrifying beasts started getting back to their feet. One lashed out with a clawed hand, but Keene deftly sidestepped the attempted blow. He and the little white dog were beside the other companions in moments.

Nearra raced up the stairs with her sister beside her. Her legs ached with the strain; her lungs blazed from Kirilin's dark spell and from the effort to climb the steep staircase. No one spoke as they bounded through the darkness. Sounds of the table being shoved aside and the draconians getting to their feet echoed below.

"Get them!" Kirilin had awoken, and her shrill, angry voice floated up from the darkness. "Kill them all!"

When they burst into the upper hall of the library, Nearra covered her mouth in shock. The front desk was overturned, and the bald dwarf lay unconscious or dead next to the trunk, sheaves of paper scattered around him. Kayla lay slumped in the corner, the pieces of her shattered spectacles in her lap.

"Oh no," Keene said. "We have to help Kayla!"

Tearing his eyes away from Kayla's fallen form, Icefire opened the trunk. "There's no time." He hefted Nearra's staff. "Good. Kirilin didn't spot the trunk." He tossed the staff to Nearra, and she caught it with both hands.

As quickly as possible, they gathered their weapons and Nearra's pack. From the staircase they heard claws on stone and guttural battle cries.

Not daring to take a second longer, the companions bounded out onto the library's front steps. The two Solamnic guards were nowhere in sight, but Nearra saw a smear of red marring the once white walls. She closed her eyes and gasped.

"Come on!" Davyn yelled. She felt his strong hand grab her own and pull her forward. Opening her eyes, she leaped over fallen blocks and between crumbling arches. Her pack thudded against her back, its straps biting into her shoulders, and the staff felt much too heavy. But she did not stop to think about the weight or the pain. She could sense the draconians behind them, and she imagined their swords biting into her flesh, their claws shredding her face. She ran.

Icefire was ahead, with Keene and Pip at his side. They wound past crumbling walls overgrown with vines, heading straight toward the nearest alleyway that led back to the living part of the city. Nearra couldn't see Jirah, but she could only hope her sister was keeping up.

And then, they were in the alley. Davyn still clutched Nearra's arm, dragging her. The dark brick walls became a blur as they splashed through murky puddles and piles of trash. The clacking and thudding of heavy clawed feet echoed behind them.

"No!" Jirah screamed. Nearra stopped immediately, wrenching her arm free of Davyn's grip. He didn't seem to notice the urgency in her movements and instead continued to follow Icefire and Keene.

Nearra spun around to see her sister sprawled on the street, covered in mud and scratched from her fall. Strands of black hair fell past her terrified eyes. She looked up at Nearra, pleading with her.

Behind Jirah, the shadow of a draconian loomed. It rounded the corner, walking slowly toward her. It held a battle-axe high, ready to bring it down and cleave Jirah's head from her shoulders.

"Get down!" Nearra shouted. Immediately Jirah dropped face-first into the muck of the alleyway, her grazed arms covering her head.

Nearra took a breath, then held the staff high. The crystal clutched in the carved dragon claw at its end glowed with blue and orange light.

"*Gedeng sihir*," she said, remembering the words Icefire had taught her. "*Api sihir*."

With a whoosh, the orb flared like a torch. Blue and gold fire swirled together, growing in power as it pulsed to the rapid beat of Nearra's heart.

The draconian grew closer. Its wide open jaws revealed yellow fangs. Its beady black eyes were on Jirah's neck as it raised its axe high.

"*Api anak!*" Nearra shouted.

With a roar like the sound of an avalanche, flames exploded from the end of the staff. Nearra screamed as she aimed the staff at the draconian's heart. Magic energy pulled from her gut and pulsed through the staff. Heat scorched her bare hands and dried her throat, sparks flew back and bit into her cheeks, but she did not let go.

The whirling tornado of flame soared above Jirah's cowering form and hit the draconian square in its chest. Howling in agony, the creature was consumed by the flames. Fire melted its armor and blackened its scales. In moments, the draconian turned into a statue covered in soot.

Feeling her energy completely sapped, Nearra stopped screaming. The flames stopped, and she collapsed.

The spell had been much larger than she had intended. She'd had no idea the staff could be so powerful. She lay there, gasping for air. Distantly she heard someone calling her name. But she was tired, so tired.

Strong arms gripped her shoulders to lift her up and guide her down the streets. Slowly she began to regain her senses, and she saw Jirah racing alongside her. Turning her head, she caught flashes of sandy-brown hair next to her face. Davyn was helping her move forward.

Another wave of exhaustion washed over her. Even as she realized they weren't safe yet, she couldn't help but close her eyes.

"It was so powerful," she whispered.

Then she collapsed into Davyn's arms.

CHAPTER

5   Cornered and Captured

The door to the inn flung open. The startled barkeep stopped washing the counter as Icefire raced in.

"Come on!" the elf urged. Behind him Jirah flew into the fire-lit room, clutching the leather-bound book they'd stolen from the library against her chest. Keene bounded in behind her, a look of excitement on his face even as he almost ran into one of the tables. Pip barked as he, too, followed.

Davyn came last. He carried Nearra in both arms, the girl's head slack and draped over his broad shoulder. She clenched the staff of fire against her chest even though she was unconscious, and her pack hung awkwardly from her back. The weight seemed too much for Davyn to carry, and indeed, veins bulged on his forehead with the strain, but he didn't seem to care.

Icefire scanned the inn's nearly empty common room, frantic. Three wiry men in a shadowy alcove studied them warily, while two young elf maidens, obviously nobles judging by the fine gowns they wore, watched the scene with disgust.

"Jirah, come on." Davyn's voice sounded strained as he shoved past Icefire and headed toward the stairs. The black-haired girl followed him up the steps.

"You!" Icefire said. He raced toward the barkeep and slammed his hands on the counter. "Bezzil, right?"

The barkeep furrowed his brow. His fleshy biceps bulging, he dipped his new rag into a bucket of soapy water and wrung it out. "Yep," he said. "Ain't you the elf that lost my rag?"

"It's not lost!" Keene piped up. He leaned his hoopak against the bar and leaped upon one of the barstools, placing his hands atop the counter in a mimic of Icefire. Beneath him, Pip stood on his hind legs and yapped urgently.

"I actually just pocketed the rag and pulled out some fake flowers I already had hidden up my sleeve. You can have it back now." The kender reached inside his vest, and a look of confusion came over him. Pulling out his hand, he revealed a tarnished metal doorknob. "Huh," he said. "How'd that get there? I know I have that rag here somewhere."

"Keene, now's not the time," Icefire warned. Knowing he must look frantic, he leaned closer to the barkeep. "I have a friend upstairs. She's hurt and I'm going to need Avina to bring up some boiling water to our room. Someone may come here asking for us. She'll look stately and old, and she's wearing red robes. If so, *we are not here.*"

The fleshy barkeep nodded, finally sensing the urgency in Icefire's tone. "You're not here. Got it."

Not wasting a second more, Icefire spun from the bar and raced toward the stairs, Keene and Pip right behind.

"Do you think Kirilin will follow us here?" Keene asked as they thudded up the steps, hoopak now back in hand. "There are knights everywhere. They wouldn't let her get five steps with those big draconians, would they?"

"I don't know, Keene," Icefire said. Skidding as he reached the second floor, he made a sharp turn down the hallway. "She wouldn't be stupid enough to attack us in the streets. But she did manage to get herself and those draconians into the city, so we're not safe here. We need to get Nearra well and get out of Tarsis."

Icefire, Keene, and Pip raced past open doors in the narrow, dim hallway. Icefire caught flashes of men and women talking and laughing and brushing their hair, oblivious to the imminent danger he and his companions faced.

"Why do you suppose Kirilin looked so *old?*" Keene asked. "I was hardly lying when I said her face looked like a dead pig. Isn't she the Stealer of Souls? Couldn't she just steal a soul and make herself young again?"

"She steals souls for Hiddukel," Icefire said. "She can't do it for herself. No, if we can break the curse, she'll be done for."

Finally they reached Nearra's room. Bounding inside, they found Davyn and Jirah leaning over the girl on her bed. She seemed almost peaceful as the hazy daylight from the single window shimmered over her skin. Pip leaped onto Nearra's chest to lick her face.

Gasping, Icefire stopped and put his hands on his knees. "What happened?" he asked. "Did one of the draconians get her? Did Kirilin cast a spell?"

Fierce and sudden, Davyn rounded on Icefire, his eyes accusing. "No," he spat. "She used a spell—a spell *you* taught her. It knocked her out."

"Davyn, it wasn't like that," Jirah muttered. She hugged the book even tighter, smearing mud from her fall on its cover. "She was saving me."

"Doesn't matter," Davyn said, his eyes not leaving Icefire's own. "If I hadn't been there to carry her to safety, then the draconians or Kirilin could have caught up. Then what would have happened?"

"Looks like she knew how to take care of herself," Icefire shot back, his tone just as stern. Shoving past Davyn, he went to kneel at Nearra's side. Gently he rubbed her hand between his fingers, his other hand reaching up to clutch at the gold hoop earring dangling from his right ear. Comprehension flashed in his mind and he sighed with relief. "She must have overdone the spell. It wore her out, but she'll be fine."

"We don't have much time," Davyn growled. "Kirilin will be on us at any moment."

"I'm taking care of it, Davyn," Icefire said with a dismissive wave of his hand. "Start gathering our things. We need to head out, fast."

"I won't leave her!"

The elf surged to his feet. Seeming to tower above the human boy, he moved to stand chest to chest with him. "What do you plan to do, Davyn? Heal her? How is being at her side going to help her if you can't do anything?"

His chest heaving, Davyn did not step back. His brow was furrowed in anger as his brown eyes scanned Icefire's own.

Without saying a word, he turned and walked out the door, his boots thudding heavily against the wooden floor.

Shaking his head, Icefire turned to kneel by Nearra. Jirah stood above him, her hands clenched so tightly as she gripped the book that her knuckles were white. "Can you really do something?" she asked.

"Yes," Icefire said. "But you can't. Go help Davyn get our things."

Jirah did as she was told, scurrying into the hall. Pip barked and raced after her, and Keene made to follow.

"Keene," Icefire said, clutching at his arm as he passed. "In my room, in my pack, there's a pouch filled with bluish green herbs. Get them for me."

The kender beamed and put his hand up in salute. "Aye aye!" As he raced into the hall he almost ran right into Avina. She swished out of the way, holding a pot of steaming water above her head. Heavy drops sloshed to the floor with the quick motion.

"Whoa there," the serving girl said with a grin.

"Sorry, Avina!" Keene cried as he disappeared into a room across the hall. "No time to chat. Icefire needs his herbs!"

With a shake of her head, the curly haired girl lowered the pot and turned to Icefire. As her eyes found Nearra, her smile fell.

"Oh, your friend," she said. Setting the pot on a low table near the door, she lifted the hem of her skirt and knelt beside Icefire. "Is she all right?"

"Yes," Icefire said. "She'll be fine. Thank you for hurrying with the water. It was very kind of you."

A blush spread over her cheeks and the girl ducked her head. Curls of black hair fell in front of her face. "Oh, it wasn't anything." Her hands fiddled with her skirt nervously. "I told my boss about your singing and Keene's jokes. She said if you could pack the house full for dinner, then she'd consider letting you all stay free of charge. I told her—"

Icefire wiped his sweaty forehead with the back of his hand and grinned. "Thank you, Avina. But I'm afraid we'll have to pay this time. We're going to have to leave in a hurry."

The serving girl's mouth opened and closed several times, as though she meant to speak but couldn't remember how. Finally, she said, "All right. I'll . . . I'll just let her know." Her eyes seemed to keep glancing back and forth between Nearra's limp form and the window. Her dress rustling, she got to her feet and ducked her head. "Do you . . . do you need anything else?"

Icefire nodded. "Clean cloth would be good."

Avina smiled and bobbed her head. "Right away."

She spun and sped out of the room, right past Keene.

"Hello again, Avina!" he called over his shoulder. Without turning around, she held up a hand in greeting before heading down the hallway. "And, well, good-bye again." With a shrug, Keene jumped to Icefire's side.

"Is that the right stuff?" Keene asked as he handed Icefire a small pouch.

Icefire tilted the pouch and shook some of the tiny turquoise leaves onto his palm. "It is," he said. "Perfect."

With one last reassuring rub of Nearra's hand, Icefire let her arm fall back to the blankets and turned to the pot of boiling water. He was just starting to sift the herbs into the water when a shadow fell over him from the doorway. Out of the corner of his eye he caught a flash of curly black hair.

"That was fast," he said with a grin. He tilted his head to look up. "You—"

Her face pale with fright, Avina trembled in the doorway. Only then did Icefire see the cloaked figure standing behind the serving girl. Only then did he see the shimmering steel of a dagger pressed against the girl's slender throat.

Shoving her from behind, the figure forced Avina into the room. "Shut the door," the figure hissed. Icefire immediately recognized the voice.

"Kirilin."

"Shut the door!"

Calmly, Icefire stepped behind Kirilin and Avina to do as commanded. The cleric turned the serving girl, keeping an eye on Icefire.

"Lock it."

Trying to control his breathing, Icefire did as he was told. He caught Keene's startled eyes as he did so. The kender seemed ready to leap forward and attack Kirilin, but Icefire slowly shook his head, warning him to stay back.

Holding his hands high to show he didn't intend to hurt her, Icefire sidestepped through the room to position himself between Kirilin and Nearra. The blond girl rustled in the bed, muttering something under her breath. The motion was enough to reveal just a glimpse of a shimmering gem cut into the shape of a key hanging about Nearra's neck.

"Oh, Icefire," Kirilin said, her tone singsong. "Dear, dear Icefire. I should have known better than to try a frontal assault. I had no idea your friends would prove so . . . inventive without any weapons." In the shadows of the hood, Icefire saw a glimmer of white as Kirilin smiled.

"I-Icefire," Avina whispered, wide-eyed. Her black curls shuddered as her whole body trembled in fear. Kirilin clutched the serving girl tighter, pressing the dagger's edge harder against her throat.

Icefire took a tentative step forward, his hands still raised. "Let her go," he said. "She's just an innocent bystander. She has nothing to do with this."

Kirilin let out a bark of laughter. Muttering words Icefire couldn't understand, the cloaked cleric gently let go of the dagger and stepped away from Avina. Only now, a sickly green light seemed to glow around the serving girl. The dagger stayed suspended in the air against her throat. Avina let out a sob as tears began to form in her eyes.

"That's cheating!" Keene cried. Narrowing his eyes, he made to leap forward. "You wretched hag, I ought to—"

Icefire's hand shot to the side, clutching Keene's shoulder. Without looking down at his little friend, Icefire once again shook his head.

Kirilin raised her wrinkled hands and removed the hood of her cloak. Her now hideous face was pulled tight into a mimic of a smile. Drying blood marred her gray and blond hair.

"'Innocent bystander'?" Kirilin said as she strode past Avina to stand before Icefire. "Oh, Icefire, you naïve young elf. There are no innocents in this world. Everyone is just waiting for the right person to come along and offer them the best price for their soul."

She brushed his cheek with the back of her blue-veined hand.

In a flash, she gripped the back of his head, her sharp nails biting into his scalp. Her false smile shifted into a sneer. "I'm still not quite sure what yours is."

Icefire did not give her the pleasure of reacting. Instead he kept his eyes locked calmly on her own, trying very hard not to glance at Keene and alert her to the kender, who was now tiptoeing toward the door.

"I won't give you the key, Kirilin," Icefire said. "I won't let you keep us from breaking this curse. No matter what you think you know, I do not have a price."

Kirilin leaned close, tilting her head back to whisper in his ear. A faint stench of decay masked by flowery perfume met his nose, and he tried not to gag.

"You promised me a song," she whispered. Her voice was still velvety and alluring. Age had not changed *that*. "You promised me your soul. Instead you seduced me and stole the key to my eternal life. But I know what's deep inside you. The darkness blazes inside you like a beacon. Be mine, Icefire. Be mine and maybe I'll let your friends live."

His jaw clenched, Icefire looked over Kirilin's head. He saw Keene tiptoeing toward the pot of boiling water near the door. He saw Avina, still frightened as the blade hovered, ready to cut her jugular.

"Never," he whispered.

"But can't you taste how wonderful it would be?" Kirilin leaned in closer, her withered flesh brushing against his arm, her sagging chest pressed against his. He could feel her heartbeat, steady and calculating. She let go of his hair, her fingers tracing a line from his cheek to his pressed lips.

"*Taste it*," she cooed.

Shadowy magic burst from her fingertips, shrouding his vision.

Tendrils of dark magic slithered into his nostrils, his eyes, his pores. Icefire gasped as it flowed inside him. The immense power of it was more intoxicating than the finest glass of wine he'd ever tasted, and the magic's voice called out to him in deep, melodic baritones.

Heavy footsteps and the clink of armor reverberated through the walls. Icefire dimly heard an authoritarian voice calling through the halls. The door handle jiggled, and then someone pounded.

"Open up! Sir Astin uth Hargoth demands the kender Keene be turned over at once!"

"Huh?" Keene said.

Icefire couldn't respond. "Give in," Kirilin whispered in his ear, her tone suddenly urgent. "You must know you have no choice. You were born a dark elf."

The pounding at the door grew louder, and he realized someone was trying to kick the door in.

"Icefire!" Keene cried.

Kirilin shrieked. She flailed away from Icefire, taking her dark power with her. Gasping for air and blinking to clear his vision, Icefire fell back against the bed—and Nearra. She stirred as his hand brushed her leg.

Keene stood proudly, holding what had once been the pot full of boiling water. Drenched, Kirilin clutched at the wall, shuddering with rage. Distracted from her dark magic, the cleric's hold on Avina fell. The dagger clattered to the floor.

Immediately the serving girl reached up to rub her throat. Tears streaming down her face, she spun and fumbled to open the door.

"We demand the kender be handed over to us!" the knight's voice called. The door shuddered as once again someone tried to kick it in.

"They're in here!" Avina cried, her voice hoarse. "The kender and the . . . the dark elf, they're in here!"

"No!" Kirilin screeched. Consumed by her rage, the cleric pushed herself off the wall. Muted cloak and red robes flowing behind her, she jumped at Nearra's unconscious form, her hand clutching for the key hanging around the girl's neck.

Just as Avina got the door open, Icefire tackled Kirilin, and the two of them fell to the floor. Her sharp nails scratched at his face as she fought to free herself.

"Hey!" a deep voice cried. "What's going on?"

A strong hand gripped Icefire's shoulder, pulling him off Kirilin. The person who'd grabbed him shoved himself between the elf and the cleric, holding the two of them apart.

The knight, in full plate armor, looked over his shoulder at Avina with his judgmental blue eyes. The girl trembled in the doorway as Keene stood beside her, watching the scene with excitement.

"What's going on here?" the knight demanded.

Avina opened her mouth, ready to speak. Instead, seeing something the knight didn't, she screamed, turned, and ran out the door. Green light flared, and the knight stumbled backward.

Her hands clenched with fury, Kirilin climbed to her feet. Divine magic blazed around her fingertips. "Don't you dare touch me," she seethed. "I am a cleric! I am a noble!" Pulling her medallion of faith free from beneath her cloak, she raised her free hand and aimed it toward the knight. "And I will not let some know-it-all Solamnic ruin my plans!"

Icefire's fist flew. It met the side of Kirilin's head with a sick thud. She spun from the force of the blow, landing headfirst against the wall. Unconscious once more, she fell in a heap.

Icefire let himself collapse back once again onto the bed next to Nearra. His eyes drifted from Kirilin's fallen form to Keene in the doorway, and then to the Solamnic Knight.

WIZARD'S BETRAYAL

67

"What in Paladine's name is going on!" the knight roared. He ripped off his helmet and stood to his full height, revealing furrowed, bushy eyebrows. He was younger than Icefire had expected.

"Well," Keene said, stepping forward. "It's a long story. It started back when we met Jirah, Nearra, and Davyn in an inn. Or did it begin when Icefire made a deal with Janeesa? Or maybe when—"

"You," the knight said. His polished steel armor shimmered in the window's light as he tore his attention from Icefire and Kirilin. "Are you Keene Waverider?"

Keene blinked his wide eyes and tilted his head. "I am. Why?"

More footsteps sounded from the hallway, and Icefire looked past Keene to see Jirah and Davyn run up to the door, concern in their eyes. Davyn opened his mouth to speak, but he didn't get a chance. Another knight, this one without a helmet, shoved between the two. Icefire recognized the gray-flecked hair and the much-too-serious gaze right away. It was the knight from earlier that day.

"Astin," the young knight said with a bow of his head. "I found the kender." Tilting his head over his shoulder, he gestured toward Kirilin. "And I got attacked by that wench of a cleric at the same time."

The older knight, Astin, nodded. His gaze stern, he strode past Davyn, Keene, and Jirah to stand in front of Icefire. "Remember me?" he asked.

Icefire nodded. "Of course."

The knight nodded. "There was a skirmish at the Library of Khrystann. Two of my knights are unconscious in an infirmary. So are two Aesthetics."

Icefire tensed. He'd almost forgotten about Kayla. "The Aesthetics? Are they all right?"

"They're alive." Sir Astin began to pace back and forth. "But one of them, the woman, she was muttering something about a kender.

Muttering something about keeping a kender named Keene away from the books."

Icefire leaped up from the bed. "Sir—"

The knight raised his hand to stop him and shook his head. Behind him Icefire saw Davyn take in the scene with an unreadable expression while Jirah bit her lip.

"I warned you, elf," Sir Astin went on. "I warned you to keep your kender out of trouble. Now we have a half-destroyed library and several people hurt. I suspect you and your friends were there too, but I have no proof. So you four get to be thrown out of the gates. The kender, however, is going to be held here until we get everything straightened out."

"No!" Jirah cried. She looked on the verge of tears.

Keene nearly knocked over the table and the now empty pot in his anxiousness to explain his side of the story. He popped up, right in front of the knight, his eyes wide. "But see, it wasn't my fault!" he said. "That woman there, she's an evil cleric named Kirilin. She brought some draconians and *she's* the one who destroyed everything."

"So you *were* there?"

Keene shrugged. "Well, yes, of course I was."

Astin turned and nodded toward the younger knight. Returning the curt nod, the young knight grabbed Keene about the shoulders.

"No!" Jirah cried again. Dropping her pack, she shoved herself between the knights to stand by Icefire's side. "Icefire, do something! We can't let them take him!"

Icefire looked past the knights to find that Davyn had crept into the room as well and was leaning back against the wall. His expression hadn't changed.

For a moment, Icefire hesitated. Keene was his shipmate and old friend. But an idea popped into his head, one he figured Davyn was thinking of as well. Kirilin had attacked a Solamnic Knight. The knights would certainly be arrogant enough to think that brick and bars would hold the cleric too. Of course she'd escape, but it would take time—time that the companions could use to get to the second wizard and free her. Otherwise, she'd never stop. She'd come at them until they were all lying dead at her feet.

If they put up a fight to save Keene, then they'd probably get taken too. And then everything would be lost.

"You're taking the cleric too, I imagine?" Icefire said after a moment.

Sir Astin nodded. "Of course."

The elf took in a breath and tried to ignore the pleading look in Jirah's eyes. He lowered his head, unable to look at her.

"We'll come back for you, Keene," he said. "Don't worry. We'll come back."

Unable to speak, Jirah stepped backward and sat down on the bed beside a still unconscious Nearra. "We can't . . ." she started. "We can't just leave him."

Keene's face fell. "I don't get to go with you to the mine? But we've come so far!"

Icefire didn't bother explaining himself as he stepped away from the knights. He couldn't risk Kirilin hearing something, even though she appeared well knocked out. Glancing to the side, for a moment, he caught Davyn's eye. Still the human boy's look told Icefire nothing.

"Escort us to the gates, good knights," Icefire said. "We don't want to cause anymore trouble than we already have."

Jirah started to cry in frustration as the young knight led Keene out the door. Pip popped up beside them as they trotted down the hallway, following the kender as always. "Don't worry, Jirah!" Keene called as he disappeared from view. "I'll be here when you get back!"

Icefire waited silently at Nearra's side as Sir Astin called more knights upstairs to haul off Kirilin's unconscious form. He ignored Jirah's and Davyn's looks as he gathered his belongings. He tried very hard to hide how much all Kirilin had said and done had affected him.

Then, with Nearra in their arms and without Pip or one of their friends, Icefire, Davyn, and Jirah followed the knights to the southern gates to be cast out of Tarsis and onto the untamed plains.

CHAPTER

6   CLIPPED WINGS

I cy, bitter wind bit at Nearra's cheeks. She was sitting on something hard and cold, and she was leaning against a wall. Slowly coming back from the darkness, she opened her eyes.

"Icefire?" she whispered. Louder, she called out again. "Icefire?"

"I'm here." His voice was warm and comforting, and Nearra looked up to find him standing above her. "How're you feeling?"

A dull throb pounded in the back of Nearra's head, but she could sense it fading. "I'm . . . I'm fine, I think. What happened?"

"Here." Icefire put his arm under hers and helped her stand.

It was twilight, and the last rays of the sun cast long shadows across the rocky, desolate plains. In the distance, jagged cliffs jutted toward the sky.

Behind them was the twenty-foot fortified wall that closed off access to the city of Tarsis. Two towering wooden doors were closed, guarded on either side by round towers that thrust up into the sky ten times a man's height. Fires blazed on braziers above the doors, and Nearra could see the shadows of soldiers keeping watch atop the towers.

"We're outside the city," Nearra said. Shivering, she hugged herself.

"That we are." Icefire pulled her close. Body heat flowed from his chest into her arms, and her heart fluttered. She couldn't help but smile as she curled into his embrace.

"The knights didn't take too kindly to what happened at the library," he went on as he led her along a rocky path away from the wall. "Just as the one at the inn promised, we've been thrown out of the gates."

"Oh no," Nearra whispered. Then, with a start, she clutched at her back, trying to find something that wasn't there.

"The staff," she said. "And my pack. They're gone."

"Don't worry," Icefire said. "Davyn's keeping them safe."

Davyn. Cold seeped beneath Nearra's cloak, snapping her fully awake. She remembered everything clearly now—the chase from the library, blasting the draconian with the staff, Davyn carrying her to safety.

Nearra clutched at Icefire's side, her teeth chattering. With the endless and massive wall to their right, they climbed over piles of sharp stone and past the black hull of some unlucky ship that had long ago sunk near here. Ancient crusted barnacles clutched at the fossilized wood.

In the orange light of a torch in the distance, she saw Davyn and Jirah. "Where's Keene?" Nearra asked. "And Pip?"

Icefire scowled. "The knights put Keene in a cell. Pip followed him, as always. But don't worry, we'll go back for them." He looked up at the ancient, impenetrable wall. "Somehow."

"What?" Nearra asked. She pulled away from Icefire's grasp, determined to rush back toward the gates. "We can't just leave them! What if Kirilin finds them? She could use them to get at us. We have to go back."

"Nearra, we can't," Icefire said. Gently he gripped Nearra's shoulder and pulled her to face him. "We can't get back in, for one. More importantly, before throwing us out, the knights took

Kirilin too. They locked her up, and though I don't believe for a second that stone and mortar will hold her for long, we have to take advantage of this. We need to get to the mine as fast as possible before she gets free and gets there first."

Swallowing, Nearra lowered her head. Her mind raced, unsure of what to do.

The thought of leaving behind poor Keene and Pip troubled her deeply, and every instinct she had told her that it was best to get them. But she barely even knew how to handle herself, let alone lead a whole group of people. Icefire had more experience, as did Davyn. It was her quest, these trials to free the wizards and end the curse, but she still felt unsure that she was even able to do it. Davyn certainly didn't seem to think so.

Icefire studied her with his lovely blue eyes. "Nearra, I'm not your leader, remember. We can find a way to go back if you feel we should."

Warmth filled Nearra even as the icy winds lashed against her chest. Icefire believed in her. He'd always believed in her. That had to mean something.

But she still wasn't sure she knew the right choice to make.

With a sigh, Nearra rubbed her forehead. The remnants of the headache were still there. "No, you're probably right. Keene . . . Keene will be fine. We have to get to the mine before Kirilin escapes, and I need to free the second wizard."

Concern clouded Icefire's face as she continued to massage her temples. "Are you sure you're all right? I was going to make you a medicine, but I didn't get a chance."

Nearra stumbled slightly as they jumped down to a lower rocky ledge. Icefire caught her arm as she steadied herself. "It's nothing, really," she said as he once again pulled her close. "Just, that spell I did with the staff. I think I overdid it." She shook her head. "I wish we had more time to train so I could do this right. What good am I if I overuse Asvoria's power and pass out?"

His arm around her, Icefire rubbed her shoulder. He looked up at the lavender sky, where the first glimpses of stars were appearing. "You're being too hard on yourself," he said. "I see it in you, Nearra. One day you will be a great white-robed wizard. It's no wonder that you are destined to break your family's curse. But you're still learning. Magic takes time. Very few mages in this world are even capable of casting a spell as powerful as the one you did, even if it perhaps was a bit overboard for the situation."

"We'll have to study more, then," Nearra said, lifting her chin high. "Because I don't intend to be carried around like a sack of grain after the next time we fight."

Icefire let out a laugh. "Aye aye, Nearra."

With another step down, they finally drew close to Davyn and Jirah. Both were wearing heavy cloaks made of some sort of animal fur, and at their feet were sacks bulging with the new supplies Davyn had purchased earlier in the day.

"Nearra!" Jirah called as they drew near. Hands kneading against one another, she rushed toward her sister. "Nearra, they took Keene and Pip! We have to go back! We can't just leave them there."

Behind her, Davyn shook his head. "Nearra, don't listen to her. There's no time. We have to be on our way. Kirilin—"

"I know, Davyn," Nearra interrupted. "Icefire told me what happened."

In the shadows dancing across his face, Nearra saw Davyn scowl. Guilt wormed its way through her, and she pulled away from Icefire. The elf gave her an inquisitive look, but he let her go.

Jirah's lip quivered as she glared back at Davyn. "I don't care about Kirilin," she said. "I don't care! Our friends are in a filthy prison, and none of you seem to care at all!"

"I care." Nearra gently rubbed her sister's arm. "I wanted to go back too. But I talked to Icefire about it, and I think he and Davyn may be right. We have to move as quickly as possible or Kirilin could kill us all."

Jirah looked down and said nothing. She seemed to be trembling.

"We should find a place to rest until morning," Icefire said, rubbing his earring gently. "Kirilin's likely exhausted herself with all she did today, so we need to take advantage of this time and rest."

"Yes," Nearra said, her eyes on Jirah's trembling form. "We'll also need time to study that book we got from the library before we head anywhere."

"Fine." Speaking between clenched teeth, Jirah met her sister's eyes. "Whatever you say."

Clearing his throat, Davyn stepped forward. "We went to the ships on the western edge of the city," he said. "I've been trading with a merchant there. He's a bit rough, but he could probably take us in for the night as long as we pay."

Icefire shrugged, then knelt to dig through the sacks. "Fine. Couldn't hurt. Here, you should put this on." He thrust a fur cloak toward Nearra, and she grabbed it.

As Icefire put on his own cloak and everyone began gathering their things, Davyn came to Nearra's side. In his hands he held the staff of fire.

"You should probably take this," he said, his voice quiet. "I saw what you did to save Jirah back there. You've been learning a lot." The way he said it, Nearra couldn't tell if he thought her newfound knowledge was a good thing or not.

"Yes," Nearra said. She took the staff, her eyes drawn to the sparkling crystal orb clutched in the carved dragon talons at its end.

"Thank you for keeping it safe," she whispered.

Davyn grunted in acknowledgment, then turned away. With a sigh, Nearra looked down and fingered the carvings of the staff.

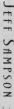

With everyone ready, Davyn led the way with the wall to their right. They seemed to be walking into a valley, Nearra realized. The farther forward they went, the more the makeshift path sloped down. Half-eroded aquatic bones were scattered among the stone as they left higher ground.

Darkness smothered them as night fully fell. The only light was from the torch Icefire held behind her—he was in the rear, so as to not ruin Davyn's night vision—and from the occasional flaming braziers along the wall and its guard towers. Stars twinkled above them in the formations of the gods' constellations, though the slivers that were the red and silver moons were shrouded by drifting clouds.

Then, as they rounded the westernmost tower and headed deeper down the incline, Nearra saw flares of firelight. Orange flame flickered from windows, and Nearra could barely make out the odd shapes of dozens of small buildings. They seemed to be oblong and rounded, ending in sharp points. In fact, they appeared very much to be like ships lying on their sides.

"The white-winged ships," she whispered.

Icefire came up beside her and nodded. "There they are. The famed Tarsian fleet itself." A sad, faraway look came to his eyes. "They must have been glorious once, riding the waves with sails of pure white. I can only hope their captains died with the Cataclysm, for seeing their ladies battered and useless like *that*." He thrust his free hand toward the ships. "Aye, it'd kill a man, it would. A ship without the sea is like a bird without the sky, or a deer without the forest."

Or, Nearra thought, like a boy without a family. Her eyes flickered past Jirah to watch Davyn in the front. He'd seemed so alone lately, so very distant from the other companions. He hadn't been this way in Icereach, where he'd found remnants of his family. But he'd still come with her, despite everything.

She longed to reassure him, to take away his pain. But she wasn't sure she was even capable of doing so anymore, or if he would even allow it.

She shook her head, trying to keep her mind on her conversation with Icefire. "It's all very sad," she whispered. "It all could have been stopped, if only Anselm . . . " Looking at the staff in her hand, she sighed.

"What's past is passed," Icefire said. Slowing his gait, he took the rear again, and they walked on in silence.

Their forward march took them from the stony incline to, inexplicably, silty sand. The frozen grains shifted beneath their feet, making it harder to walk. Above them now, beginning where the fortified wall ended, was a seawall that enclosed what had long ago been a seaport. Crumbling docks jutted above their heads, beyond which lay the old marketplace.

The white-winged ships lay haphazardly on their sides in the sand, mostly near the ancient seawall. Farther north, Nearra could see dozens and dozens more ships, though little light flickered from their depths.

As the companions neared the ships, Nearra sensed people watching them from behind the broken slats, whispering suspiciously. Down here, a constant wind blew, and the few tattered sails that still existed fluttered constantly.

The air stank of filth, as though unwashed animals lived here, and not people. Makeshift signs hung from some of the hulls, and in the distance, Nearra heard a dog bark. She caught a glimpse of a rail-thin man watching her, his beard tangled and clothes ragged. It seemed only the poorest of Tarsis's residents lived here in the Lower City.

Davyn led them between the broken hulls to a smaller ship with a hanging sign that read in Common, "Supplies for Cheap." What had once been a hatch that led to the lower levels of the ship was

JEFF SAMPSON

now the main door. Behind a square-shaped hole cut into what was long ago the ship's deck, Nearra caught sight of lamplight and the shadow of someone moving about.

Davyn knocked on the door. Immediately the shadow stopped moving.

His eyes narrowed, Davyn knocked again. "Hello? Arkenon? It's Davyn. I was here a few hours ago. We traded for some gear."

No answer.

Davyn pounded again. "Ark, your light is on. I know you're in there."

From deep inside, a gruff male voice called out. "All sales are final!"

Davyn rolled his eyes. "Ark, we're just looking for a place to spend the night. I have steel. We can pay."

The hatch opened just a crack, and Nearra could barely make out someone's shadowy head. Shaggy dark hair fluttered in the wind. "Steel, you say? How much do you have?"

"How much do you want?" Davyn asked.

"How much do you have?" the merchant asked again.

Again Davyn rolled his eyes. "I can part with—"

Icefire stepped forward. "How about we haggle about this *inside*?" He raised an eyebrow and looked at the shadowy face.

The merchant laughed. "As long as you pay, sounds fine to me."

The sign shuddered above Davyn's head as the door opened all the way and the merchant stepped out. At first Nearra thought he was just unusually tall and his torso much too long. Then he stepped all the way into sparse moonlight and she saw that he was, in fact, a centaur.

Nearra had ever met only one centaur in her life. They weren't exactly common back near her home in Solamnia. But that centaur—a girl named Ayanti who had been a friend of Davyn's—was small, well-groomed, and carried herself with a gentle regality. This centaur was the exact opposite.

He towered above them, his equine hindquarters taut with muscle. The dark brown hair of his horse-like body was shaggy, and knots tangled his black tail, the remnants of old braids.

His biceps bulging, the centaur crossed his arms in front of a massive bare chest that jutted up from where a horse's head would usually be. His face was square and chiseled, and he smiled a cocky grin. Long, shaggy black hair fluttered about his shoulders. Most unusual of all were the jagged scars crossing from his forehead down beneath a black eye patch that covered his left eye.

For a moment, everyone except Davyn stared.

"Wow," Jirah whispered.

Davyn rolled his eyes. "Can we come in?" he grunted. He held up a little leather pouch and shook it. Steel coins clinked against one another.

Smiling sociably, the centaur stepped aside to reveal the cozy, well-lit interior of the ship. "Ladies first?"

With a nod of thanks and a smile, Nearra ducked into the ship. Jirah was right behind her.

Lamps blazed between rickety, haphazard shelves overloaded with weapons, furs, and other traveling supplies. Larger gear was piled in heaps in the far right corner, and near the door, dark shapes floated inside a barrel that appeared to be full of salt water. There were a few chairs and a low table against the back wall to the left of the door, and in the corner beyond them was a mound of furs and blankets.

It was rather odd, Nearra noted, being inside the ship. It was exactly as she had remembered Icefire's ship to be, only sideways. The wide beams of the hull curved up and above them to meet the completely flat front wall—the underside of the deck. The floor beneath her was broken in places, covered in piles of sand.

"Take a seat," the centaur said as he clomped in behind Davyn

JEFF SAMPSON

and Icefire. "Welcome to my humble home. The name's Arkenon. But you can call me Ark—all my customers do." Trotting to the pile of furs, he began sorting them and creating makeshift beds.

"Thank you," Nearra said. She gave Jirah a pointed look and, after rolling her eyes, the black-haired girl helped her sister pull the chairs out and arrange them near the table. Everyone took a seat.

"So," Ark said as he turned back around. "Tell me a bit about yourselves."

"You first," Icefire said, his look wary.

Tail slapping at unseen flies, Ark snorted, laughing. "It's all right," he said. "I'm a big creature. I'm used to being mistrusted. Ever since I moved here, all the people have been afraid I might do something dangerous—been keeping in at night and whispering amongst themselves. Tarsians aren't too good with outsiders, I've found. But they're sure to come around once they get to know me."

Settling back against the main pile of furs and blankets, he crossed his arms. "My story's simple. Lived here on the plains all my life. Fought in the war, hence the eye." He gestured toward his eye patch. "Decided to settle down and become a merchant, and been at it ever since. How about you?"

Icefire began the story, with Davyn filling in bits and pieces. Nearra listened intently at first, then felt her eyes droop. She'd need to rest soon.

Her gaze drifted to Jirah, and she saw anger clouding her sister's face. Jirah noticed Nearra staring, then scowled and turned away from her sister. It seemed Jirah was still upset about leaving Keene behind.

Waking up to find everything so different, Nearra had shoved aside thoughts of Keene and Pip. Now, watching her sister, worry began to tug at her again. Keene was brave, but he was also a kender—small and much too curious. Pip too. They could get into so much trouble in a prison. They could be hurt, or worse.

But Icefire seemed to think it was best they leave the two behind, and he hadn't been wrong before. Besides, his and Davyn's point made sense. Kirilin was locked up, if only temporarily, and taking advantage of that lead was only sensible.

Nearra shook her head, trying to shake off her doubts. She had to trust that everything would be fine, or else they'd get nowhere. She turned her hazy attention back to the conversation at hand and waited for sleep to consume her.

Later that night, as the four companions lay sleeping inside the ship, the centaur Arkenon crept out of his home and onto the sands. Dark clouds writhed high above him as he searched the distance for the messenger.

Then he caught sight of a hulking creature wearing a brown cloak. The winds blew the cloak aside and Ark caught a glimmer of bronze, a flash of sharp claws and teeth. It was one of Kirilin's draconian soldiers.

"I've got four travelers inside," Arkenon said as the draconian approached. "Two girls, a boy, and an elf, just like you said."

In guttural Common, the draconian responded. "Good. The Stealer of Souls is working on escaping. She says wait until they are alone in the plains, where they will have no chance of escape. Then attack and take whatever you want." The creature's thick tail lashed back and forth beneath the cloak. "Don't kill anyone," it added, almost as an afterthought. "She wants to be there to see them die."

With a smirk, Arkenon nodded. "Tell her I will do as she commands. Oh, and let her know that I appreciate the take-what-I-want part. She sure knows the quickest way to my heart."

With a nod of its fearsome lizard-like head, the draconian

turned and bounded back toward the city. Arkenon watched as it disappeared in the distance.

"All hail Hiddukel," he whispered.

Then he turned and trotted back to the battered ship that was now his home.

CHAPTER

7 BEASTS

They've been reading that book all morning," Jirah whispered into her mirror. "Icefire has a map out, and he's plotting our trail. He and Nearra have been working at it since before sunrise."

Her reflection raised an eyebrow. "Oh really?" Janeesa's voice asked. "Icefire and Nearra? Still close, are they?"

"Y-yes," Jirah said. "He's still helping her to learn magic."

There was a long, uncomfortable pause. Then Janeesa cleared her throat. "I thought I told you—" She stopped abruptly, then let out an aggravated sigh. "Never mind. It's not important at this point. Anything else?"

Jirah looked up from the mirror and peered around the petrified beam she was hiding behind. Far in the corner, sitting at the table with a lamp lit between them, Nearra and Icefire flipped through books. Icefire had a quill in hand and was marking a map. Davyn sat on the furs, sharpening his sword and glancing furtively at the girl and the elf. The centaur Ark was nowhere in sight.

Not one of them, Jirah noted with anger, seemed the least bit concerned about their missing friends.

"Hello?" Janeesa said. "I asked you a question. Jirah?"

Jirah twisted back behind the beam. Pots jangled on the curved wall as she leaned heavily back in the pile of sand in which she was sitting. "Sorry," she said as she lifted the mirror up. "I . . . I think I told you everything. The attack at the library, the centaur . . . "

She let herself trail off. Should she tell them about Keene? Maybe he would be safe in the prison, from the Messengers at least. But Kirilin was back there. Maybe if she told the Messengers about his capture they'd demand she keep him by her side since they knew getting at him was a good way to get at *her*. Either way it went she'd be helping the kender.

"There's Keene too," she added quickly. "He was captured and put in jail."

"Was he?" It was Tylari's voice drifting from behind Jirah's reflected face.

"Y-yes," Jirah whispered. "It's just me, Nearra, Davyn, and Icefire now."

"You planned it," Tylari said. "You got him locked away in a prison to protect him from me, didn't you?" His voice rose. "DIDN'T YOU?"

Jirah stiffened as he shouted. The elf continued to rant as she stuffed the mirror under her cloak and peered back around the beam.

Icefire and Nearra were still flipping through their books, and Davyn was still working on his sword. No one had heard.

With a sigh of relief, she leaned back and pulled out the mirror. Jirah heard muffled arguing from the mirror as Janeesa scolded her brother.

Jirah's reflection blinked and its lips curled into a smile. "I apologize for Tylari," Janeesa said. "He's been . . . unwell as of late. But he makes a good point, Jirah. You don't think that just because Keene is out of our reach now that we won't be able to kill him should you betray us? Because you would be very, very wrong."

"Yes, Janeesa," Jirah whispered. The mirror shook slightly as her hand began to tremble. "Maybe . . . maybe I should get them to go back into the city and get him, then."

Her reflection smiled knowingly. "Oh, Jirah. Now, that doesn't seem the best use of your time, does it? Kirilin is a powerful cleric and could escape any moment. Restoring the Trinistyr is far more important than saving some little kender. No, should you betray us, and Tylari and I need to kill Keene, a little prison won't stop us."

Defeated, Jirah slumped down. "All right," she muttered.

"Now, you're certain that you told us everything?"

"Yes," Jirah said. "Everything is . . . everything is fine. The second wizard will be free, and we'll have her weapon."

Her reflection nodded. "Very good. Now, I must run. Tylari and I are making travel arrangements. Contact us again after you reach the mine, got it?"

"Yes, Janeesa."

"Give Icefire my love," Janeesa said, her tone cold. Then Jirah's reflection stilled. The Messengers were gone.

Shoving the mirror into the pack at her side, Jirah gathered her new fur cloak and stood. Tylari had seemed insane from the moment she'd met him, but clearly he was getting worse. Janeesa had almost always been able to control him with a word or two after an outburst. But lately, she wondered even if she did follow the Messengers' instructions precisely, whether Tylari might just hurt her anyway for the joy of it.

Now Keene was trapped, and no one but she seemed to care—not even Icefire, the kender's supposed best friend. And if the Messengers were telling the truth, they could still hurt him. Every day, things just seemed to get worse. If only she'd never met Janeesa. With a breath, Jirah shook her head and tried to compose herself, then walked out to the others.

Icefire's hand moved in quick, fluid motions, and Nearra watched, enthralled, as he connected all the points they had charted across their detailed map of the Plains of Dust. He had various metal tools out, which he'd been carrying in his pack and which she'd seen in his office on his ship.

As he drew, he hummed under his breath, an intricate melody so catchy that she found herself humming along. It distracted her from the book of magic she'd been studying.

"What song is that?" she asked.

Startled from his work, Icefire looked up and met her eye. Then, with an unusually shy grin, the elf ducked his head.

"It's another song I've been working on," he said quietly as he resumed his work on the map. "For you."

"Another song for me? Icefire, I—"

Jirah ran past them, clutching her pack to her chest. A smile flitted across her face, but it quickly fell away. The girl plopped down next to Davyn on the furs.

Nearra reached a hand forward and gently touched Icefire's forearm. "You wrote another song for me?" she murmured. "Thank you."

Icefire shrugged. "The longer I know you, the more there is to sing. This one is not quite done yet. A work in progress, you might say."

"Well, you'll have to sing it for me one day," she said. "I'd love to hear it. I already know the first one by heart."

Behind her, Davyn cleared his throat. "You two almost done up there?"

Quickly Nearra pulled her hand away. "Yes, Davyn," she said. "Almost."

With another expert line put on the map, Icefire lifted the quill up with a flourish. "Actually, we're completely done." Grinning, he turned in the chair and looked at Davyn. "The book spoke of many landmarks that we found on a current map. The mine actually isn't that far. We should be there by midafternoon."

Sheathing his sword, Davyn stood to his full height. "Well, then, if you're done whispering sweet nothings, we should set off."

Not waiting for a reply, he pulled his cloak closed around his neck, hefted up his pack, and thrust through the front door.

Icefire flashed a grin even Nearra knew was cocky. "What's with him?"

He's doing it on purpose, Davyn raged in his thoughts. Icefire's flaunting their little romance right in front of me to upset me. Well it's not going to work, Icefire. It's not going to work!

Storming from the ship, his feet kicking up sand, Davyn didn't notice the centaur until he almost ran into him.

"Whoa there," Ark called down.

The massive centaur held a broadsword in his hands, its hefty blade flat and dull. Dozens of sharp daggers hung from a broad leather baldric that was strapped across his chest.

"Sorry," Davyn grunted.

"In a hurry?" the centaur asked. A strip of leather tied back his black hair, and the scars on his face stood out stark and plain. If it was possible, he was even more frightening in full daylight.

"Yes," Davyn said, hefting his pack to readjust it over his shoulder. "We have to be on our way. Thanks for letting us stay here."

Ark nodded, then reared back on his hind legs. He thrust his sword into the air, practicing attack maneuvers. Davyn watched the massive creature in awe. It always surprised him how an unusually shaped creature like a centaur could move with such precision and grace.

"You know, young traveler," Ark said as his hooves clomped to the ground and his sword chopped down in an arc, "the Plains of Dust are not safe. Dangerous creatures roam and hunt." He thrust with his sword again, his hooves dancing in an intricate pattern. "You ever fight a giant scorpion? Nasty buggers."

Davyn shrugged, then crossed his arms. "You ever hack your way through an army of undead before fighting a zombie dragon, a mind-reading shapeshifter, and a two-thousand-year-old sorceress in the body of yet another dragon?"

Ark stopped midthrust and met Davyn's eyes with a sidelong glance. After a moment, he lowered the broadsword and let out a hearty laugh. "No," he said. "Can't say that I've done that. But it's likely I've seen far more battles than you have, young ranger. I'm not doing much business lately. In fact, you're the only customer I've had in a week. Surely another man—or centaur, as the case may be—couldn't hurt. As long as you can pay, it'd be nice to get back to my roots as a centaur for hire."

Davyn studied the centaur's wide eye. It bore into Davyn's own eyes, sharp and aware. Still, something about the centaur bothered him. It wasn't just his appearance—good people often came in frightening packages, just as evil ones came in deceptively beautiful ones. He'd been fine with staying with the centaur for one night. But now he was wary. Ark seemed much too eager to trot off with them, and memories of Maddoc's lessons on the gods had started to tug at Davyn's thoughts. Wasn't Hiddukel, whom Kirilin served, a god of corrupt *merchants*?

"Thanks for your hospitality," Davyn said after a moment. "But we paid you in full for the night, and we don't have enough steel to pay you further. We'll be fine on our own."

Turning his back on the centaur, he tromped further away from the ship. Behind him hinges creaked as the boat's door opened.

"Actually," Icefire called after him. "I think having Ark along is a good idea."

Of course he'd been listening in, Davyn realized. Elf hearing.

"He knows the plains," Icefire continued. "It's always good to keep around companions with skills you lack, especially when they offer so politely. Besides, I have enough steel. I can pay."

Davyn clenched his fists and dropped his pack with a heavy plop. He spun around, ready to lash out with a biting retort—why did Icefire always contradict him!—but then he saw Nearra and Jirah waiting at the elf's side. His broadsword held propped against his shoulder, Ark raised a questioning eyebrow.

"You're right," Davyn said through clenched teeth.

"I knew you'd come around," Icefire said. A cocky grin creasing his face, the elf came to Davyn's side. "Now, how about we set off." He held forward the map he'd just drawn. "Care to navigate?"

The map was a confusing mess of black lines and numbered coordinates. Davyn looked up from it and met Icefire's eyes with a steely gaze.

"Why don't you go ahead, Captain Icefire," he said. "Seems you get to call the shots today."

Icefire's eyes flashed and he grinned again. "Well, if you insist."

Nearra and Jirah came to their side, Ark trotting beside them. For a moment Davyn stood by his fallen pack, grinding his teeth in anger as he watched them begin their course west, away from Tarsis and into the Plains of Dust.

Calm down, Davyn thought. One day, Icefire will get his. Focus on the task at hand. The faster it gets done, the faster I can get away from him.

Davyn pulled his cloak tight around his shoulders and hefted up his pack. Then he raced to follow the others.

The companions and Ark traveled for hours across the plains. Icefire consulted his map as he led them across the sands and over rocky hills. He was following some trail Davyn couldn't discern. Davyn had spent years learning to follow the land, letting it guide him, but as he looked around, all he saw was desolation.

The sun grew high in the sky, hitting them harsh and unfiltered. There were no trees out here, no plant life of any kind. But despite the lack of shade, it was still blisteringly cold. Bitter, icy winds met them face on. Davyn's skin dried and froze, but he forged on, his teeth chattering.

Icefire seemed to be leading them to an inexplicably large boulder in the center of a flat, stony field. Jirah and Nearra huddled together for warmth as they walked behind the elf.

So far, as the hours drew on, they had managed to avoid any sort of confrontation. Earlier in their trek, Arkenon had spotted a shadowy creature skittering along the horizon, and he called for them to halt. But whatever the beast was, it did not come close, and the centaur warrior signaled that it was safe to move on.

Davyn shuddered as they neared the boulder. He was chilled, but not just from the cold of the plains. He knew nature; he'd been tracking and hunting since he could walk, and he knew that nature was always alive, even in a desert. Bugs crawled through sand, predators and scavengers stalked between rocks, birds cawed overhead as they scrounged for scraps of decaying meat.

But here, it was silent. The mournful song of the wind was all Davyn could hear beyond the rustling of the companions' cloaks and the sound of their boots meeting rock and sand. For a moment Davyn longed for Keene and Pip to return. With the two of them around, it was never quiet.

He scanned the blank scene around him. No, something was definitely not right.

"Here," Icefire called back. He turned around to face them and wave them forward, and the wind blew the black waves of his hair over his face. "This boulder, it's been here since before the

Cataclysm, if you can believe it." He ran up to the giant stone and patted its side. The oblong stone was as high as two men and was eroded to a perfectly smooth surface.

"The book said that this used to be an area of higher ground," the elf went on as the others drew near. "An island perhaps, more likely a peninsula. The mine was located north of here. The ocean water dripped through the stone and left the mineral deposits. The ancient dwarves picked it clean long before our friend the wizard was cursed there."

"Fascinating," Davyn muttered.

"It is!" Nearra said, smiling broadly. "Icefire, you guided us straight here. Thank you. We'd have been lost for weeks without you."

Davyn rolled his eyes.

Ark shifted back and forth from hoof to hoof. The silk of his black eye patch shimmered in the afternoon sun.

"We should keep walking," the centaur said in his deep voice. "Stay still too long and something's bound to jump out at you."

Jirah gulped and moved to stand closer to Nearra.

"Hey, don't worry, Jirah," Icefire said as he came to her side. "You're a natural born athlete, and you're getting skilled with a sword. You'd be able to take them."

"Of course I could," Jirah said. "But if it's all right with you, I'd rather not have to." She gestured north. "The mine?"

Icefire bowed his head. "But of course."

They moved past the boulder and began heading north. They were on rocky ground again, though there were still drifts of sand. In fact, the winds seemed to have blown some of the sand into dunes.

"It's a good thing you four got here at the end of summer," Ark said as he trotted at Icefire's side. "In a month or so the entire plain will be covered with snow. I'd imagine that'd make your quest that much harder."

"No doubt," Icefire said.

Davyn squinted as they walked past the mounds of sand. There were smaller boulders littering the landscape between the dunes, each one about as long as a man lying on his back. The boulders were shiny and tan and almost perfectly round. For a moment, Davyn thought he saw one move. He clutched the hilt of his sword.

"Icefire," he said in a low voice.

The elf didn't hear him—or, perhaps, ignored him—and continued walking past the mounds of sand and the shining brown and gray boulders. Nearra and Jirah spoke to each other in small, excited voices, oblivious.

Another boulder moved.

"Icefire!" Davyn called, his sword in his hand.

All around them, the dunes exploded outward. Grains of sand hit Davyn square in his eyes, though he tried to shield his face.

A dozen men and a few women, all dressed in heavy black clothes and sporting vicious tattoos and scars, leaped from the mounds of sand that had been their hiding spots, jeering. They'd hidden beneath large woven baskets under the sand.

"What the—" Icefire said as his hand flew to his own sword.

But the bandits didn't race toward them. Leaping and screaming, they chased the boulders.

That was when the boulders came alive. Startled by the bandits' shouts, they lifted up from the ground on dozens of short, spiky legs. Faces appeared, terrifying insect faces dominated by serrated mandibles and covered with beady black eyes. Armored tails slid out from their backsides, barbs jutting up from their ends.

"Skrit!" Ark called above the bandits' hollering. "Run!"

Davyn didn't hesitate. The man-size beetles swarmed toward them, mandibles snapping open and shut with voracious hunger. Venom dripped from the serrated edges.

Jirah, Nearra, and Icefire raced forward, following the galloping

Ark. Davyn was at the rear, pumping his arms and legs with all his might. He'd heard of skrit. One bite would paralyze a grown man, and then the monsters would swarm, dragging their prey away from the protection of its companions to feast on it.

Davyn forced himself to run faster.

Two of the bandits raced alongside the stampeding skrit, whooping shouts of bloodlust. Foul liquid sloshed in buckets that they carried in their arms.

The two bandits bounded ahead of the skrit, tossing the liquid from the buckets in front of the line of giant insects. It splashed against the dirt, and a sick stench filled the air.

Immediately, the skrit stopped their chase. They did not pass the unseen barrier that the bandits had apparently put up.

Hardly believing what he was seeing, Davyn stopped. Gasping, he put his hands on his knees. He sensed the others huddling behind him.

The bandits strode to either side of the skrit, unafraid of being attacked. Strangely, the creatures did not try to bite them. A woman with honey-colored skin and a shaved head strode forward. A black tattoo of a skull completely covered her face, marring what had once been lovely features.

"Now, what do we have here?" she taunted, hands on her hips.

A shadow flew above Davyn's head, and he heard Ark bellow. The centaur had leaped over them to land right in front of the sneering woman.

Ark lifted his sword and pointed it at the woman's heart. Her face devoid of fear, she held her head high. Behind her, a sea of tan carapaces writhed in hunger.

"What did I say?" Ark growled. "Didn't I tell you to wait to attack until I gave the signal? They were supposed to lead us to the mine. Lady Kirilin's maps led only to the boulder. She will not be pleased."

Nearra gasped. "No," she whispered.

Turning to face them, and smiling his good natured grin, Ark shrugged. "Sorry, friends," he said. "But I've made a promise to Lady Kirilin, and I almost never go back on my word."

Turning to meet Icefire's eyes, Davyn shook his head. "I knew it!"

CHAPTER

8   MINE

Icefire clutched at his earring as he tried to take in the sudden betrayal. The gold hoop was granted with the power to provide him foresight; he'd relied on this ability many times to gauge his situations.

Icefire knew that the way Nearra listened to his advice over Davyn's bothered the human boy. Davyn's attitude toward him and *especially* toward Nearra had started to grate on Icefire's nerves, so he'd done what anyone would have—tried to bother the boy even more. He'd figured inviting the centaur along after Davyn turned him down would be harmless. Besides, he hadn't been lying— someone like Ark would definitely be useful on the plains.

But the earring had failed to tell Icefire of Ark's true allegiance. Something had nullified its warning power.

"Kirilin," Icefire whispered, remembering the magic she had cast through him back at the inn.

Ark swaggered back toward the companions. "Pheromones," he said, gesturing to the streak of wet dust splattered in front of the terrifying insects. "Funny stuff I got from some wizard. Bathe in it once and the skrit won't go near you. Downright repulsed by the stuff they are, so much so that it'll stop a whole stampede right in its tracks."

Behind him, the skrit climbed atop one another, trying desperately to surge forward and kill the four companions. The tattooed bandits still stood on either side of the creatures, hemming them in and keeping them from swarming around the invisible line that kept them at bay.

"Gods, Ark," the female bandit called from behind him. "Must you always chat up our victims?"

"Staite, watch your tongue before I cut it out." Ark's look lost none of its good cheer.

Icefire trembled with anger. "Why are you doing this?" he demanded. "Why pretend to want to help us?"

Ark shrugged. "It's what I do: lie, cheat, and steal. I find it really increases my profit margins." Behind him, the other bandits chuckled and murmured.

"That's not it," Nearra said, her voice steady. "You said Kirilin's name. You're working for her."

Ark scowled and pawed at the ground. Hoof met stone, sending up sparks. In one swift move, he had one of his daggers in hand and pointed it at Nearra's chest.

"I work for myself, girl," he said. "Don't forget it."

Icefire walked past Davyn. "You sold your soul to her, didn't you?" the elf demanded as he came to face the centaur. "You're just one of the many conquests of her and her god."

The grin once again appeared on Ark's scarred, chiseled face. "Well, yes, I did. Had to do *something* after the war."

"You didn't fight in the war," Davyn said with a scowl.

Again Ark shrugged. "Never said *which side* I fought on, kid."

With the centaur momentarily distracted, Icefire's hand shot up and clutched his earring as he spat ancient words of power. He could only hope Kirilin hadn't been able to nullify all of the earring's magic.

"Spellcaster!" the female bandit shrieked. She leaped past Ark and barreled into Icefire's chest. They fell against the harsh stone.

Her eyes raging behind the black skull tattoo that marred her face, the woman raised a dagger high. Icefire tensed, waiting for her strike.

Twin pairs of powerful equine hind legs met the bandit's side. Icefire heard her ribs crack, and the woman flew off him.

"Lady Kirilin does not want them killed!" Ark bellowed. Aiming the point of his sword at Icefire's gut, the centaur shrugged. "But she never said anything about maiming."

"Aargh!" Jirah raced forward, a blur of fur cloak and black hair. Her short sword was raised high and she brought it down hard against Ark's flank. The centaur bellowed in pain, rearing back.

Icefire leaped to his feet. "Thanks."

Jirah took in quick, frightened breaths. "I'm starting to really hate two-faced liars," she wheezed.

The other bandits took the attack on Ark as their cue. Hefting bloodstained maces and dull axes, they ran past the mound of writhing skrit.

Again Icefire clutched at his earring.

"Davyn, Nearra, Jirah!" he called. "Get back!"

Not waiting to see if they complied, he cast his spell.

The power surged within him, the music of it swelling to a vicious crescendo. Around him, he felt the familiar sensation of air stirring against his skin.

"Vile elf," Ark spat. His hair had fallen loose from its tie, and the sneering centaur leaped forward. At that exact moment, Icefire finished the last words of his spell.

The bandits didn't know what hit them. Wind roared, swirling the sand that had once hidden the bandits into a tornado of fury. The sandstorm caught Ark in its grip, blinding him, and muting him with mouthfuls of dust.

Within moments, Ark, the bandits, and the skrit were completely lost from sight. Icefire could barely hear their frightened and angry cries over the roar of the wind and the whoosh of swirling sand, and that was with his superior elf hearing.

The spell cast, Icefire felt his energy ebb. He turned to run to his companions' sides, then stumbled and fell to one knee.

"Icefire," Nearra cried. She ran to his side and offered her arm. Davyn and Jirah were behind her.

"Here!" Icefire called over the howling wind. He pulled the map he'd drawn from his belt and handed it to Davyn. "We're almost there. Lead the way."

"Aye, aye," Davyn said, his tone clearly mocking. They grabbed their things and raced away from the writhing mass of sand, giant insects, and wild warriors.

Icefire pushed himself, following as Davyn directed them north. The elf's legs threatened to give out, his muscles slackened when they should have tensed, but he had to keep moving. Stopping would mean death.

Davyn peered at the map, then veered west. "Doing all right back there?" he called to Icefire over his shoulder.

"I'm fine," Icefire wheezed.

"Liar," Nearra whispered. She clutched at his side and helped him move forward. Her heartbeat echoed in his pointed ears, a comforting rhythmic sound. As her power grew, so did the music of her personal magic. He hadn't told her yet, but the new song he was composing was inspired in no small part by the melody of her soul.

"Davyn," Jirah called as she sped up to race at his side. "Are we almost there? Those bandits could be on us any second!"

"Yes." Davyn scowled, then turned the map sideways. "It should be around here somewhere."

Icefire took a step forward, then another. That was when he felt it.

"We're there," he whispered.

Magic seeped from the ground beneath his boots, rising and falling in lapping waves of power. The unseen force met his shins as he waded through it, sending energy coursing up through his limbs.

"Oh," Nearra gasped beside him. The power touched her too, though he could tell not as strongly. She met his face with shocked eyes. "Is it . . . ?"

Icefire nodded, feeling the magic rise through his veins before bursting into his heart. "It is. The wizard's magic."

Davyn spun to face him, still scowling. "Wizards," he muttered. Then louder, he said, "Would you care to let us know where this mine is? Jirah's right. Ark could be on our trail, and it sounds like he expected Kirilin to be here too."

Pulling free from Nearra's supporting embrace, Icefire stepped forward, searching the landscape.

"Faster would be better," Jirah said. She hugged herself and bit a trembling lip.

Icefire pointed. "There."

It was hard to see at first; the entrance seemed little more than a cleft in the endless gray of the stony ground. But as they grew closer, they saw that it was a narrow black opening that led into the earth. Others might assume it was a sinkhole or the home to one of the giant beasts that roamed the Plains of Dust. But as Icefire grew closer, he moaned with pleasure. The magic rolled out of the opening in waves, overwhelming him with a swelling song of sorrow.

"The mine," Icefire gasped as the others approached. Sparks of blue energy tingled at his fingertips, but he ignored the sensation. "We're here."

Above them, gray clouds roiled to cover the sky, hiding the sun and chilling the companions even deeper. Still shaken up by their sudden betrayal, no one bothered arguing. Davyn was the first down the hole and, with his call of confirmation, the others were quick to follow.

Hazy gray light did little to pierce the darkness. Icefire lit a torch and crept forward as Davyn helped Nearra and Jirah down into the small entrance.

Craggy gray stone walls spread out to reveal a vast circular cavern. Spiraling along its side was an ancient wooden track that led to the bottom far below. The track flattened into platforms at different levels, behind which were shadowy holes that led to other sections of the mine, but Icefire didn't dare delve into them.

Feeling a bit refreshed, Icefire silently took the lead once more. The wood of the track felt soft and decayed beneath him, but it held. He ran his slender fingers over the wall to steady himself, feeling the grooves where minerals had once resided. It was an empty, desolate place—the perfect place for a tomb.

They crept down the track, Nearra clinging to the back of Icefire's cloak, Jirah to hers, and Davyn following at the rear. The wood beneath their feet creaked in protest, threatening to crumble.

The darkness above grew thicker as they made their way slowly, deep into the mine. A sliver of gray light pierced through the blackness from the opening far above, but it didn't reach far. As they passed old torches in wall sconces, Icefire set them ablaze with his torch, trying to chase away the dark as much as possible. As an elf, he could see fine, but his companions did not share his night vision.

On the floor below, old metal and wood carts were piled in a heap of dust-covered wheels and boards. They'd have been too big to fit through the mine's opening, Icefire realized, so someone must have decided to leave them here when the mine was abandoned. Beyond that, the floor beneath them was bare.

"Here." Icefire thrust the torch toward Davyn as they stepped down to the dusty stone floor. "Light any torches or braziers that you find. You have peat in your pack, right?"

Davyn crossed his arms. "You're giving me a command?" he demanded.

Nearra shook her head and touched Davyn's arm gently. "Davyn," she said. "Not now."

He shrugged her aside and stepped into Icefire's face. "I don't think you should be giving anyone commands," he said. "Not after what just happened out there. I *knew* something was wrong with Ark, but you insisted he come anyway. Why? Just to upset me? Or did you know who he was already?"

Icefire trembled with anger. The magic pulsed within him, sending sparks flaring over his clenched fist.

"My earring," he said in a low voice. "Kirilin did something to nullify my foresight. I didn't know. I'm sorry."

Davyn snorted. "Your earring?" he said. "Your *earring*?" He threw his hands in the air. "Well, maybe if you didn't rely so much on your blasted magic, Captain, then we wouldn't have a bloodthirsty centaur out there chasing us. Nearra could have been killed!"

"Davyn," Nearra said, gently pressing his shoulder. "And you too, Icefire. Please, don't—"

"You mean your earring isn't working?" Jirah interrupted. "You mean you wouldn't have been warned if Keene was going to be in trouble when they took him away? What if we were wrong to leave him? What if—"

"It's done, Jirah!" Icefire said. "This isn't about Keene. This is about me and Davyn." Shaking now with rage, Icefire dropped the torch. It clattered to the floor and rolled away.

"Not a fan of my magic?" Icefire seethed as he stepped toward Davyn. Lifting his hands, he felt dark power pulse through him.

Davyn's hand shot to his sword. "Coward," he growled. "Going

JEFF SAMPSON

for magic, like always. What happened to good old-fashioned brawling, like the sailor you're supposed to be? Or was that all a show to hide your lust for magic? Well, it's not so hidden anymore, now is it?"

Baring his teeth, Icefire let the power roar forth. The melancholy song of the magic waves now shrieked as a tempest of fury. Lightning flared over his fingertips.

"Both of you, enough!"

Nearra leaped between the two, her staff clenched in both hands. She brought it down hard against the floor. Wood met stone with a loud clang that echoed around them.

The orb clutched in the carved dragon claw at the staff's end burst with orange light. Fire flared around the walls as the torches erupted with flame.

Nearra stood between Icefire and Davyn, trembling slightly but unmoving. She met both of their eyes, one by one. Jirah lifted her head, the expression on her face awed.

Weary, Nearra lowered her head. "Enough," she whispered. "We're here now. We're alive. That's all that matters. I have a quest to complete, and we don't have time for you two to prove who's the better man."

Icefire lowered his hands and let the power drain from his limbs. As it did, he began to shake with fear. What had he been about to do? He was supposed to control the magic, not the other way around. He'd fought its siren call for years to avoid something like this. Was he really going to hurt Davyn?

Ashamed, Icefire looked past Nearra at Davyn. The ranger refused to meet his gaze.

"Nearra," Jirah said, taking a half-hearted step forward. She put her hand on her sister's shoulder and turned her toward the northern wall. "Look."

Set in a shadowy alcove was a block of stone, sheared flat. Like the walls, it was brown and gray. Unlike the rest of the cavern, black minerals streaked across its unnaturally smooth surface.

"The tomb," Icefire said. Taking a breath to compose himself, he went to Nearra's side. "Do you need to rest first?"

Nearra shook her head and refused to meet his eyes. "There's no time," she said. "Jirah and Davyn are right. Those bandits could be after us. I need to do this now."

Icefire nodded. "It's your quest," he said. "And so it is your call."

Brushing past Davyn, Nearra went to Jirah. She handed her sister her cloak and her pack. "Hold on to these for me," she said.

Jirah murmured her consent and clutched the items close.

Nearra reached beneath her bodice and pulled free the shimmering key-shaped gem that hung around her neck on a silver chain—Kirilin's key, the reason the cleric was after them. It was with this key that she had sealed the cursed wizards in their eternal tombs, and it was this key that had given her their life-force.

Now, the key was to be Kirilin's undoing.

Holding her head and staff high, Nearra strode toward the sheared rock of the tomb. Icefire, Davyn, and Jirah watched from a distance. They stood in a silence colder than the winds above.

As Nearra approached, the glowing forms of two soldiers in ancient armor appeared on either side of her. They unsheathed phantom swords and pointed them at her neck. Nearra spoke to them and showed them the key, though Icefire couldn't hear what she was saying. They bowed their heads and let her pass.

Without looking back, Nearra pressed her hands against the rocky wall, then stepped through the stone into the wizard's tomb.

CHAPTER

9   DEPRIVATION

Nearra clenched her eyes closed as she stepped through the rock wall. It flowed around her, thick as mud. As she stepped all the way through, she turned around and opened her eyes.

The wall of stone rippled as though molten, seeming to shudder with each breath that she took. The mineral veins that snaked through its surface were still opaque, but the slate gray stone had become transparent, almost like a window covered in frost. She could barely make out the shadows of her companions watching her.

Icefire and Davyn glared at one another still. Feelings raced through Nearra, feelings of sadness and anger all at the same time. They both loved her, they both wanted the best for her, but why did they always have to bicker over her? Why did Davyn insist on implying that she was incapable of handling herself despite everything she'd done? And why did Icefire allow himself to get drawn into arguments about it if he was really so certain of her strength?

She wasn't a general, nor was she some royal trained from birth to lead anyone. But she was certainly capable of handling her own quest. And the more she thought about it, the more she wondered if maybe Jirah was right, if maybe she should have trusted her instinct and not just listened to Icefire about leaving Keene behind. If only she could make them—all of them—understand that she wasn't a damsel in distress waiting to be told what to do.

She shook her head. It was time to focus. With a steeling breath, she turned to face the second wizard.

As she turned, ripples of reflected light washed over her. Brackish water surged upward like a pillar, filling the cave and refracting the warm glow from the mine into a blue haze. It seemed to pulse in waves, and it was as though the ocean had somehow turned on its side to stand in front of her.

Only this ocean had no sound. There was no lapping of waves against a hull, no sailor chants, no salty breeze rustling through sails, no sea birds calling out overhead, just the sound of her breathing. And beyond that, utter silence.

Confused, Nearra took a reluctant step toward the pillar of water, then another. There was something dark within it, a vague shadow in the shape of a person.

"Hello?" she whispered. Before, when she had entered the tomb of the wizard encased in fire, he had spoken to her. He had beckoned for her and had told her what to do.

"Hello?" Nearra said again, louder. "I'm here to free you. Can you hear me?" For a moment she wondered if perhaps this was the wrong place. But this was where Anselm's map had told them to go. The spectral guardians had stood outside the tomb, just as before. This had to be right.

Nearra grazed the watery pillar with a trembling hand. It was pleasantly warm, not the blistering cold of the sea as she had expected. Silent waves crashed into her fingertips and crested in foamy white.

Nearra swirled the magical liquid into little whirlpools and studied the shadowy mass within, which had to be the second wizard. Still, the wizard did not move.

"I hope I'm doing this right," she said. With a deep breath, Nearra closed her eyes and walked into the pillar of water.

The water enveloped her in its warmth, and for a moment she reveled in the comfort that it brought her. She remembered the few times in the past few years that she'd been allowed the luxury of a hot bath, and for a moment she wished that Jirah and the others could join her, to know what this was like. Inadvertently, she breathed in contentment, only to find that she didn't choke on the brackish liquid. She could breathe just fine, in fact. The water that passed her lips seemed like soupy air. It was a strange sensation.

Nearra opened her eyes. Darkness surrounded her, a deep, impenetrable darkness. She spun around, her movements sluggish and slow under the water's weight. She couldn't see the cave. She couldn't see the wizard either. Lifting her hands, she found she couldn't even see herself.

This isn't so bad, she thought. It's warm, and I can breathe, and it's quiet.

Nearra couldn't help but let out a laugh. A flurry of bubbles burst past her open lips and out from her nostrils.

This is torture? she thought. This is a holiday!

Nearra closed her eyes and raised her arms. She let herself float in the dark waves and let the world go away. Here, nobody was trying to control her or kill her. Nobody was fighting over her attention or arguing about decisions *she* should be making. They were all outside this little tomb—and still bickering, no doubt. Finally, she had a moment to breathe.

Blue light flared, and Nearra's eyes snapped open.

Before her, the second wizard had appeared. White robes billowed around the wizard as she floated in the dark water. Strapped to her back was an ornately carved longbow capped at each end with jewels that cast the blue glow.

Bloated by the water, the once feminine features of the wizard's face were deformed. Waterlogged, the flesh of her face swelled and her glassy eyes bulged fish-like. Mineral-encrusted hair flowed around her head in branch-like tangles.

The woman seemed very much dead, and Nearra's heart pounded in her chest. She floated in front of the wizard's drowned corpse, unable to move away.

This was a good wizard, Nearra reminded herself. She met a bad fate. I am doing this to save her. There's nothing to be afraid of.

The decaying body bobbed in front of her, swaying gently. Nearra tried to calm her breathing, tried to keep her hands from trembling.

The wizard blinked.

The scream left Nearra's lips without her choosing to do so. A flurry of bubbles created a curtain between Nearra and the wizard, and she flailed, trying to escape the undead creature before her.

One of the deformed woman's hands shot out and clenched Nearra's wrist. Cold lanced through her arm. Stunned by the chill, she stopped screaming.

Descendant. A voice whispered in her thoughts, sounding distant even as it echoed through her head. *End suffering. Become him.*

Nearra couldn't tear her eyes away from the woman's empty, doll-like gaze. The wizard's skeletal hand gripped her wrist tighter, and her nails bit into Nearra's flesh. The voice came again, echoing louder.

Remember.

The blue light blinked out, and the world was once again shrouded in darkness. Nearra felt the heaviness of the water disappear from her shoulders. The bony fingers of the cursed wizard no longer encircled her wrist. The pillar of water was gone. She, or at least a part of herself, was somewhere different.

A pinprick of light appeared in the distance, a lone star in a shrouded night sky. The light shimmered and wavered. Nearra tried to gain her bearings in this new, dark plain. This had happened before.

With a flash, the light flared and seemed to race toward her. It grew immense, blazing like a sun until it enveloped her in a surge of white light that hurt her eyes.

With a cry, Nearra collapsed to the ground. Her palms met gritty stone with a loud slap, and she felt gravel cut into her flesh. She looked down to find that the hands were not her own. They were large, thick, and wrinkled with age. When they lifted, they moved of their own accord.

Anselm, she realized. She was being shown the past through Anselm's eyes, just as she had when she was freeing the cursed wizard Rudd.

"Get up." The cruel voice was familiar even in the ancient Istarian tongue, which Nearra understood only by virtue of sharing Anselm's mind. Anselm turned and looked up. As he did, Nearra saw Kirilin— or, at least, what Kirilin had once looked like.

She wasn't the young beauty Nearra had first seen when Kirilin attacked them by ship, nor was she the raging middle-aged woman they'd fought in Tarsis. This Kirilin was older, her hair pure white, her skin marked with liver spots and covered in wrinkles. She wore white robes, and though she was clearly old, she moved with speed and grace.

In the last vision, Kirilin had appeared to be middle-aged, only gaining true youth once the wizard Rudd had been cursed in a tomb of fire. Nearra realized immediately what was going to happen— Anselm was about to curse the female wizard in the pillar of water, after which Kirilin would be granted the wizard's life-force and transformed from her crone-like appearance into middle-aged form.

Nearra could only imagine how old Kirilin must have been before she'd forced Anselm to curse the first wizard.

Guilt flooded Anselm's mind as he stood. The guilt was so heavy that Nearra could hardly bear it. She wanted to cry out, to reassure him that this was not all his fault. But even as she watched through his eyes and dwelled in his mind, she realized that if Anselm hadn't cursed these wizards, if he had let himself die instead of betraying his companions, she would never have been born, and she wondered what the world would be like now. Would Krynn be a place of peace? Would her friends' lives have been better?

She knew what she would have done. She wouldn't have succumbed to Kirilin. She would have let herself die rather than curse the world, because who was she compared to the rest of the world? Wouldn't it have been an easy choice?

"I am up, Kirilin." Anselm's deep voice reverberated through Nearra's head as she felt his lips move. "I am up."

Kirilin pursed her red-painted lips and raised an eyebrow. "Of course you are. Don't forget your children, my dear Anselm. One word from me . . . "

She didn't have to finish. Nearra saw flashes of Anselm's memories of his wife dying. She remembered the tortures she had experienced during her first visit into his mind. And she saw his memories of his children, who were frightened and chained in a dank cell.

The children, Nearra thought. They changed everything. Could I have let them die to keep the world from its destruction?

She didn't know the answer. But the past had long since passed, as Icefire had said. She had no say in the matter, so she watched.

Kirilin gestured to someone standing behind Anselm. As he turned, Nearra saw a soldier clad in outdated and ornate armor, just like the spectral guardians.

They stood in the bottom of the abandoned mine. The wooden

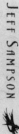

JEFF SAMPSON

tracks lined the walls, and the unused carts were still piled in the alcoves, just as they were in Nearra's present. No one had entered these mine since this remembered day, the day Anselm cursed the second wizard.

A flash of magical insight coursed through Anselm's mind, and he clenched his eyes tight. "She comes," he whispered.

When he again opened his eyes, Nearra saw Kirilin standing over the soldier's body. A long dagger jutted from the dead man's chest.

"Good," Kirilin said. She knelt and grabbed the hilt of her dagger. "Prepare yourself."

Anselm blinked, and suddenly the scene shifted. Kirilin and the fallen soldier were nowhere in sight. But Anselm wasn't alone in the cavernous mine. He faced someone carrying an intricately carved longbow capped at each end with blue gems.

"Flomana," Anselm said as she approached him. She was young, Nearra noticed, not much older than she and Davyn were in the present. Flomana's long brown hair hung in a braided coil down her back, but for efficiency, not style. Curly strands of untamed hair fell over a round, friendly face. Despite looking in the corners warily, she still smiled in warm greeting.

"Anselm." She nodded respectfully. "An odd place to meet, but I suppose we have enemies everywhere."

"That we do."

Nearra saw a deep intelligence in the young wizard's gaze. That awareness had been stolen from her. When the pangs of guilt lanced through Anselm as he considered what he was about to do, Nearra felt a sense of despair she never knew she could feel.

Flomana gestured toward the quiver of arrows on her back. "I have the weapon, just like we were instructed. It's odd that I am to be the one using this particular one, seeing as I cannot stand the sea. I am not looking forward to our voyage south."

"But it must be done," Anselm said. Weariness tainted his voice. He was tired of the lies.

Please, Nearra thought. Please don't do this.

As she watched, the lovely young wizard turned her back on Anselm. There was a flash of shadow in the corner. Kirilin.

No, Nearra thought, even as she knew what was to come could never be changed. Please no.

"I am sorry," Anselm whispered, though Flomana didn't hear him. Raising his hands, he began to intone the first bitter phrases of the curse that would entomb her forever.

Then, darkness.

Nearra blinked her eyes several times. She tried to move, only to find she was back in the watery void. The decaying wizard—Flomana—was gone. Even knowing who the wizard had been before, Nearra still felt chilled. Prickles ran up her spine, and she expected the decimated body of the wizard to leap at her from behind and pull her farther into the watery depths.

No one came. She was alone. She had been shown the past, and now she was to relive the wizard's suffering. Still Nearra was unsure of what was to happen. This wasn't unpleasant, not exactly. What was it that had driven Flomana so far beyond insanity that all spark of life had been wrenched from her gaze?

Nearra floated in the dark void, breathing slowly as she trod the water. It was so very silent. There was no sound at all outside of her, and so every rush of blood through her veins, every beat of her heart, every gurgle of her stomach seemed to echo inside her head.

There was nothing touching her but the warm water. It didn't even seem to lap at her flesh anymore. There was no breeze touching her, no bristling of the fine hairs on her arms that let her know her limbs were still there. She could feel nothing.

Taste and smell did not exist, for the magic water flowing past her lips had no taste and no scent. The darkness was so complete that she soon could not tell when her eyes were open or closed.

Nearra floated in the darkness, completely alone for the first time in her life. She bobbed in the water, existing but experiencing nothing. Time was nonexistent here. She could have been inside the tomb for mere minutes, or it could have been hours.

She sang Icefire's songs for her in her head. She recited childhood limericks. She remembered everything she could possibly remember.

Despite her efforts to distract herself, she was much too aware that she was stuck here and had no idea how she was going to get out. Only then did she realize the torture that Flomana had endured, the torture that was now hers to relive, for how long she couldn't know. The first wizard's torture had been endless pain. He had at least *felt*.

Flomana had felt nothing. Time for her had inched by, achingly slow.

I can't do this, Nearra thought as she began to thrash in panic. I can't do this!

Nearra opened her lips and screamed for help. Even as she did, she realized it was futile. There was nothing out there to help her.

Nothing at all.

CHAPTER

10   A Deadly Bargain

"What's taking so long?"

Davyn paced back and forth as he waited for Nearra, his look stern. Jirah's hands fidgeted together as she watched him. He was making her nervous.

Icefire crossed his arms and leaned back against one of the craggy, pitted stone walls. Torchlight flickered above him. "She'll be fine," he said. He shook his head, sending waves of black hair tumbling over his shoulders. "Davyn, haven't you noticed by now? She's not a helpless waif."

Davyn's lips raised into a sneer and he stopped midpace to round on Icefire. "I know, Icefire," he growled. "I've known her a lot longer than you, let's not forget."

Icefire's look grew cold. "Wouldn't seem that way by how you act toward her, Davyn." He stood up to his full height and straightened his shoulders. "After all she's said to you, you still don't seem to understand that she has to make these choices herself. I hadn't had you pegged as this dense."

Davyn took two large steps forward and jabbed his finger into Icefire's broad chest. "*You* still don't seem to understand that this isn't your quest, and you're not our leader, mine or Nearra's.

You're a dark elf, and for all I know you planned everything that happened up above."

Icefire seethed. "How dare you call me that!"

Jirah crossed her arms and hugged herself. The boys were fighting, as she knew they would. It had been building to this ever since Tarsis. Boys like them would never get along; she saw it all the time back at home.

With a shudder, Jirah remembered old conversations with Janeesa. She'd wanted this. She'd wanted Icefire and Davyn to fight, for one to kill the other. Weaken the bonds between the companions so that the Messengers could easily take the Trinistyr and the mystical weapons when the curse was completely broken. Now it was happening at the worst possible moment, and there was nothing Jirah could do to stop it.

"I call it how I see it," Davyn sneered. "And I can say whatever I like."

Trembling, Icefire seemed to have to force his hands from shooting forth deadly magic or throwing a dagger. He took several long breaths.

"Look," Icefire said. "Look what we have let ourselves become. Fighting will get us nowhere, especially not with Kirilin pursuing us. I thought we had made some peace, Davyn. I respect you as a fighter and, yes, as a leader. I just think your feelings are shrouding your opinion of Nearra."

"And yours aren't?" Davyn said. He snorted. "Your plays of power, your fake confidence, it's what got us into this. Kirilin is after you more than any of us. She sent Ark to capture us, and he'll be here any minute." He shook his head. "Nearra's taking too long."

Icefire sighed again. "Just wait. If she's not out soon, we'll find a way to help her."

"Yes, *Captain*," Davyn said. With one last dark glare, he turned on his heel and resumed his pacing.

Jirah hugged herself tighter. It was warmer down here in the mine than outside, especially with the blazing flames on the walls, but something chilled her deeply. Maybe it was the eerie silence. Every step seemed much too loud.

She watched the tomb, waiting. The spectral guardians were gone, but she could still sense the vileness of their presence. It was the same feeling she had gotten when she was around Asvoria's undead beasts, the same she felt every time Tylari's fetch popped out of a mirror. The dead should not walk, she thought. And when they did, they disrupted even the air around them.

She wasn't quite sure what she was supposed to see, but the tomb was still dark gray and streaked with black minerals. At any moment she expected the tomb to dissipate and a mystical wind to carry away the spirits of the dead wizard and the spectral guardians, like with the wizard Rudd.

She waited, counting in her mind. Davyn paced behind her, his steps a steady rhythm. Icefire hummed to himself, some song she didn't know.

The wind did not come.

Then far above, the wooden tracks creaked.

Icefire stiffened. Immediately his slender fingers clutched his earring, and his eyes darted to look up into the hazy gray light above.

With his sword unsheathed in an instant, Davyn rounded into a fighting stance. "It's Ark and his men," Davyn said. "They've come back to finish us, just like I said."

"No," Icefire whispered. "It's Kirilin. She's here!"

Davyn narrowed his eyes and let out a deep sigh. "So she finally caught up to us. We never should have spent the night at the ships."

"She'd have found us eventually anyway, Davyn."

Trembling, Jirah fumbled with her own sword as she backed

116

toward the boys. "What do we do? How do we stop her? Nearra's not done yet!"

Icefire shook his head. They heard the noise clearly now. At first it was just Kirilin's steady footsteps. But then, bits of thick, guttural speech drifted down. Heavy clawed feet pounded against the ancient wooden tracks.

"Put me down!" a familiar voice cried out. A dog barked, the tiny yap echoing in the cavernous mine.

"Keene," Jirah whispered, clutching at Davyn's sleeve. "No! I told you we couldn't leave him! She's going to hurt him!"

Neither Davyn nor Icefire responded, though a quick flash of some emotion—guilt?—seemed to appear on Icefire's face. As one, the two boys began to back toward the broad stone wall behind them, their eyes never leaving the track. Gulping in her fear, Jirah followed their lead.

Keene's voice echoed again, but whatever he was saying was suddenly cut short. Another voice called out.

"Icefire," Kirilin called, her tone singsong. "My dear elf Icefire, I know you are down there. And I have something that you want."

The footsteps grew louder as the flickering firelight lining the tracks cast long shadows against the three companions. Then Kirilin walked into sight.

The cleric looked much as she had in Tarsis, only now her hair was tangled and knotted from heavy winds. Her eyes were wide with manic rage, and her red robes were torn. But she walked down the rotting spiral track with long, regal steps.

She smiled as she caught sight of the three of them. "I knew it," she crowed. She turned and studied the picked-clean mine, the pile of carts, and the stone tomb.

"Just like I left it," she said as she took another step down the track. She pressed her finger against the wall, then looked at her fingertip. "Dustier than I remember, though."

Behind her, shadows loomed. As the creatures came into sight behind the cleric, Jirah couldn't help but let out a small cry of despair. Davyn clutched at her hand reassuringly.

The four remaining draconians from Tarsis walked behind Kirilin, two by two. The one in the lead, its face scarred and burned from the flaming oil Icefire had thrown at it in the library, held a struggling Keene in its bulging leathery arms. One clawed hand was around the kender's mouth while the other held his hoopak, shortsword, and pack. The draconian beside them held the little white puff of fur that was Pip. The tiny dog trembled with fright.

Kirilin stopped midway down the track, watching the trio with a defiant, crazed smile.

"Seems I have you cornered," she called down, putting her withered hands on her hips. "And outnumbered at that."

Icefire and Davyn said nothing. Both boys clenched their weapons tight. Jirah sensed Icefire's free hand start to rise to clutch at his earring.

"Now, now, Icefire," Kirilin said. "Play fair." She held her hands high and muttered. A pulse of black shot toward the elf. He made to move out of the way, but it was too late.

"My magic," Icefire whispered as the cloud of misty black dissipated around him. "She made it so I can't use magic."

"Guess you'll need to get back to brawn, then, won't you," Davyn whispered back.

"I want only one thing, and it's very simple," Kirilin went on from above. "This little curse you're so intent on breaking must stay intact. And I will not stop chasing you until all of you are dead or have given up."

Stepping to the side, she gestured toward Keene and Pip, who were still struggling to break free from their monstrous captors. "Now, you know what I want," Kirilin said, then smirked. "And

I know what *you* want—for your friends not to be dead. So let's do as Hiddukel is so fond of doing and make a bargain. Pull your little friend Nearra from that tomb and give me back my jewel. In exchange, I will hand over your friend and his mongrel. I even brought along the kender's things so that he won't have to buy anything new. You can all go free." She tilted her head. "Well, except for Icefire, of course. You are to be at my side for the rest of your very long life."

Jirah glanced at both Icefire and Davyn. They met her eyes with sideways glances. Kirilin was most assuredly lying. And with her cocky manner and crazed look, it seemed she wasn't even trying to hide it.

"Never," Davyn growled, taking a step forward and brandishing his ornate sword. He clenched his jaw and met Kirilin's gaze with a look of steel. "We won't let you hurt Nearra."

"Give it up, Kirilin," Icefire called up in his cocky drawl. "You've been alive for four hundred years now, and I hate to break it to you, but I don't date older women."

The cleric took a deep, exaggerated breath, then smiled, tight lipped. "Very well," she said. "I tried to be reasonable."

Turning to the draconian holding Pip, she flicked her wrist in command. It nodded, then gripped Pip by the neck with one of its obscenely large hands. Pip barked, his tiny paws scrabbling at the air in a futile attempt to escape as the draconian lifted him high.

"No!" Jirah screamed, tears forming at her eyes.

Keene tried to yell and reach out for his little friend, but it was useless. The draconian holding Pip tossed the dog into the air and opened its fang-filled mouth wide in preparation.

With a gasp, Jirah turned away and dug her head into Davyn's side. Pip's barks ended, deathly abrupt, and she let out a sob. Davyn put his arm around her shoulder and pulled her close.

"I warned you!" Kirilin called down. "Now, give me the girl!"

Crying out, Icefire sprinted forward, holding his sword up like a javelin. His knuckles were white from the strength with which he gripped his sword; his sinewy muscles moved in perfect form as he threw it.

Kirilin dropped belly down to the wooden tracks. The sword whizzed above her and pierced the flame-scarred draconian's face right between its beady black eyes. Immediately the creature turned to stone, trapping the sword in its skull and a still-struggling Keene in its grip. Fresh tears fell down the kender's cheeks.

"There's your answer," Icefire called. His voice was steady and even, but it echoed around them with the force of an ocean wave.

Kirilin's head shot up. Mud and mold streaked her cheeks and the front of her gown. She bared her teeth and clutched at the track.

"Kill them," she commanded.

Bellowing, the draconians bounded past their dead companion and leaped to the ground below. Kirilin slowly stood, shaking. As she muttered another prayer to Hiddukel, she clutched at a silver medallion of faith that dangled from her neck. Jirah knew exactly what the cleric was doing—using her minions to keep them at bay while she prepared to cast a powerful dark spell that would destroy them all.

"Jirah, your sword!" Icefire called back. He turned his head and held out an expectant hand. With a nod, she tossed her short sword forward. It spun through the air before the elf caught it. Not losing the momentum, Icefire twirled forward, prepared to defend himself.

"Get back." Davyn clutched Jirah's shoulder and roughly shoved her toward the tomb where Nearra still relived the second wizard's curse. "Stay in the shadows; we'll protect you."

Jirah did not argue. She was weaponless, and all she wanted to do was curl up and cry. They'd killed Pip, innocent little Pip who'd never done anything wrong.

As Jirah backed up, she saw Davyn come to Icefire's side. Grim faced, the two boys waited. In front of them, sharp teeth glinted and wings shuddered in the orange light as the three draconians stalked forward. In their claws they clutched maces and axes.

A puff of white fur stuck to the scaly cheek of one of the draconians, and fresh blood stained its teeth. Jirah let out a gulping sob and slid down the wall behind her. In the shadows near the tomb, she clutched her knees and let the tears come.

The draconians grew closer, their claws meeting the stone floor with precise, deadly clicks that sent chills down Jirah's spine. One swung its axe and growled a laugh.

High above, Kirilin watched as green and black energy built up around her hands, blazing like ghostly bonfires.

Behind the cleric, Keene was still struggling to escape his stone bonds. Around him, the statue began to crumble as the dead draconian started to decay into dust. Finally the claw that had covered Keene's mouth fell away, and he cried out so loud and so full of rage that, for a moment, everyone in the cave turned to look up at him.

Keene fell to the track, dust clinging to the tears on his cheeks. His belongings and Icefire's sword fell beside him with a heavy thud and a resounding clang. Immediately the kender gripped the hilt of Icefird's sword and swung the blade at Kirilin's side with all his strength.

Steel met silk and then flesh, and the cleric tilted back her head to let out an anguished cry. Blood oozed from the wound and down her leg, and she dropped her arms. The dark magic dissipated into the chill air.

"Pip!" Keene cried as more tears flowed down his cheeks. "How could you! How could you!"

His arm muscles straining, Keene lifted the sword for another attack. Clutching her side with one hand, Kirilin turned to face him. She mumbled prayers, her free hand once again encircling her medallion.

"You Killed Him!" Keene cried. He brought the sword down.

Sickly green light flashed from Kirilin's hand, and Keene was thrust backward off the decaying tracks. He flew through the air before landing with a loud crack in a pile of old carts. The sword slammed against a wall and clattered to the floor. A few feathers that had torn free from the kender's topknot floated through the air.

"Keene," Jirah whispered.

The draconians attacked. Icefire and Davyn blocked their blows with expert swings of their weapons. One of the monstrous creatures lashed out with its foot, clawing through the green leather of Davyn's armor. He stumbled backward.

Icefire ducked and jabbed with Jirah's short sword. But one of the beasts managed to get a blow in, a punch to the elf's gut that sent him sprawling to the floor.

Up above, Kirilin clutched at the wall with a bloodstained hand, leaving red streaks. Again she muttered, again she attempted to bring down some spell from her dark god.

Oh gods, Jirah thought. We're all going to die. We're all going to die!

One of the draconians fell against the craggy wall, mere feet from where Jirah hid. She yelped in fear, but the monster ignored her. Bounding to its feet, the draconian leaped back into battle.

Frantic, Jirah stood up, her eyes on the tomb before her. She had to get out of here. She could get Nearra. Nearra had magic and could protect her.

Though unseen, the spectral guardians still guarded the tomb, waiting to strike. One touch from them would kill her, Jirah knew.

And the thought of their cold, undead touch made her want to retch.

But she had no choice.

Leaping from the shadows, Jirah raced to the front of the tomb. She reached forward and touched the stony wall. It rippled as though molten. She could still pass through.

Immediately the ghostly soldiers appeared. They glowed misty blue and held up their long swords.

Behind her, Jirah heard Davyn let out an angry cry, then the sound of steel meeting steel. Again Kirilin shouted, commanding their deaths.

Jirah leaped through the stone wall.

CHAPTER

11   Touch

I am alone, Nearra thought.

Nearra floated in the same black void. She'd been trapped for what felt like hundreds of years. Long ago she'd forgotten why she was even here, in this dark place of nothing. She'd forgotten why she wanted out.

No one was coming to help her escape or even to tell her why she'd been forced here. No one ever did, and no one ever would.

It will never end, she realized.

It wasn't a thought of despair so much as a statement of fact. She considered it for a few moments, then thought it again.

This will never end. I am to be trapped here forever.

Letting out a sigh of release, Nearra closed her eyes. It was at that moment that Nearra did what she'd vowed never to do—she gave up.

I am alone, Nearra thought.

And then, she thought nothing more.

Jirah gasped as she burst through the stony wall that guarded the tomb. Immediately she turned around. She was startled to find that she could see through the stone, as though it were cloudy glass. Davyn was on the floor, his sword held high to protect himself from attack. Icefire had somehow recovered his original sword and now fought with two. But all three draconians were still alive.

Then Jirah saw the spectral guardians. They floated silently in front of the wall, skeletal hands stretched toward her. She backed away, her arms trembling.

They can't see me, she thought. I'm inside the tomb now, they can't see me.

Still the ghostly soldiers came forward. Their hands pierced through the stone wall.

With a yelp of fear, Jirah turned to run, only to find herself face to face with a towering pillar of water. Only then did she notice the hazy blue light trickling around her.

The water seemed to surge upward in waves, but there was no sound. It was also blocking her way. A chill crept up her spine, and she realized that the spectral guardians were right behind her.

Fear clutched at her heart. Behind her lay death by the hands of the undead guardians, evisceration by the draconians, or a crushing spell sent down by Kirilin. Before her lay a void of uncertainty. She couldn't see anything but endless blue blackness within the void. Where was Nearra?

Turning, Jirah screamed again. The glowing skeletal fingers were mere inches from grazing her skin. Harsh winds, even more blisteringly cold than up above in the Plains of Dust, seemed to rush at her. She met the guardians' dead eyes, so empty and black that they reminded her of the deep wells near her home in Solamnia.

She had no choice.

Jirah leaned backward and let herself fall. The water enveloped her like a warm blanket, wrapping her in comfort as it pulled her deeper into its depths. The spectral guardians stopped as their fingers reached the edge of the void. Within moments, the water shrouded her vision with darkness, and they faded from sight.

Thrashing, Jirah tried to turn around in the water. Her lungs ached as she held her breath. Still there was no sight of Nearra.

She wanted to be angry at everyone else for everything that was happening. Nearra, Icefire, and Davyn—they had all decided to leave Keene and Pip behind. It was their fault Pip was dead, their fault that Kirilin had been able to use their friends to get the upper hand.

Except that wasn't right. Jirah was the one who had started this blasted quest. She was the one who had lied to everyone at Janeesa's request. It was all her fault.

I'm going to die in here, she thought. I'm not the chosen one, and I'm going to drown. This is all hopeless.

A calm descended over her, then a peacefulness that came with a frightening realization: death was her escape.

She'd realized it before, after they'd freed Rudd. Tylari's fetch had been inches from touching her and ripping the life from her body, and she was going to let it. Only when Janeesa threatened Keene's life did she agree to take up the quest again.

They wouldn't know, she thought. Janeesa and Tylari, they would think her death was an accident. They would leave Keene alone. Kirilin and her minions would stop chasing her. All the lies and the fear could go away.

Floating gently in the warm embrace of the black water, Jirah opened her lips to let the water rush in to flood her lungs and drown her.

Then, something touched her arm.

Something's touching me!

Nearra's eyes snapped open. For a moment, warm flesh had grazed her arm and someone else's thoughts had lanced through her mind. Someone else was here. Someone had come for her!

She tried to call out to whomever it was beside her in the void, but all that emerged from her lips was a cloud of bubbles. Splashing through the water around her, she reached out to grab whomever it was.

Then she felt the warm limb again. She clutched onto it with all her strength.

Nearra? a voice cried in her head. *Nearra, it's Jirah. Is that you? Please say it's you!*

She had to think for a moment, but yes, that was it: her name was Nearra. The thoughts that had been torn from her in the centuries that she'd been floating here began to bubble back up in her mind.

Yes, Nearra thought back. *It's me. Jirah, it's me!*

They fumbled for each other in the dark, and soon Nearra felt her sister's arms embracing her. She wanted to cry and laugh at the same time. It had been so long since she'd felt anyone's touch.

Nearra, we need to hurry and break the curse. Kirilin found us in the mine, she . . . she killed Pip and maybe Keene. She's casting a spell while Davyn and Icefire are fighting her draconians, but they're outnumbered.

No! Nearra thought. *I knew we should have gone back for Keene, I should have trusted myself, I should have . . .* She shook her head. *Jirah, thank you for coming to get me. It's been so long . . . .*

I'm . . . I'm here now. You're not alone. We can finish this, can't we? We need to hurry. And—how come I can breathe underwater?

Magic, Nearra thought as she rested her forehead against her sister's. *Magic, just like you'll someday have. We can do this together, Jirah, and then you can be what you want to be.*

Yes, Jirah thought. *What I want to be.*

What is it you always said? "Magic is life—"

"—And life is magic," Jirah finished. A feeling of uncertainty crept through Jirah's arms and into Nearra's body. Nearra furrowed her brow, not understanding her sister's lack of passion.

They clung to each other in the watery void. Nearra caressed Jirah's black hair just to feel its unique texture. She listened as Jirah rambled off every childhood story she could remember. She sang Jirah songs she made up on the spot.

Years flowed by, the time suddenly feeling tangible among the waves. Bit by bit, Nearra began to feel herself again. She wiggled her toes, she shook her head, she flexed her fingers. She imagined that she could taste the slight acridness of the water that they breathed.

With Jirah's touch giving her new strength, the final years of torture flashed by in an instant.

Nearra, Jirah said, her body trembling. *Nearra, look!*

Flomana appeared in front of them with a flash of blue, her body still ravaged by the years of underwater torture. But her features were changing right before their eyes. Her skin tightened and healed, glowing with renewed youth. Her hair untangled and braided itself. Her ivory robes repaired and flowed free.

Brown eyes now sparkling with sentience, Flomana smiled.

Nearra, the wizard's voice whispered in her mind. *Descendant of Anselm. You have again proven your purity and strength. Thank you. Your sacrifice has released me.*

The wizard turned her head to look at Jirah. *And Jirah,* she went on. *You shouldn't be here.*

In the blue glow from the wizard's magic bow, Nearra saw Jirah's eyes open wide with fear. *I—I'm sorry. I didn't know what else to do.*

You, too, have proven that you hold some strength. Continue on this path, and perhaps you shall also be rewarded by the gods.

Floating gently, her robes flowing around her like the wings of a pure white butterfly, Flomana unstrapped the quiver of arrows from her back. She held the arrows and the gem-capped longbow forward—to Jirah.

What? Jirah thought. *I can't. I'm not allowed to touch the weapons—they'll kill me.*

No longer, Flomana replied.

Letting go of Nearra, Jirah reached forward and grasped the bow and arrows in both hands. As the petite girl took them, Flomana closed her eyes. A peaceful calm seemed to settle over her.

Thank you, she whispered.

Then, like a flurry of snowflakes in a winter storm, Flomana exploded into dust that swirled through the waves before dissipating and floating away.

Around her, Nearra felt the water begin to tremble and she heard a dull, distant roaring. Above, she could see a hazy gray glow as the top of the watery pillar rapidly grew closer.

Nearra clutched Jirah's arms. *Hold on to me,* she shouted in her sister's mind. Jirah grasped her wrist just as the water crashed around them, taking with it the magic that had let them share thoughts.

The girls splashed to the floor, unharmed but drenched from head to toe. Jirah started to scream, but her cries quickly turned into hacking coughs. Nearra looked up to see what had frightened Jirah and saw the twin spectral guardians standing over them. Their gaunt hands were held forward to kill them with an undead touch.

But a wind arose then, swirling around the tomb and bringing with it a scent of roses and damp leaves. Nearra's hair whipped around her face as the breeze swirled up the remnants of the watery pillar and soared toward the cavernous ceiling. With cries of rapturous joy, the two spectral guardians closed their eyes and let the wind carry them away.

After a moment, the wind was gone. Nearra and Jirah sat huddled together in complete silence.

"Thank you," Nearra whispered. "Jirah, you've grown up so much."

Jirah didn't respond.

Distant clangs sounded and the two girls' heads snapped up.

They heard Davyn and Icefire shout in anger and pain. They heard the draconians' terrifying war cries.

"The battle," Jirah whispered.

Ahead of them, the tomb's veined stone wall crumbled away in chunks. Nearra jumped to her feet and held her staff ready. Holding her new weapon awkwardly, Jirah stood as well.

Her face stern, Nearra turned to her sister. "Let's go."

Jirah watched Nearra leap ahead, seemingly fearless. Her sister seemed to become more capable by the minute. However, Jirah didn't feel jealous. For the first time she could remember, she felt . . . pride.

Trembling, she studied the longbow. It was almost as tall as she was, carved at its ends with images of waves that splashed into dragon claw that held the two blue orbs. A silver bowstring ran from end to end.

A weapon. A magical weapon, given to *her*. It seemed to tingle in her hand, but not unpleasantly. There was something new inside of her, something deep and powerful that fought to surface.

Was it magic? Did she even want magic?

"Icefire, watch out!"

Jirah heard the scream from the cavern and it snapped her out of her thoughts. Strapping the quiver to her back, she held the longbow with both hands and leaped out to join her sister.

One of the draconians stood still. Two swords jutted from its side and the draconian had turned to stone. Weaponless, Icefire ducked and rolled beneath another draconian's wild blows. A barbed mace struck the ground right where his face had been moments ago, sending chips of stone flying.

Beside them, Davyn slashed with his sword, his movements calm and precise. The draconian he fought roared and lashed out with its clawed fists, but Davyn was ready for it. Somehow he'd managed to tire the beast out.

Nearra stood in front of the tomb as Jirah ran to join her. Nearra, too, showed no signs of fear as she held her staff at the ready.

"Die already!" Davyn bellowed. The draconian lunged, and Davyn ducked. He rolled between its legs, coming up directly behind it—and right in front of the piles of carts. His eyes darting between the carts and the draconian, Davyn smiled.

As the draconian reared to turn, Davyn reached behind him and grabbed one of the ancient metal wheels and let it fly like a discus. The wheel spun through the air before colliding with the draconian's forehead. The beast roared as it fell backward.

"Davyn, here!" Icefire held his hand out expectantly. The draconian attacking him had maneuvered the elf right next to its fallen comrade.

For a moment, the ranger hesitated. Then, with a shake of his head, he tossed his ornamental sword. The silver blade swirled through the air before Icefire caught it. With an expert flourish, he spun around and sliced the blade right through the fallen draconian's neck. The draconian coughed and sputtered, giving Icefire just enough time to pull the blade free before the monster turned into stone.

Spinning in the same move, Icefire brought the blade up to attack the final draconian, only to be met with its fist. The elf flew to the floor, losing the sword.

The draconian loomed over Icefire.

That was when Nearra fired.

"Api anak!" A fireball exploded from the tip of her staff. It blasted through the air, meeting the draconian's chest. Flames consumed the creature. The draconian shrieked in pain, then fell silent.

Nearra lowered her staff, a hint of a smile at the edge of her lips.

Davyn ran to Icefire—then leaned past him to pick up his sword. Rolling his eyes, Icefire stood to collect his and Jirah's swords from the pile of dust that had once been a draconian.

A flash of red silk and gray-blond hair caught Jirah's eye.

"Kirilin!" Jirah shouted.

Icefire and Davyn spun around as the dark cleric flew at them from the dark. Screaming as she ran, the woman had both her hands held taut at her side. Green and black power swelled in her palms.

The cleric's scream turned into a word of divine power, and the green energy exploded. Icefire and Davyn flew backward.

"No!" Nearra ran forward, her staff held high. But Kirilin was still racing forward, straight toward Icefire. Black magic darkened the air around the cleric. Nearra would never make it in time.

If there's a god up there who likes me, Jirah thought, please help me now.

Her hands trembling, she held up the ancient longbow. She had very little experience with a bow and arrow, but she hoped it was enough. With one eye closed, she nocked one of the mystical arrows and aimed it directly at Kirilin's chest.

She let loose. The silver bowstring twanged, scraping along her bare forearm and rubbing her skin raw. She yelped.

But the arrow was flying.

As it flew, splashes of blue light seemed to burst backward from the arrow's tip. It looked very much like a dolphin diving through ocean waves.

As it neared its target, the arrow exploded into a powerful pillar of water. Kirilin barely had time to register the inexplicable waves that pounded toward her before she was caught in their powerful grip. Shrieking in fear and rage, the cleric flew backward through the torch-lit cavern, sputtering as the water filled her nostrils and seeped into her mouth. She crashed through one of the beams supporting the spiraling wooden track, then slammed into a stone wall with a satisfyingly loud thud.

Unconscious and soaked head to toe, the dark cleric slumped to the floor. Only then did Jirah notice that Kirilin's hair was now pure white, that her skin was more wrinkled and withered than ever. The freeing of the second wizard had stolen more of her once eternal life.

"Are you all right?" Nearra ran to Icefire's side.

The elf sat up, rubbing his head. "Bruised, and my magic was nullified, but I'll be fine."

Davyn dusted himself off and stood. "I'm fine too, if you care."

Jirah raced forward. "Did you see that?" she said. Holding the longbow high, she stared at it with awe. "Did you see what I did?"

Nearra laughed, then jumped up and pulled Jirah tight in a hug. "I sure did." Pulling back, she held Jirah by her shoulders and beamed. "We're doing it, Jirah. We're really doing it!"

Groans sounded from behind them, in the carts. "Oh," Jirah said. "Keene!" Then, remembering, she let out a gasping sob. "Pip," she whispered.

Icefire's face fell. "Gods," he said. "Keene." Then, meeting the others' eyes, he snapped to attention. "Gather our things. We need to get out of here before Kirilin wakes up. I'll get Keene."

"Yes, Cap—" Davyn started to say in his usual sarcastic way.

Then they all heard it—a terrifying rumbling, the creaking of timbers under strain.

All eyes turned to the ancient wooden track. Rocks fell from the wall as the wood splintered.

The track—their only way out of the mine—was about to collapse.

CHAPTER

12   THE FINAL PATH

G o!" Icefire screamed.

Nearra, Davyn, and Jirah sprinted toward their packs. Rocks smashed into the ground around them as dust fell like rain.

Spinning on his heels, Icefire scanned the hill of carts. He strained his pointed ears to listen over the ominous rumbling for the sound of Keene's breathing.

There. Toward the top of the pile. Sheathing his sword, he ran furiously, veering around toppled carts and jumping over piles of dirt.

He saw another beam against the wall splinter and give way.

"Keene!" he called. Clutching at the rusted cart edges, he hauled himself up. He balanced on slender edges, avoiding spinning wheels. "Keene!"

Behind him he heard Davyn yelling for Nearra and Jirah to hurry up. They were already on the tracks and racing high. He heard someone yelp as they almost fell.

"KEENE!" Icefire bellowed. The torchlight shuddered as the rumbling grew louder.

"Icefire," a small voice wheezed.

Heart pounding, Icefire ducked through the slats of a broken cart and, finally, he found the kender. The little sailor lay unmoving in a cart bottom, surrounded by layers of dust that had been disturbed by his forceful landing. Wren feathers that had torn free from Keene's topknot lay haphazardly around his fallen form.

"I'm here," Icefire said. Gripping his friend's shoulder, he hefted the little kender up and turned toward the tracks.

The tracks near the bottom swayed. Kirilin lay unmoving where she'd landed, though Icefire knew she wasn't dead. Nothing would kill her until the final wizard was freed.

Another timber gave out. In a flurry of dust and wood chips, the track started to collapse.

"Icefire!" Nearra called from above him. "Come on!"

Nearra, Jirah, and Davyn stood on a platform near the top of the mound of carts. Blood smeared the wall behind them. Jirah stared wide eyed as the tracks farther down gave way and fell to the cavern floor.

Not waiting a second more, Icefire bounded up the mountain of debris, clutching at awkward edges and bent wheels to pull himself forward. When he was only a few feet away, he hefted Keene with all his strength, tossing him high. The kender thudded against Davyn's chest.

More timbers cracked and fell, the noise deafening. With only moments to spare, Icefire leaped. He landed hard against the edge of the platform, the wood punching him in the gut and knocking the wind out of him. Hands clutched at his shoulder, hauling him up.

"RUN!" Davyn screamed.

With Davyn carrying Keene, the companions bounded up the tracks. Mud and mold flung from their feet as they scrambled up the wooden beams.

Ahead, Icefire saw the hazy gray light of the afternoon sky. His lungs blazing with pain, his muscles screaming from the strain, he forced himself forward.

The companions climbed out of the hole, gripping at the stone and pulling themselves up. Adrenaline gave them all the strength they needed, as beneath them, the ancient tracks finally collapsed. The thunderous sound of crashes enveloped them as clouds of dust mushroomed up from the small opening, scratching at Icefire's face.

Everyone collapsed on the cold, stony ground. For a long moment they lay there, gasping for air. The rumbling faded away like thunder, and Icefire watched as the wind carried the cloud of dust into the evening sky.

Beside Davyn, Keene coughed.

Nearra sat up, rubbing dust out of her eyes. The key-shaped gem swayed at her throat. "Is everyone all right?"

Icefire murmured that he was, then looked around. Thank Zivilyn everyone appeared unharmed.

His legs trembling with strain, Davyn got to his feet. "We can't stop now," he said even as he heaved for air. "The bandits . . . "

Jirah shook her head and crawled across the frozen ground to Keene's side. "I can't," she said. "I need to rest." She clutched Keene's hand in her own, squeezing it gently. Icefire swallowed as he saw his old friend staring blankly up at the broad gray sky, no expression on his face.

"Nearra," Icefire said. "What do you want to do?"

She shook her head. "Rest. We have to. We won't be able to travel far in this condition. The battle, the magic . . . It was too much."

"But Ark!" Davyn protested.

Nearra shook her head. "If he comes back, he comes back. We'll fight him then. And we'll be more ready to do so if we're not completely exhausted."

Letting his pack fall heavily to the ground, Davyn turned to scan their surroundings. The black dot that was the ancient boulder sat on the horizon. Far to the south were the distant hills and cliffs. Wind flowed past them, freezing the sweat that poured down Icefire's face. There was no sign of any life at all, let alone Ark and his bandits.

"They'll be back," Davyn grunted.

Icefire got to his knees and scooted nearer the others. Davyn sat down at Jirah and Keene's side, leaning against his pack. Still, Keene lay unmoving.

"Jirah?" Icefire said. "You went into the tomb. You got the weapon?"

Jirah did not look away from Keene's face. She stroked his cheek with a gentle finger, a look of guilt clouding her features.

"Jirah?"

Shaken from her thoughts, Jirah turned and nodded. "Yes," she said, her voice low. "The wizard, she gave me the weapon. For helping."

Icefire reached for the longbow. Its carvings were intricate, its design sleek and deadly. The arrows strapped to Jirah's back glowed with blue light. Strangely, though she'd fired one shot, the quiver seemed full.

As his fingers neared the bow, he heard the bow's voice calling to him. It was feminine and sorrowful, and also deeply powerful. He noticed Davyn giving him a hard look and he stopped reaching for it, his hand shaking.

"I'll have to take a look at it later," he said. "Magnificent design."

Nearra offered a weak smile. "We did it, everyone," she said. "We got past Kirilin again. Thank you so much, all of you."

No one said anything and, after a moment, Nearra's smile fell and she looked down.

"Pip," Keene gulped. His chest shuddered with sobs, and his lip quivered. Sadness overcame Icefire then. Pip had been a constant companion to them since he was a puppy. He was Keene's partner in comedy. And now the little dog was gone. The joy had been torn from Keene's face, and the sight of it filled Icefire with despair.

Keene's eyes shifted, meeting Icefire's own. "You said you'd come back for us," he whispered. "You said you didn't leave a man behind."

"We were going to," Icefire said. "Keene, we had to hurry. We knew the prison wouldn't hold Kirilin for long and—"

"It didn't hold her," Keene sobbed. "She and her draconians killed people, and she broke down the door of my cell, and they took me and Pip. I thought it was you coming for me, but it wasn't you." He looked away. "Pip was so scared. I'd never seen him shake so much."

"We were going to come back," Icefire said.

"You didn't," Keene said. "You didn't even fight to keep me out of prison. It's all your fault, Captain. Pip would be alive if it weren't for you, I know it."

Icefire reached forward and gripped Keene's shoulder. The kender wrenched it away and tilted to his side. Facing away from the group, the kender continued to sob silently as he stared over the desolate scenery.

For a long while, no one spoke. They huddled beneath their cloaks as night fell, clinging to one another for warmth. They didn't dare light a fire, for doing so would lead any enemies directly to them.

As the last rays of light spread across the plains, Nearra remembered Anselm's magic map. She pulled it from her pack, and the companions spread it out in front of them. As before, the enchanted parchment now revealed a new path—the path to the final wizard, whose freedom would break the curse, kill Kirilin, and end their quest once and for all.

"I don't recognize that area," Nearra said. "It looks like it's part of Solamnia, but that can't be right, because look here." She pointed to a chain of mountains. "That's the Vingaard Mountains. That area to the southwest doesn't exist."

Icefire shook his head. "No, it does still exist. This was before the Cataclysm, remember. That's Ergoth of old."

"Southern area," Davyn said. "So, Southern Ergoth, I presume?"

Icefire nodded. "Looks like we are to go to the homeland of the Kagonesti and—" he shook his head, rueful "—the Silvanesti. This was where we migrated during the war."

Tilting the map to study it in the hazy light, Icefire thought hard. The positioning of the last tomb seemed very specific.

"I think I know where this is," he said. "I'd have to do some charting, but I'm almost positive about the location."

Nearra grabbed his hand and squeezed. "Would you be able to guide us, Icefire?" she asked.

He nodded. "Of course. We'll need my ship, though. I'll cast a spell in the morning—perhaps the seeing spell I used in Icereach—and speak to Tu. I'll have her meet us, but we'll have to travel west."

"West?" Davyn asked. "Why not south? Ice Mountain Bay is closer."

Icefire squeezed Nearra's hand back. "Tu's making trade runs north by now, so getting the ship to the bay would take too long. And I don't know about you, but I'd rather not be in this frigid weather any longer than we have to."

"Fine," Davyn said. His mouth set, he watched Nearra and Icefire clasp hands. "We should set out when the sun rises. Let's get this quest over with."

Still stroking Keene's arm reassuringly, Jirah looked away. "The final path," she muttered. Casting off her cloak, she stood and turned toward the others. "I'll be right back," she said. "I need to . . . go."

"I should go with you," Nearra said, starting to rise. "It's dangerous."

Jirah shook her head. "No," she said. "I'll be quick." She patted her side. "I have my sword."

"Jirah—"

"I'll scream if anything happens, all right?" Jirah snapped. Without waiting for a response, she turned and bounded into the darkness, her pack over her shoulder.

"Don't worry," Icefire said. He squeezed Nearra's hand again. "I'll keep an eye on her. I'll . . . er . . . turn away when she does her business."

As she ran into the dark, Jirah seemed to glow with a misty red light. His elf heritage gifted him with night vision. As he suspected, he saw her pull a mirror from her pack.

Janeesa, he thought. Still biding your time. What are you up to?

With a questioning look from Nearra, Icefire turned away. His eyes came to rest on Keene's tiny form, huddled beneath a cloak of furs. Guilt flowed through him once more, and Icefire lowered his head.

"Yes, Jirah?" Janeesa asked through the mirror. "What is it?"

"We did it," Jirah whispered. "We freed the second wizard. We have the second weapon and Kirilin is trapped below in the mine."

Her reflection's eyebrows raised. "Really? Well, that was fast. Do you know the final location?"

"I do," Jirah said. "It's in Southern Ergoth, some place in the south. Icefire said he might know it."

"What luck," Janeesa cooed. "Tylari and I are on a ship bound for Southern Ergoth as we speak. We have . . . business to take care of. This is perfect. Once you're there and know the final location, you must contact me at once. Then we can be there when the curse is broken. We will have the weapons, and we can help you kill Nearra and claim your birthright as the descendant of a powerful wizard."

Jirah stiffened. She turned from the mirror, glancing over her shoulder to look behind her. The huddled shadows of Nearra, Icefire, Davyn, and Keene were only a few yards away.

Again guilt wormed through her. She'd been with Nearra in the tomb. She'd felt only moments of the torture that Nearra had to endure. But those moments were enough.

Her sister had gone through so much: Maddoc removing her memory, Asvoria possessing and violating her body, reliving the centuries-long tortures of two cursed wizards. And she wasn't even doing it for herself. She was doing it for Jirah!

Bits of magic swirled in Jirah's gut, but the feeling sickened her. She didn't deserve this. So many people were being hurt because of her lies and her obsession to regain magic for herself and her father.

"Janeesa," Jirah said. "I can't do it. I—I won't. I won't kill Nearra."

Steely silence was her only response. Jirah braced herself, waiting for Janeesa to snap at her, or for Tylari's dark voice to rage from the shadows of the mirror.

"I see," Janeesa said, her voice strangely calm. "Fine, Jirah. I see you have made your choice. We will take care of everything."

Jirah swallowed. She didn't like the sound of that.

"Is Tylari there?" Jirah whispered. "Did he hear?"

"He heard," Janeesa said. "Luckily for you, Jirah, we are both much too busy with other matters to worry about you at the moment. You haven't been living up to your half of our bargain. Icefire is not a slave to magic. Davyn is not dead. You keep changing your mind about exactly how far you are willing to go to become a wizard. But it doesn't matter anymore, as long as the curse is broken and the Trinistyr is restored. If you follow through and finish at least that, then Tylari and I will reconsider how to handle your sister."

There was a long pause.

"Maybe."

Again Jirah swallowed. She felt hot all over, despite the chill air flowing past her. "Yes, Janeesa," she whispered.

The mirror stilled. Jirah studied her dark reflection in what little moonlight seeped through the writhing clouds above. Sweat-soaked black hair twisted across her face in the endless winds.

For a moment, she crouched among the rocks and sand, consumed with her thoughts. Then, shoving back her fear, she made a decision.

Gingerly, she set the silver-framed mirror on the ground. She picked up the largest stone that she could find. Hefting it up with all her strength, Jirah brought the stone down hard.

Glass shattered. Slivers of the broken mirror exploded outward, slicing her hand, but she didn't care.

Feelings she couldn't describe raced through her. Still clutching the stone, Jirah hefted her pack over her shoulder and stood. Trembling, she stared at the scattered pieces of the broken mirror.

Then she dropped the stone among the mirror's remains and turned around to walk back toward her sister and their friends.

CHAPTER

13   MADNESS

The prison was small, a gray stone structure no bigger than a peasant's shed. Covered in ivy and nestled between dense trees, it seemed as though it had always existed in this untamed forest.

But, Janeesa knew, there had been no prison before the War of the Lance began six years back, when the Silvanesti had migrated to Southern Ergoth.

Six years ago. That was when her father's madness had grown too big a liability. That was when the other elf mages had cast the spells that inadvertently destroyed his mind.

Janeesa crouched beneath the trees, anger rising within her as she watched the small prison through the bushes. Those elf mages—her father's *friends*—had failed to heal him. Rather than try to set things right, they had locked him in this dank cell in the middle of nowhere until the war ended and he was, as they had told Janeesa then, "no longer a threat."

Now, they were gone. The war over, many of the Silvanesti had returned home to try and fix the destruction brought on by Lorac's Nightmare. The elves would rather hide in the withered, deformed trees of the homeland forests than mingle among the wild Kagonesti elves. And really, who could blame them?

But the Silvanesti had left her father behind. Those know-it-all fools had left him in this prison to rot, a forgotten casualty of their magical experimentation.

Not that he was alone here, not entirely. The prison was near some Silvanesti artist colony called Aerendor, a town that had existed on Southern Ergoth for years before the great migration. The town was there still, though when Janeesa sneaked past it only moments ago, she saw that it had fallen into ruin. A faded stench of dark magic had wafted from the burnt buildings, though she didn't particularly care why a wizard would have bothered attacking a bunch of simpering elf artisans.

Now the only thing done for her father was that a few healers from the colony still traveled to the prison daily to feed him and make sure he was well. They refused to put him out of his misery even as they looked at him with disgust, because they naively believed that the white-robed elves would return with some cure.

Janeesa knew better. No one besides her and her brother cared about their father, not really. And for that, they would pay.

"I am tired of sitting in these brambles," Tylari muttered beside her. Janeesa turned and saw her brother through the underbrush. A drab brown cloak—the same kind as she wore—covered his robes, its hood drawn to cast his face in shadow.

"I am not some filthy Kagonesti," he went on as he scratched irritably at his side. "There is no one outside the prison. Let's go already. Or are you making me wait on purpose, to make me itch? You are, aren't you?"

"Yes," Janeesa drawled. "That was my plan all along—to make you itch."

"I knew it," Tylari muttered, and Janeesa was unable to tell if he was serious or not.

With a sigh, she stood and pushed through the branches. Leaves rustled as Tylari followed.

Midday sunlight streamed through the canopy above, bathing the prison in golden light. As she neared, Janeesa saw that purple flowers had bloomed along one of the vines clutching at the small fortress. With a snort, she reached into a pouch at her waist. Muttering arcane phrases, she flung a handful of dark powder at the flowers and watched as they withered and blackened.

"Nice," Tylari said.

A small window was cut into the stone wall, just at a grown elf's height. Rusted bars filled the opening, keeping anyone from coming out—or going in. At the base of the wall, below the window, was a narrow opening where the healers shoved in her father's plate of food. Grass rustled as a rat scurried out of the opening.

Besides the window and the hole for the food, there was no other way into the squat, square building. It was perfectly sealed, a cell from which there was no escape without much firepower—and the elf mages had made sure that her father had no firepower.

Janeesa lifted her two slender hands and gripped the rusty bars. Peering between them, she looked into the cell. "Father?"

The stench met her in a wave. It was the smell of wet animals and sewers, and she nearly gagged. She released the bars and clenched her nose closed.

"Father?" she said again.

Still, nothing. She looked closer, scanning what little she could see by the light that made it past her head to fill the room. She saw the rotting pallet her father had to sleep on, the bubbling stream from which he drank course up in the corner, the strange charcoal markings scratched onto the walls.

"*You.*" A face loomed in front of her, eyes wild, teeth bared, its hair a tangled and matted halo. Janeesa jumped back.

The creature—her father—clutched at the bars with torn and

bloody fingers. Bloodshot blue eyes shot back and forth, studying Janeesa and Tylari. "My meal. MY MEAL!" he screamed.

"Father," Janeesa whispered. She reached forward a trembling hand.

Like an animal, he snapped at her fingers, and she pulled back.

"He smells," Tylari muttered. Tangles of hair fell in front of his face, and he looked almost bored. Janeesa felt a surge of anger toward him. Did he not care?

With a shake of her head, she turned back toward her father. "Father, listen," she said.

"The factors are misaligned," the insane elf growled. His pointed ears quivered as he freed one hand from the bars to scratch urgently at his wrist. Around it was a braided metal band that glowed with a magic aura. "There are MEALS to be had, you *beasts*, and they must be had by the factors!"

Tears stung Janeesa's eyes. "Listen to me," she said, her voice quaking with rage. Her father snorted and looked away, but did not move from the bars. "Listen to me!"

"The gods frown," he whispered. His look was far away as he once again met his daughter's eyes. "They frown because of the factors. They—"

Janeesa swallowed. "We've come to free you," she said, resting her palms against the cool stone of the wall and leaning close. "We have found a cure. I *will* heal you, and we will destroy those who hurt our family. It won't be long now. I'll have the Trinistyr, and then I can use it on you and Tylari. We—"

A hand clenched her shoulder, and Janeesa jumped back. Her brother glared at her.

"What?" she demanded.

Tylari's hood had fallen, and the breeze blew his hair from his face. His look was unusual, like some mix of pity and hatred.

"Again," he muttered. His fingers dug into Janeesa's shoulder, and she cried out in pain. "You said it again! You mean to take away the divine power that is my right!"

Wrenching free from his grip, Janeesa scowled. "Tylari, hush," she hissed. "Just stop it with this 'god' nonsense. Stop it!" She flung a hand toward the wild face of their father, who still peered at them between the bars. "Is *this* what you want to happen to you? Do you want to be thrown in some prison and forgotten about because you can't control yourself?"

"You would do that to me, wouldn't you?" he seethed. "Wouldn't you!"

His teeth bared and his fingers crackling with power, Tylari stepped forward, forcing Janeesa back against the prison wall.

"Tylari," she said, holding her hands high. "Brother, think for a moment. Just *think*. I know your mind is not ravaged yet. I know it. What you are saying is madness. I would never hurt you."

"*Lies.*" Tylari took another step closer.

High-pitched giggles sounded from the window, and Tylari and Janeesa both turned to see their father, a manic grin searing his cheeks. He pointed toward the forest behind them, his fingernail cracked and caked with dried blood.

"There are factors," he said, his eyes meeting Janeesa's. "I have been charting the course of the backward Etat. It might be . . . behind you."

Then Janeesa heard it: twigs crunching, voices murmuring.

"Tylari," she whispered, trying to move past him. "We must go. Someone is coming. We'll have to come back for Father later."

"No!" Tylari shouted. Again he raised his hands. Sparks flew between his fingers as magic energy coalesced into some new spell. His lips moved rapidly, though he made no sound.

"Tylari," Janeesa whispered as she shoved gently against his chest. "Snap out of it, now. I don't want to hurt you, but I will if I am forced."

Too late. Janeesa stiffened as she saw two figures move in the trees behind Tylari. The Messengers weren't supposed to be here. They couldn't be caught, not now, not when they were so close to fulfilling her plans.

The figures were two Silvanesti elves from the colony. One was a male dressed in an archer's leather armor. Long blond hair was tied back at the nape of his neck, and dark blue eyes did not leave the face of his companion.

The other was a younger female elf that Janeesa recognized immediately. Golden curls hung past her shoulders, and her green eyes sparkled. Gloves covered her delicate fingers, and she wore leather pants that disappeared into high boots.

"Rina," Janeesa whispered.

It was the elf girl who had traveled with Davyn back when they were still fighting to free Nearra. It was the girl Jirah had been commanded to kill, because Rina knew who the Messengers were.

And she was here.

As one, the two elves caught sight of Janeesa and Tylari fighting near the prison. Immediately the older male elf reached for his bow. Rina's hands hovered over the daggers strapped to her side.

"Who are you?" the male called. "What are you doing here?"

Tylari did not move from his position. His steel-colored eyes did not leave Janeesa's, and he continued to cast his spell. Janeesa ducked beneath his arms and held her hands high.

"We are travelers," she said. "Just passing through. We saw this building and wondered what it was."

"Aerendor was attacked recently," Rina said, her hands relaxing. "We are rebuilding, and we are not welcoming visitors."

Janeesa bowed her head slightly. "Our apologies. We shall be going. Brother?"

Tylari stopped chanting and turned to face her. Madness flashed through his eyes. "You would betray me, Janeesa? You would ruin my life's work?!"

Rina stiffened at the mention of Janeesa's name. Immediately she reached for her companion's arm. "Fiernan," she said. "Go back to town. Get help. I know these two."

"Rina," he said.

"Go!"

The archer nodded, then turned and raced back through the trees. Rina's hands once again hovered over her daggers.

"Janeesa," she said. She took a tentative step forward. "And Tylari, right?"

"My name," Tylari intoned, "shall be worshipped by all."

"That's right," Janeesa said, ignoring her brother. She took a step toward Rina. "Fancy seeing you here."

Rina's eyes flashed with realization as she sidestepped over a fallen log. "The Messengers," she said. "You helped Davyn back at Forestedge when we fought Asvoria. I knew that I knew you. Dark elves, banished from the Silvanesti after their father fell mad, and they chose red and black robes. I thought there were three of you." Confusion creased her features, and she shook her head, sending golden curls bobbing over her shoulders. "But that doesn't make sense. Why did you disguise yourselves as humans to help us?"

"The girl," Tylari muttered. His shoulders stooped, he came to stand beside his sister. "It was for the girl."

Janeesa stiffened. *Careful Tylari,* she thought. *Be careful.*

Janeesa held her head high, letting her sleek golden hair fall back over her cloak. "We'd heard tales of the sorceress inhabiting Nearra's body. We knew how catastrophic it would be to everyone were she to complete her plans. Most don't trust dark elves, so we disguised ourselves. That's all."

Her daggers now in hand, Rina rounded on Janeesa. "No," she

149

said. "That's not it. I heard tales, remember. I know what you two are like. And you two don't go helping people out of the kindness of your hearts."

"*You,*" Tylari seethed. "Jirah was supposed to kill you. You know too much."

"I knew it," Rina whispered. "Jirah was trying to hurt me, and at your command, wasn't it? What is going on?" Her dagger aimed at Janeesa's heart, she scowled. "Tell me!"

In a flash, Tylari was in front of the elf girl. His eyes bulging with manic fury, he raised his hands. "I am to become a god, and you are to know nothing! Davyn is coming here and he cannot be told of my power, of my divine destiny!"

Rina reeled back. "What are you—"

"*Daya belit!*" Green light exploded from Tylari's fingertips. Screaming, Rina flew backward through branches that snapped with the force of her passing. Her head snapped back with a heavy crack as she slammed against a tree, then crumpled to the ground.

"You will die," Tylari sneered. His hands arched like a raptor's talons, he stalked forward to finish the job.

"Tylari!" Janeesa shouted. "Control yourself! That other elf saw us, and he will be back soon with help. We have to go."

The mad elf spun, his finger pointed directly at Janeesa's chest. "*Santet!*"

Prickling pain shuddered up her back, and Janeesa gasped. The jabs continued to course up and down her spine, slicing deeper and deeper, forcing every nerve in her body to scream in pain. Unable to stand the agony, she fell to her knees.

"You will command me no longer," Tylari seethed. "I will stand no more of your lies while you work with that human girl to destroy me!" With two large strides, he came to stand before his crouching sister. Kneeling, he put his hands on her shoulders. His blue-gray eyes flashed with anger. "You will not use that unholy relic on me."

"Tylari," she pleaded. "You're hurting me."

In one swift move, Tylari stood and spun around to stand behind her. Janeesa tried to cry out, tried to move so as to cast a counter spell. But she could not think through the pain in her body, could not move even if she could summon the thought to do so.

She sensed his hands hovering on either side of her head. Her temples pulsed and pounded, and she screamed. Through vision blurred with pain-induced tears, she saw Rina stand and run away.

"*Aku calang mu daya,*" Tylari intoned, ignoring their fleeing enemy. "*Perubahan dari ente ke saya!*" White light flared around her, searing her eyes with its brightness.

Tylari continued to chant, casting his spell, but Janeesa could no longer hear his words over the sound of her own shouts of agony. Her mind seemed to boil inside her head, melting into a slimy mess that would surely pour out of her pointed ears. Her reserves of magical power pulsed backward through her veins until they were pulled up and out through her mouth, her nostrils, her eyes. Outside magic tore through her to ravage her insides. Her screams became piercing howls that rubbed her throat raw.

Then finally, Tylari stopped incanting. The magic ceased tearing through her, and Janeesa fell to the dirt at his feet.

She lay there, shivering, her knees clutched to her chest. Even as the memories of the spell drifted away, she sensed the last of her coherent thought fading. The image of the woods around her blurred. Decades of her life's knowledge flashed through her head, fighting to surface from the bog in which they had been drenched, but they seemed foreign, and she forced them down.

Tylari's boots walked into her line of vision. With tremors pulsing through her body, she looked up.

The young wizard stood above her. Though once he had walked stooped and broken, now his back had straightened with new strength. Though once his eyes had held a dark cast, now they were quick, focused. Always the follower, always incoherent, he was now imbued with her magic and strength. Tylari shone with an aura of golden power.

Janeesa stared up at her brother as he was now, born anew. As the only distinct image in the murky, incoherent world that now surrounded her, she felt that she was seeing a god.

"Get up." His voice was different—louder, confident. "We have big days ahead, dear sister. We have to save Father and take vengeance upon his betrayers, don't we?"

"Father," Janeesa muttered. "We must avenge . . ." But even as she spoke the words, she felt confused. There was something important that she was supposed to do. Something . . . hard. There had been much planning. There were names. Icefire? Jirah? She couldn't remember who they were.

Tylari knelt down and offered Janeesa a smile. "That's right," he said, his broad grin seeming to blaze as bright as the sun. "There's vengeance to be had." He grabbed Janeesa's hand and lifted her up. She looked at him with rapture flooding her heart.

"But first," he said as he led her away from the prison, "I have a few stops to make."

CHAPTER

14 QUICKENED

"S omeone's following us."

Davyn stiffened and halted, his sword held high as he prepared to hack through another cluster of vines blocking their path.

Icefire stood behind him, staring at the forest canopy above. His slender fingers clutched his gold hoop earring.

Nearra circled, looking wary, the staff of fire clenched tight in both hands. "Are they close?" she asked the elf.

Icefire nodded. "I'll give you three guesses who they are."

"Kirilin?" Keene growled.

Icefire shook his head. Davyn scowled. "It's Ark and his bandits."

It had been weeks since they had freed the second wizard in the Plains of Dust. They'd managed to survive that first frigid night near the old mine and had set out the next day. As the others had gathered their things on that early morning, Icefire had called forth a shimmering blue orb of magic and had spoken through it to Tu, the first mate of his ship.

More magic, Davyn noticed. Icefire had claimed, often and forcefully, that he wasn't a wizard, that he was nothing but a sailor. But Davyn knew for certain now—the elf was tapping into that power every chance that he could. If it hadn't been for Nearra breaking up their argument, Icefire would have cast some spell on him deep in the mine. He was sure of it.

Icefire was still teaching Nearra magic, dragging her deeper and deeper into a world that he was now certain was inescapably dark, no matter the color of one's robes. Davyn wanted to stop it, wanted to keep Nearra from a dark path, but she refused to listen to him, and so there was nothing he could do.

They'd traveled west, with the icy winds still freezing their faces and whipping their hair. They'd seen a nomadic tribe of centaurs and a few unsettlingly large creatures, but they had managed to avoid any further confrontation. As summer grew ever closer to its end, the skies had started to grow darker. Snow would surely fall upon the plains before too long.

Davyn was surprised at how warm it was as they climbed to higher ground and trekked through the forests near the foothills of the Kharolis Mountains. They rested in towns along the way, selling their cold weather gear for more pressing supplies.

The entire time they traveled, Jirah did not leave Keene's side. The little kender was startlingly quiet, his grief a potent reminder of all the darkness they'd experienced so recently. It seemed unnatural for a creature so unrelentingly cheerful as a kender to withdraw as Keene had. It was like seeing all the fun kicked out of a once lively puppy.

Jirah, too, seemed even more quiet than usual. She kept looking over her shoulder, as though expecting to find someone looming behind her. Dark circles rimmed her eyes, and Davyn noticed that she seemed to avoid any and all reflective surfaces.

Davyn didn't have much time to worry about the two of them, though. As the companions rested and ate at the inns, using up even more of what little steel they had left, Icefire and Nearra flipped through spell books. Icefire especially seemed interested in

JEFF SAMPSON

the mystical longbow that Jirah clutched protectively everywhere they went. The elf had yet to try to grab it, as he had every other magical artifact they'd come across, but Davyn saw a dark gleam of anticipation in his eyes.

Now, days into their journey since the last town, and deep in an overgrown forest, Icefire made his startling announcement of Ark's proximity.

Davyn lowered his sword and backed toward his companions. They were in a clearing, but around them was heavy woodland. Pines and oaks rose to cluster above their heads, a green canopy that filtered the midday light. Birds called to one another, and animals scurried through bushes. Insects of the normal size zipped around his sweating forehead.

"I don't hear anyone approaching," Davyn announced. He slackened hold of his sword. "A centaur Ark's size would make a lot of noise clomping through here."

Icefire shook his head and grabbed for his own weapon. "No, he's close. And it's definitely our old friend the centaur bandit."

"Do you think Kirilin is with him?" Jirah asked. She sidled up to Nearra. "Could he have helped her escape the mine?"

Icefire shrugged. "I don't know. I hope not."

To the north, near a cluster of boulders at the base of a tree, Keene tossed stones from the sling at the end of his hoopak and watched them soar through the leaves. "I never got to meet Ark," he said, his voice sounding unusually tired. "A centaur merchant bandit sounds interesting, especially one who sold his soul to . . . to *Kirilin*." He spat the cleric's name, then tilted his head and thought for a moment. "I wonder if he'd scream a lot if I cut him with my sword?"

Davyn saw Jirah shudder.

"Well, if he's on his way here," Davyn said, "then we need to go. We're not far from the port. If we get there and meet Tu quickly, then we have a good chance of losing him."

Nearra nodded. Coming to Davyn's side, she gestured forward. "Lead the way."

Davyn raised his sword again, ready to slice through the vines and forge their path forward, when they all heard it.

Heavy thudding gallops thundered as a large equine creature raced through underbrush. Branches snapped as something heavy burst between trees.

Then there came the whooping shouts of several bandits.

Icefire met Davyn's eye and raised an eyebrow. "Seems my earring was right after all," he said. As Nearra tensed for battle with her staff held at the ready, and Keene pulled free his short sword, the elf spun toward Jirah, his hand held out expectantly. "Jirah, give me the bow and arrows."

Jirah looked confused. "What?" she asked. "Why?"

"Don't question, just hurry!"

"No," Jirah said, clutching the bow against her chest. "The cursed wizard gave me the weapon. It's mine, just like the staff is Nearra's."

Icefire let out an exasperated sigh. "Jirah, I've been researching these weapons in the book we got from the library. In the hands of an experienced mage they have much more potential than just shooting a ball of fire or a pillar of water. I'm going to teach you the spells to enhance the power of your weapon like I taught Nearra, but we don't have time now. Give me the bow. I'll be able to use it better."

"No!" Davyn shouted, much louder than he intended. He leaped forward between the girl and the elf, keeping them apart.

"Do not give him the bow," Davyn growled, his eyes on Icefire's. "Don't let him near that magic. You remember how he acted when he touched Nearra's staff back in Icereach?"

Jirah hesitated. Icefire once again sighed in exasperation. The

thudding hoofbeats grew louder, as did the war cries.

JEFF SAMPSON

"Are you insane?" Icefire shouted at Davyn. "I need the bow! I've been preparing spells for it, ones that Jirah doesn't know how to cast. This is our chance to stop the centaur from following us."

"I don't care," Davyn said. "You're taking your magic too far. It's bad enough that you're teaching magic to Nearra, but—"

Nearra shoved between the two boys, scowling at Davyn. "'Bad enough'?" she asked.

"Icefire's magic is out of control. Don't you see it?" Davyn pointed at the elf's face. "Look at his eyes. He's manic. I'm just trying to protect you."

"Well don't," Nearra snapped. Then, eyes softening, she shook her head. "Davyn, please, just stop it. Now is really not the time."

"Nearra, listen to—"

Caterwauls echoed, a rising din that terrified the animals around them. Birds cawed and flew from the trees, and small creatures skittered beneath the bushes.

An arrow flew from the trees, slicing right past Keene's cheek. It thunked into a tree, quivering from the force. The kender blinked.

"Jirah!" Icefire roared. "I need—"

Nearra raised her hand, silencing him. "She's right, Icefire. She proved herself. The bow is hers. But help her. Stay with her. Teach her the magic." Turning to meet Jirah's eyes, she smiled. "I know she can do it."

Jirah lowered her head, the emotions running across her face unreadable. Shoving past Davyn, the black-haired girl stood in front of Icefire and nocked an arrow.

"I'm ready," she whispered.

Resigned, Icefire nodded. "I will tell you what you need to do." Leaning close, he whispered instructions in Jirah's ear.

Davyn ignored the noise of the approaching bandits, his eyes on Icefire. Even as the elf continued to whisper to Jirah, Davyn was certain Icefire was looking at the bow, anticipating eventually making it his own.

Fine, Davyn thought. I see you've made your choice, Nearra. Now you get to live with it.

Always before, he'd imagined going back to Icereach to get to know his newfound family with Nearra at his side. Now, for the first time, he realized maybe he didn't want Nearra with him anymore. Maybe he wanted to leave *all* of them behind. Maybe . . .

Shaking his head, he, too, tensed, his sword held at the ready. His chest heaved beneath his leather armor, and he heard Jirah breathing just as heavily beside him. Icefire, Nearra, and Keene, however, all seemed completely unafraid.

The bandits' cries swelled to a crazed peak. Ark leaped from between the trees, his hair matted and his scarred face sneering. Behind him, four of his bandits leered as they crept between the towering tree trunks, their weapons raised. The woman with the skull tattoo on her face held her bow at the ready, an arrow nocked and aimed toward Keene.

"Well, look what we have here." Arms crossed, Ark smirked and nodded sociably to the five wary companions. "It's my old friend the spellcasting elf and his little band of adventurers. And I see you found a kender along the way."

Icefire unsheathed his sword with a flourish. "Hello again," he said. "Fancy seeing you here, so far from home. I don't suppose you brought your skrit with you?"

"Ark!" the skull-faced bandit shrieked. Veins throbbed with anger on her forehead. "Why must you always do this? This was how he got the best of us last time!"

The centaur ignored her. "No skrit this time," he said. "Just me, my best warriors, and this." Reaching over his shoulders, he unsheathed his own weapon, the massive broadsword that had been strapped to his back. His biceps flexed with the weight of the weapon as he held it in a high attack position.

"No skrit?" Icefire said. "Good to know. Jirah, why don't you show them what *we've* got."

Quick as lightning, Jirah turned to aim the arrow at the skull-faced bandit. She let it fly, and a pillar of water burst forth more forceful than a towering wave during an ocean storm. Her eyes wide, the bandit screamed as the water washed over her and threw her back into the trees. Dripping wet, she landed with a heavy thud and fell silent.

"Now!" Davyn cried. His ornamental sword held high, he raced toward the nearest bandit, a tall and scrawny man with scraggly chin hair and rotted teeth. The man bellowed and swung a club at Davyn's skull. Davyn dodged, rolled beneath him, and got to his feet.

Above him, vines hung in tangled ropes. Before the bandit could turn around, Davyn grabbed the thickest vine, wrapped it around the bandit's throat, then pulled hard. The bandit dropped his club, his fingers scrabbling at the vine that strangled him. Green peeled from the vine and stuck beneath the bandit's already dirty fingernails. Finally, with a gasp, the bandit fell unconscious, and Davyn let go.

Dirt flew as Davyn spun around. Nearra fought the two remaining bandits near the boulders as Keene hollered and flew between a rearing Ark's legs, his sword a blur.

Strangely, Icefire and Jirah stood exactly where they'd been. Icefire's eyes blazed with magical fury as he spoke words of power to Jirah. The girl had another arrow nocked and aimed toward the centaur's hooves, and she repeated the words as she heard them. The arrowhead glowed a misty blue.

Nearra landed a bludgeoning blow to the back of one of the bandit's heads and sent him sprawling. The bandit smacked headfirst into a boulder, then slumped to the ground.

In the same move, Nearra spun around faster than Davyn had thought her capable and jabbed the end of her staff into the remaining bandit's fleshy thigh. She shouted a word of magic, and his trousers burst into flame. Shrieking, the bandit dropped his sword and scrambled back into the woods.

"Get back here!" Ark roared. Holding the hilt of his broadsword in both hands, he thrust down hard, piercing the ground. Soil flew as the blade barely missed Keene's flailing auburn topknot. The kender rolled, landing at Davyn's feet.

As Davyn watched, Icefire put his hand around Jirah's own and helped her pull the bow taut. As one they mumbled a phrase of magic and shot into the dirt.

The arrow landed between Ark's front hooves with such force that it burrowed deep into the ground. Hefting his sword back up, Ark looked between his legs curiously.

"Aargh!" Keene cried. He leaped to his feet, ready to race back and continue his useless strikes against the centaur. Davyn grabbed his topknot and yanked him back.

"Never," he scolded, "run toward magic."

For a moment, nothing seemed to happen. His usual good-natured smile gone, the centaur lifted his head and glared at Icefire and Jirah with his one remaining eye.

Then the ground began to shift beneath the centaur's hooves. The soil beneath him had muddied and turned into quicksand, and Ark began to sink. He tried to bound forward to lop off Icefire's head with his sword, but the movement only made him sink farther.

"Vile elf!" Ark spat. Lifting his sword high with one hand, he aimed it at Icefire's heart.

"*Api anak!*" Nearra aimed her staff and a fireball burst from its tip. The flames hit the sword, knocking it from Ark's grip as it seared his hands. The blade spun away and sliced into a tree. Bark exploded, and the sword stuck.

Nearra came to stand beside Icefire and Jirah, holding her staff proudly. Icefire smirked.

"So those were your best warriors?" the elf asked.

Ark sighed and shrugged. Slowly he sunk deep into the earth, the muddy mess almost to his flanks. Seeming to realize that moving would only make him sink faster, he remained still.

"Those were the best," Ark said. "Bet you can imagine how good the rest of them are. They're excellent at corralling skrit, though."

"I bet."

Davyn walked forward, Keene trailing behind. "Kirilin," Davyn demanded. "Did you go to the mine? Did you free her?"

Ark rolled his eye and slapped at his flank with his tail. "Do you really think I'm going to tell you anything?"

"Kirilin *was* the one who put you in this situation," Icefire pointed out. "I can't imagine that inspires much loyalty on your part."

Ark's nostrils flared, and he didn't respond.

"Also, you seem to be helpless at the moment," Icefire went on. "Your 'best warriors' are all unconscious or have fled. You can either help us, or we kill you before they get back to help you out. Your choice."

"Good point." Sighing, the centaur crossed his arms. "We found the mine, yeah. We sent some of my men down there on ropes, but Kirilin wasn't in the rubble. She must have found a way out. She's probably following you again."

"That seems to be all she does anymore," Keene muttered.

Ark shrugged. He was enveloped up to the base of his human torso now, and was still sinking much too slowly. "Well, kender, you're trying to murder her. There aren't many that would take kindly to that."

Davyn pointed his sword at the centaur's neck. "You're lying. Why would you follow us if not at Kirilin's command?"

Ark shook his head. "You blast sand in my face and escape my perfectly good plan and you don't expect me to give chase? Haven't fought many bandit leaders, have you?"

He was covered to his chest now, and seemed to have stopped sinking. Instead, he bobbed in the muddy mess that now surrounded him. Showing no fear, again the centaur smiled.

"You," he said, tilting his head toward Nearra. "You seem like a nice girl, and at least partially in charge here. Tell you what. If you keep your boys here from slitting my throat, I'll call this whole thing a wash and leave you alone to your quest."

Nearra held her head high. "I won't let them kill you. But how do I know you'll keep your word?"

Ark let out a bark of laughter and shook his head again. His straggly, unkempt hair rustled around his burly shoulders. "You do realize how fast you took me and my men out, don't you? You knew I was coming, and you were prepared. I imagine if I attacked again you wouldn't hesitate to blast me with that staff of yours. No, I'd rather return to Tarsis and get back to my usual business. Kirilin can fend for herself."

Nearra bit her lip as she studied the centaur's face. She fingered the staff, and Ark winked his single uncovered eye.

"Nearra," Davyn said, his voice low. "We have to kill him. We can't trust him."

The girl paused a moment more, then shrugged. "Probably not. But he's right—if he tries to come after us again, he'll burn. And he seems much too interested in saving his own hide to worry about some mess Kirilin got him into."

From where he bobbed in the muddy lake of quicksand, Ark grinned. "She's right, you know. I'm really quite self-centered."

Nearra tilted her head toward the forest. "Let's go."

Turning their backs on the bobbing centaur, the companions continued their course through the woods, almost, Davyn noted with frustration, as though nothing had happened.

"That wasn't smart, Nearra," Davyn muttered as he slashed through the underbrush blocking their way.

"What?" Nearra said, eyes narrowed. "I—"

"Yeah it was," Jirah spoke up, daring to meet Davyn's angry gaze. "The spell Icefire and I cast, the water will disappear soon. Ark's going to be buried in heavy soil up to his chest. It'll take his bandits ages to dig him out when they eventually wake up. By that time we'll be on a ship, and there's no way he can follow us."

Icefire nodded. "Exactly right. I think Nearra made the best choice. She has good instincts. We should have trusted them back at Tarsis, when we left." He shook his head and looked down at Keene. "Wouldn't be right to kill Ark if he's willing to leave us be. And we don't need any of his men deciding they need to come after us to avenge him if we did kill him. No, we won't have to worry about him anymore. I'm sure of it."

Davyn grunted, his muscles straining as he slashed vines with his sword. Leaves and vines flew. "But there's Kirilin," he said. "She'll be back. Like always."

"Probably," Icefire said. "But we'll deal with that when it happens."

Nearra smiled at Davyn. "See? There was nothing to worry about. Icefire knew exactly what he was doing. And, I guess, so did I."

With one last look at Ark struggling in the dirt behind them, Jirah turned to shove past Davyn, Keene at her side. Nearra clutched at Icefire's arm, and the two of them followed.

Davyn couldn't help but notice that Icefire seemed unable to wrench his gaze from Jirah's longbow.

Yes, Davyn thought as he watched Icefire take over cutting through the underbrush. He knows exactly what he's doing.

CHAPTER

15 A Farewell at Dawn

The deck of *Troubadour's Song* swayed gently back and forth to the ocean's rhythm. Mournful sailors crowded beneath the fluttering sails and between barrels. All eyes were on the prow, where Keene stood silently as beside him, Icefire raised his voice in a sorrowful song.

Jirah hugged herself as she stood between the brawny men that manned Icefire's ship. They held their caps to their chests respectfully as they watched the funeral, and some even had tears in their eyes.

Beside Keene and Icefire stood Tu, stoic as always. Her light brown skin shone gold in the light from the rising sun. Soft clouds drifted gently across the sky, colored in hues of flaming orange and blush pink.

Jirah sighed as Icefire's song ended. Keene knelt before a small, crudely carved wooden boat. In it was a ball and a rag—Pip's favorite toys—as well as an incredibly lifelike sketch of the dog that Jirah had been surprised to learn Keene had drawn himself. Sniffling, the kender sailor placed a white flower inside the tiny boat, then stood and nodded to Tu.

The first mate put a gentle hand on Keene's shoulder, then knelt and picked up the boat. As Icefire began to sing another song of loss, Tu held the little skiff over the water and let it fall. It landed with a small splash, and Jirah peered over the deck's railing to see it floating on the lapping waves. It drifted away in the current as Icefire's voice swelled to one last, mournful note.

"That was lovely," Nearra said as she came up behind Jirah. The sailors slowly began to dissipate, getting back to their work.

Jirah turned to murmur her agreement, then saw Davyn leaning back against the mainmast with his arms crossed and a scowl on his face. High above him fluttered a sky blue flag emblazoned with a golden tree bearing green leaves.

Icefire came toward them, Tu and Keene at his side. Keene was still silent, his look distant. He was dressed in his finest clothes: a bright yellow silk tunic tied around the waist with a red sash, and purple trousers tucked into his black boots. His topknot was braided with intricate knots and laced with feathers.

"It was a beautiful ceremony," Nearra said as Icefire came closer.

"Only the best for one of our finest sailors," Icefire said, solemn.

Tu nodded. She was a sailor through and through, though her practiced swagger and her outfit of breeches, tunic, and leather vest did not hide that she was still a young woman, no older than Nearra and Davyn. But she had been hardened by life, and it read in her features.

"Pip will be missed," Tu said. "He's been a member of our crew since I can remember. It's not right. If only Janeesa hadn't—"

"Tu," Icefire snapped.

Jirah stiffened at the mention of Janeesa's name. She'd tried to forget about the Messengers ever since the night she broke the mirror. She expected at any moment the fetch would pop out of a reflective surface and try to murder her or, worse, Keene. She even expected the mages themselves to descend upon the ship.

But they hadn't come. They hadn't sent warnings in any way. And that worried her even more than if they had.

"Janeesa?" Nearra asked. She sidled up to Icefire. "What does she have to do with anything?"

"Nothing," Icefire said. Squinting, he looked at Tu. "Go get Davyn. I need to meet with him, Nearra, and Jirah in my quarters."

Tu pursed her full lips and narrowed her wide brown eyes. "Aye, Captain," she said.

Keene stood beside Jirah, staring up at Icefire and trembling with rage. Without saying a word, he turned and stormed across the rolling deck toward the crew quarters.

Icefire made to follow, but Jirah raised her hand. "I'll go talk to him," she said. "You should have your meeting."

Not waiting for a response, Jirah raced across the deck after Keene. Crisp, salty air whipped her hair into her face, and long shadows from the rising sun danced in front of her.

"Keene," she said as she pushed into his room. His quarters were cramped and small, and she found him easily enough, sitting in one of the swaying hammocks against the wall. In the corner sat the hulking form of Bem, Tu's brother and the ship's second mate. He sat on a chest and leaned forward onto a small wooden table, picking at his nails with a dagger. Outside the port window, waves lapped against the hull.

"Go away," Keene muttered. He laid back in his swaying hammock and stared at the ceiling.

With a quick cough, Bem stood to his towering height. "I'll go see if they need any help on deck. You should talk to Jirah, Keene. If not, I'll hold you over the railing again."

"No you won't," Keene muttered.

With a sad look at Jirah, Bem brushed past them and headed out on deck. The door slammed behind him.

Jirah dragged the chest across the floor, stumbling as the floor beneath her moved from side to side. Sitting down on it, she leaned forward and frowned. Not knowing exactly what to say, she waited.

"Are you still talking to Janeesa?" Keene asked. He blinked, then turned his head sideways to look at her.

Jirah swallowed and looked down. "No. I . . . I smashed the mirror."

Keene raised an eyebrow and sat up. "Did you?" he asked. "Wow, Jirah, that was very brave of you."

Brushing a lock of hair out of her eyes, she looked back up. "Not really," she said. "I was scared of them. They threatened me, they . . . they threatened you, Keene. They were sending a monster from the Abyss through the mirror, so I had to get rid of it."

Keene shook his head. "That's not it at all," he said. "You know Janeesa is bad now, right? You don't want to be like her?"

"No," she said. "I don't."

"Then turning your back on her was very brave. You know she's dangerous, you know what she can do, but you chose your sister and your friends over your fear. That takes a lot."

Biting his lip, Keene leaned back. His dangling legs kicked up and down, swinging the hammock back and forth.

"I miss Pip," he said. "He was my best friend—well, aside from Icefire and you, of course." He sighed. "I'm so angry and sad, and every time I think about how scared Pip was, how much it must have hurt when that draconian . . . "

"Keene," Jirah said. She reached forward and gently grabbed his hand. "I understand. I'm so sorry. It's all my fault."

Keene narrowed his eyes. "You?" he said, incredulous. "No, it's not you. It's not Icefire either. It's a lot of things all at once. The real bad guy is Kirilin. And Janeesa too."

Jirah got up and began to pace around the room. There was the elf's name again. What had Jirah done the past year? Blindly

167

following Janeesa's commands, idolizing her, agreeing to kill people? What sort of person was she?

It didn't matter what Keene said, she knew what was true. She could help Nearra free a wizard, she could learn to work a magical bow, but that didn't mean she was brave. It just meant she was trying to make up for everything that was her fault. She didn't want anyone else getting hurt.

"You can stay here if you want," Jirah burst out. "On the ship. You don't have to help me anymore."

Keene jumped to his feet and stomped toward her. "Jirah, I could never not help you. You're a good person and a good friend, and none of the Kirilins or Janeesas of the world will keep me from finishing this quest with you. Besides, someone has to pay for what happened to Pip. And I intend to be there when it happens."

Jirah swallowed. Tears bit at the corners of her eyes, but she fought to hold them back.

He didn't know, she realized. None of them knew, not really, all that she'd done in the name of magic. It sickened her, more now that she saw the one person who had been hurt most of all, so blindly believing in her. It frightened her to think how much Nearra, Davyn, and especially Keene would hate her if they ever found out what she'd done.

His small fingers wrapped around her own, and Keene looked up at her, smiling. "Thank you for coming to talk to me, Jirah," he said. "It still hurts. I still dream about Pip, but it helps that you've been there for me. And I'll be there for you too."

"You're welcome, Keene," she whispered, her voice hoarse. "And . . . thank you."

His arms crossed, Icefire sat in a plush chair in his cabin. Beside him, set into the back wall, was a large stained-glass window.

Pieces of green, yellow, and blue glass were arranged in patterns within the piping, a stylized image of the tree on the ship's flag. Hazy emerald, gold, and sapphire light fell across an unfinished game of King's Table in front of him. Across the table from Icefire, and looking just as forlorn, was Nearra.

"Poor Keene," Nearra whispered. Her hands fiddled against each other in her lap.

Icefire nodded and sighed. "He's taking this very hard. But it's to be expected. Kender are strong folk, though. He'll be fine soon enough."

Rubbing her temples, Nearra stood and walked toward the long vallenwood table that took up most of the cabin. Leaning between two high-backed chairs, she placed her palms on the smoothed wood.

"We're almost through with the quest," she said. "But nothing feels right. Keene is grieving, Davyn is angry all the time, and Jirah is bothered too, I can tell."

Icefire got to his feet. Coming to her side, he rested a hand on her shoulder. "It'll be all right, Nearra," he said. "We have one wizard left. Kirilin's minions are all dead, and she's been transformed back to a withered old woman. We'll be able to handle this just fine. *You'll* be able to handle it."

Nearra tilted her head back. She seemed to be searching for something in his eyes. "It's you too, Icefire," she said. "Davyn may be blinded by his anger, but he's not wrong. We've been studying magic more and more, and he's right, your eyes are different. You're becoming more and more obsessed with magic."

Icefire sighed, exasperated. Not this again.

"Nearra—" he started to say.

"Why did Tu say that about Janeesa?"

Icefire stiffened. That had been a huge mistake on his first mate's part. Janeesa had been a large part of Icefire's life for a long time, and he was still beholden to her for the steel she'd lent him for this ship. Nearra knew the tales of their relationship, spat out by Keene in his innocent fashion over a meal in this very room.

But Nearra knew nothing of Janeesa manipulating him into leading Nearra on this quest. She knew nothing about Jirah's secret conversations with the two Messengers. Of course she'd assume any mention of Janeesa would be because of magic. And maybe it was, a little.

He considered telling her then, the truth about Janeesa's part in all of this. But even he wasn't sure what his former love was up to. Now that they were nearing the end of the quest, he'd have to find time to make Jirah tell him. He didn't want to risk letting Nearra feel betrayed if there was no reason.

Nearra shook her head at his hesitation. "Icefire, just tell me," she said. "I trust you more than anyone right now, and I know we all have our pasts. But please tell me—have you seen Janeesa? Are you doing magic again for . . . for her?"

Reaching forward a long and slender finger, Icefire touched Nearra's chin. "There is only one person I am doing magic for," he whispered. "And that is you."

He kissed her then, pressing her tender lips against his own. He felt her fall into him as her body relaxed. Her arms encircled his waist, pulling him closer.

They pulled their lips apart, and he rested his forehead against hers. Her breath fluttered against his chest as she smiled.

Someone cleared their throat.

Quickly, the two pulled away. Davyn stood in the cabin's entrance, his arms crossed and his face unmistakably angry. At his side was Tu, her expression unreadable.

"Here's Davyn," Tu announced as she leaned back against the doorframe. Behind her floated in the sounds of rope snapping, sails fluttering, and sailors singing and laughing as they worked on deck.

"Thank you, Tu," Icefire said. Pulling back one of the chairs, he sat down and propped his legs on the table. "Want to sit?"

Davyn scowled. "No. What do you want?"

Icefire shrugged. Beside him Nearra kneaded her hands, her head down. Her cheeks were pink with an embarrassed blush.

"I just wanted to discuss the final leg of our trip," Icefire said. "We will be reaching Southern Ergoth in a few days' time. We'll anchor away from shore, then row in as night falls. We'll find shelter, then set out early the next morning. I've been charting the course, and I have books that I've been researching on the final location. I can show you—"

"You are leading us?" Davyn interrupted. His expression did not change.

"No," Nearra said, looking up. "*I'm* leading us, Davyn. Icefire will be guiding us. He's the best one to navigate, as you know."

The ranger shrugged. "Fine." Without another word, he spun on his heels and stormed out of the cabin. Tu watched him go with a raised eyebrow.

Nearra shook her head and sighed. "I'm going to go find Jirah and tell her the plans." With a shy smile at Tu, she, too, walked out onto the deck.

Raising her chin, Tu let the door close behind her and strode toward Icefire. "I see you've managed to get yourself into more troubles of the heart, despite my warnings." She swatted at his boots. "Get your feet off the table."

Icefire lowered his legs as commanded. "As I've told you before, how I choose to handle my relationships is none of your business."

Tu lowered herself into the chair opposite him. Her black hair was pulled back tight against the nape of her neck, making her brown features seem much older than they were. "You keep acting like a fool for love," she said. "And as your first mate, I think it's my duty to point it out."

Icefire scowled, then leaned forward onto his crossed arms. "Why did you mention Janeesa in front of her?"

Tu pursed her lips and leaned away. "Why shouldn't I? Nearra already knows of her. And Janeesa is the reason we've been dragged into all of this."

"Nearra doesn't know everything," Icefire said. "Nor is she to."

With an exasperated sigh, Tu shook her head and stood. "Icefire, you are acting like a little boy. I saw you staring at Jirah's longbow when you all came aboard. It is obviously magic. And I saw the way you looked at it."

"Tu," Icefire said, his tone cold.

She raised a hand. "No, listen to me," she said. "You tell me now, Captain Icefire. Have you been giving in to Janeesa? Are you going to abandon your ship to become an elf mage?"

"Never!" Icefire stood and slammed his fists against the table. "How dare you question my principles? After all the time I've known you!"

Tu shrugged. "Give me a reason not to."

Trembling with anger, Icefire turned from her and paced. Multicolored shadows fell over him as morning light streamed through the window.

"I am only doing magic to help Nearra," he said, not turning around to face her. "I am helping her learn. Janeesa is no longer in control of this quest, even if she believes herself to be." Tilting his head to look over his shoulder, he met Tu's eyes. "So there is your reason, Tu. Nearra."

Tu shook her head. "Fine, Captain," she said. "I have work to do on deck. I will be there if you need me." She turned and left the cabin.

Icefire stood bathed in the stained-glass window's light, lost in thought. Nearra had been right. As the quest neared its end, every one of the companions seemed consumed by their own emotions.

JEFF SAMPSON

Was he going too far with magic, as everyone seemed to fear? In the mine he'd thought so, but afterward he'd felt the power of the longbow. He longed to use it, to carry it by his side.

Janeesa and Kirilin, both of them insisted he had a darkness inside just waiting to be released. Both tried to seduce him with magic's promise. And it was true—the voices of magic that spoke to him no longer seemed unwelcome invaders in his mind.

"It's all for Nearra," he whispered to himself. "It's all for her."

He could control it, he was certain. He could use it for the powers of good, no matter what Janeesa and Kirilin tried to convince him.

But there was still one wizard left to free. Janeesa and Tylari were still out there, plotting. Kirilin was undoubtedly still trying to find ways to stop them from breaking the curse. Even though they seemed so close to overcoming their foes and breaking the curse, anything could happen.

And, he feared, anything *would*.

CHAPTER

16   DUST TO DUST

Several days later, on the same dark night as the companions reached Southern Ergoth and headed inland, Tylari waited on the island's darkened southern beach. Spray from the lapping waves cooled his cheeks as he studied the stars. He made out the lines of the broken scales, only one of the many constellations of the gods.

But Tylari was not waiting for Icefire and Jirah, his betrayers. Nor was he waiting for their traveling companions, the three who were so blind to the true nature of the elf and the sister. Typical of mortals. One couldn't expect them to notice much.

No, Tylari waited for the dark cleric. He waited for Kirilin.

"Tylari, I . . . I had thought . . . "

Tylari turned at the sound of the voice. Janeesa was huddled beneath the shadowy, craggy trees that were the beginnings of endless forest. She stood hunched and slightly wavering, as though she could barely concentrate enough to stand. Her unbrushed golden hair hung down her back in tangles over her red robes. Silver and red moonlight tinted her skin the color of a pale rose; her lovely face was marred with a look of distant confusion.

Tylari met her eyes. "Shh, dear sister. Thoughts are not your friend."

For a moment, Janeesa's eyes seemed to flash with recognition. Then, as always now when she looked at him, any bit of intelligence seemed to fade from her gaze and a beatific smile graced her face.

Tylari shook his head and closed his eyes. It was a shame what had happened to her, but it had been the only way. Like the companions, she, too, had been blind. She had no idea of the potential harm the Trinistyr could have caused him. Divinity was his destiny, and she refused to believe it. At first he'd wondered if perhaps she were right, if perhaps he was descending into madness like their father.

But then, in a moment of divine insight, he'd absorbed Janeesa's power into his own and used her strength to mend what had been stolen from him by his Test at the Tower of High Sorcery. Everything felt clear once more. Now the voices of the gods whispered in his mind, telling him their secrets and promising him they would share more once he'd made his ascent.

With a sigh of resignation, he turned back to look over the water. Inky waves crested in foam that shimmered like gemstones in the moonlight. On the horizon, where sea met sky, he could make out the distant shape of a ship headed in his direction.

Is it she? Tylari asked in his thoughts.

He waited for a moment, then one of the voices came. It told him, yes, this was the ship. It told him that it was almost time, that working together they could succeed where Kirilin had failed so miserably.

This voice was louder than the others. This voice seemed different somehow, though Tylari wasn't quite sure in what way. But this voice told him things the others didn't share, and so he listened intently when it spoke.

He knew that dark magic had helped Kirilin escape the mine

that her young foes stupidly thought would be her prison. But by the time she'd awoken and dug herself free of the rubble of the fallen track, they were long gone.

He knew how she'd followed Nearra's trail at first, divining for scraps of knowledge where she could. But her body was old now, brittle and frail, and she hadn't gotten very far. Finally the voice had taken pity on her and had given her a divine vision to show her where to go.

In the state she was in, it had not occurred to her that the voice was not a god who took pity. But Tylari knew the true nature of the voice. Yes, he definitely knew. Unlike Kirilin, he would be prepared.

Now Kirilin was sailing toward him on a slum of a boat, the best she could afford with what little steel she'd had on her. As she grew closer, Tylari began to sense her presence. He closed his eyes and the voice whispered to him, showing him a vision of what the cleric was doing.

The captain of the ship upon which Kirilin sailed was named Keresh. He was an old, bitter man with grudges on his mind. He sailed with his dregs of a crew doing dirty work for pay, and even dirtier work when it came to settling old scores. And he wanted Kirilin off his boat.

They were arguing, the cleric and the captain, as his men tried to force her onto a little skiff that dangled above the waves on frayed ropes. She demanded to be taken to the docks. He told her he was not going near any shore, and her steel had only paid for him to take her this far.

In the end, Captain Keresh won. Kirilin was in no condition to argue, especially not since the voice had begun to vastly limit her power.

Tylari grinned as the voice whispered Kirilin's thoughts to him. She still dared to think that she could win back her youth even now, that she would be able to come back and make these men pay for daring to disrespect her.

If she only knew what was to come.

Tylari opened his eyes once more. The distant shadow of Captain Keresh's squalid ship remained where he'd last seen it. But a tiny dot rode the waves now, coming closer. With his superior elf vision, Tylari could make out the forms of two people on the little skiff.

It was almost time, the voice told Tylari. Almost time.

Tylari pulled his black cloak tighter around himself as he stood in the shadows. A salty breeze tangled his hair as he watched a rat-faced human sailor row the little skiff close to shore. With a look of unmistakable rage on her face, Kirilin lifted her robes and stepped into the frigid waters.

"Do sail with us again," the sailor said in a high-pitched voice. "It was a pleasure riding with the legendary 'Stealer of Souls.' Or, at least, the crone claiming to be her."

The man guffawed as he leaned into the oars. Dipping and pulling in a steady rhythm, he rowed back out toward the distant vessel.

Waves crashed against the cleric's waist as she watched the man leave, and she seemed to tremble with rage or cold, or maybe both. When she finally turned around and began to slosh her way through water and shifting sand toward shore, Tylari got a good look at her for the first time. He couldn't help but smile.

The companions had taken it all from her. Not just her beauty, but her youth. Fatigue seemed to float off her in waves, and Tylari could tell she was worthless now, her energy and strength completely sapped by her journey. Her hair was wisps of white, her withered skin hung in wrinkled folds. Her body was so frail that he was surprised it could even support the weight of her heavy red robes, let alone carry her across land and sea in search of her missing key.

The cleric reached shore and stumbled forward into the sand.

She lay there, gasping for air as she fingered the medallion of faith that hung around her neck.

"Lord Hiddukel," he heard her whisper. "I am your faithful servant. Do not forsake me now."

Now, Tylari thought, now is the time to strike.

He strode forward, his footsteps almost silent. The only sound in the cool night was of the waves crashing against the shore, and night birds that called out from the trees. It wasn't until he was almost upon her that Kirilin noticed she wasn't alone on the beach.

Groaning with agony, she hefted her hunched body forward. Green eyes that were paled with impending cataracts flitted from him to Janeesa behind him, studying the two elf mages in the moonlight.

"Kirilin," he said after he had given her sufficient time to realize she wasn't dealing with the filthy Kagonesti that usually stalked these shores.

"How do you know my name?" the cleric croaked. "Who are you?"

She sat in the sand, still clutching at her pendant as Tylari came closer. He held out a hand.

"My name is Tylari," he said. He gestured over his shoulder. "Back there is my sister, Janeesa. She is unwell, sadly, or she'd come and chat."

Uncertain, Kirilin held forward her own hand. Tylari took it in a strong grip and hauled her to her feet. She groaned with the effort.

Tylari brushed his hair back behind his pointed ears and smiled. "We've heard much about you," he said, "for we have enemies in common."

Lifting her chin high, Kirilin raised an eyebrow. "Do we?" she asked. Despite everything, the cleric still attempted to give off an air of regality. It made Tylari want to laugh in her face, and the voice whispered it wanted to do the same. She was nothing but a failure.

"That we do," Tylari responded. "Icefire. Nearra. Davyn. Jirah."

Kirilin took in a breath. "You know of them?" she asked, clutching at his arm with a wrinkled hand. "You fight them too? But why?"

Tylari shrugged. Telling the truth now wouldn't matter. "We didn't fight them, Kirilin. We helped, for they have something we wanted. The Trinistyr and the weapons of the cursed wizards."

Kirilin gasped and reeled back. Her skeletal face was contorted in a look of fury. "You!" she seethed. "You were the ones feeding them information? How dare you confront me!"

Holding his hands up in a show of peace, Tylari took a step forward.

"Now, now, Kirilin," he said. "The plan for the Trinistyr was my sister's."

"What do you mean, elf?" Kirilin asked. "Get to the point. I weary of this."

Tylari shrugged. "My sister wanted the Trinistyr. She wanted to use it to steal my power. And so I stopped her."

"You work to keep the Trinistyr from being restored?" Kirilin asked.

"In a sense, yes."

Kirilin's thin lips spread into a smile as her wispy white hair fluttered in her face. Again her pale eyes flitted back and forth, studying him. At first he thought he could almost hear her thoughts and realizations. But no, it was the voice again. It told him what was in the cleric's mind. It told him to be ready, for the voice and Tylari were mere moments away from fully joining together in their cause.

"I see." Kirilin lifted a blue-veined hand and brushed his cheek.

It was as though someone was rubbing wet parchment against his skin. "You want to work with me," she went on. "Together we can stop Icefire and his little friends, and the curse will stay intact. My god will be pleased, and you shall be rewarded greatly."

Tylari smiled broader. He clutched Kirilin's shoulder.

"I think you misunderstand me, cleric," he said. "I am not here to help you. I am here to keep you from getting in my way. If I am to become a god, I can't have you around mucking things up. You've caused enough problems already."

Rearing back, Kirilin tried to pull free of his grip. "The Trinistyr," she seethed. "You don't want it restored, and neither do I. We work for the same goal!"

Tylari shrugged. "Not quite."

Pulling hard, the dark cleric finally managed to wrench free from Tylari's grasp. With a gasp, she fell to her back on the sand. Ocean water splashed over her, filling her mouth with bitter salt water. Sputtering, she shook her head.

Tylari leaned over her shriveled form. The voice was telling him more now, exactly what to say and do to finish this step, once and for all.

"You will pay for this," the cleric shrieked as he loomed above her. Clutching at her medallion, she tensed her free hand to cast a spell. "Hiddukel will not stand for this!"

Tylari crouched down. The voice told him what to say.

"He's not your god anymore," he spat. "Who do you think gave me the visions to show me where you were? Hiddukel knows whose side to take now, Kirilin, and it is mine."

"Lies!" But even as she said it, Tylari saw a look of understanding in her eyes. He watched her intently, waiting for full realization to settle in. Hiddukel—the voice—had been with her for centuries. She'd coerced souls into his fold, and he'd repaid her with fame and power and eternal youth.

And now, as Tylari knew and the cleric was only beginning to comprehend, he had abandoned her.

"How . . . " she whispered. "How is it possible? You are a wizard, not a cleric. Hiddukel should not work with you. It is not done. I don't understand—"

"And you never shall."

The voice told him to take the symbol away from Kirilin and scatter the cleric to the winds. The cleric seemed unable to move as Tylari grasped her medallion and wrenched it free from her neck. She did not move as he hung the silver symbol around his neck. He felt a rush, a connection, forge its way through him. He couldn't help but let a thunderous laugh of triumph escape his lips.

"I have been chosen!" Tylari shouted to the constellations above. "Hiddukel sees who shall be the new god in his fold, and he has conceded to share his power with me!"

"You are mad," Kirilin whispered beneath him. She, too, stared at the stars. "The gods would never let a mortal join them." She shook her head. "Fool."

Tylari looked down upon her, disgust flowing through him. She was nothing compared to him. *Nothing*.

"They will have no choice," Tylari whispered. "My destiny is upon us."

Muttering arcane phrases as the voice whispered them in his mind, Tylari let the red power flow over his hands. Kirilin gasped in shock as her hands began to dissolve into dust that mingled with the sand.

Tylari laughed as the cleric closed her eyes, resigned to her fate. "Fool," she whispered. And then she crumbled into dust, and the waves washed away what was left of her.

"Tylari." He turned to see that Janeesa had strode forward. She watched the scene with a look of emptiness as the red robes around her waist twisted in the wind.

Rubbing the medallion between his fingers, feeling the engraved markings of the broken scale symbol beneath his thumb, Tylari walked toward her. "Everything is all right, dear sister," he said as she looked up into his eyes. "Soon everything will be ready."

The voice spoke words of congratulations in Tylari's mind. It promised great rewards if he followed instructions and helped keep the wizard's curse from being ended and the Trinistyr from being restored.

But there was something the voice didn't know about Tylari's plans. He didn't want the Trinistyr used against him, but he did have great plans for the item once it was his. The voice was Hiddukel, a god. But Tylari would soon be a god himself. He didn't plan to be taking orders from any of the others.

"Yes, Janeesa," Tylari said. He smiled down at her as he led her into the trees. "Everything is going to be ready very soon."

Joyous at the thought of his impending ascension, Tylari led his sister into the underbrush. There was only one more stop to make.

At long last, his ascension would be at hand.

CHAPTER

17   UNSPOKEN TRUTHS

The cave was dark and cramped, but comfortable compared to some of the places Davyn had stayed in. He stood at its mouth, keeping watch. Near a fire that raged in the center of the cave, Jirah and Nearra curled up against one another beneath their cloaks. The flickering firelight cast intricate patterns of orange and black over their sleeping forms. Smoke swirled up to escape through a hole in the craggy ceiling.

Keene was snoring, his small body splayed out haphazardly between two boulders. Only Icefire was awake, but he sat deep in the cave, on the other side of the fire from Davyn, reading from the book they'd gotten in Tarsis.

The voyage to Southern Ergoth had been surprisingly easy. They'd expected attacks from Kirilin, as their first voyage on *Troubadour's Song* had been plagued by such, and Davyn was certain that the cleric was still on their trail. But nothing had happened, and so instead they practiced their swordsmanship with Bem and chatted with Tu and the other shipmates. Icefire seemed forlorn as they left the ship once again to begin hiking into the forests of Southern Ergoth, but he still insisted on coming, as always.

183

Now, they waited and rested—all except Davyn.

He turned away from the fire and stared out over the untamed forest beneath. Fir trees aimed toward the night sky like the feathered shafts of thousands of giant arrows plunged deep into the black earth. A river meandered through the underbrush, a shimmering necklace of silver and rubies in the light of the full moons, on its way south to meet the ocean.

They were almost finished with this wretched quest, and then Davyn could part ways with the sisters, Keene, and best of all, Icefire. Finally, he could then head back south to meet with his newly discovered relatives—people who actually wanted him around. But somehow, as he stared over the trees and watched the distant waves crash against Southern Ergoth's shores, a deep sense of dread came over him. Something wasn't right this night. The feeling made him restless.

"Anything wrong, Davyn?"

Davyn turned. Icefire continued to read his book, flipping through the pages as though he hadn't just spoken.

"I'm fine," Davyn grunted, then turned back to face the outside of the cave.

"Sleep." The way Icefire said it, the word seemed almost a command. "We have a big day tomorrow."

Davyn gritted his teeth and clenched his fists. "I need a walk." Without waiting for a response, Davyn strode out of the cave and into the dark night. A chilling breeze flowed down the cliff face and met his bare forearms. Blinking rapidly, he tried to erase all remnant of the firelight so as to regain his night vision.

The air was cool and crisp, fresh with the scent of fallen leaves and damp soil. He was at home here in the woods. He had spent years sneaking outside of Cairngorn Keep, evading the monstrous hounds his false father Maddoc had put out to guard the grounds. He had followed the tracks of what few game animals had ventured near the keep, and had practiced his archery on faraway targets. As Davyn now followed the stony path down into the thick of Southern Ergoth's woodlands, he imagined he was escaping a present full of hard emotions and constant fear and rediscovering a past that was blissfully oblivious to the truths of his parentage and the hardships of his future.

Branches cracked beneath his boots as he crept between the tall trees. They towered above him, shadowy giants rustling in the breeze. One of the trees had a strange formation of knots vaguely in the shape of two eyes and a pursed mouth.

Smiling grimly, Davyn grabbed the ornate hilt of his sword and pulled it free of the scabbard on his belt. The blade shone bright silver in the moons' light. It was the Dragon Knight's sword, which was fitting, since Davyn himself was now supposedly that very knight—a knight of destiny, drawn to great events to aid the side of good.

"I am the Dragon Knight," Davyn whispered. He eyed the knotted tree with malice and brought his sword up into an offensive position. "I am the one who was called on to help Nearra. I am the one who is to be at her side when the curse breaks. Not *you!*"

With a shout of frustration, he brought the blade down hard against the side of the tree. Bark exploded into the air as the sword's edge cleaved the tree's trunk. Brown sap oozed from the wound.

"I was by her side for two years," he said through clenched teeth as he wrenched the sword free. "I loved her through it all." Down the sword went. More bark flew.

The knotted eyes watched Davyn, judging him silently. With a sneer, he pulled the sword free and brought it down again. The power of the blow sent a shudder back up through the blade and into his body.

Again and again Davyn hacked at the tree, scarring its trunk and sending a few small branches flying. In Davyn's mind, the knotted

WIZARD'S BETRAYAL

face grew more and more to look like Icefire. The more that Davyn saw that cocky, leering grin, the harder he attacked. His muscles ached, his lungs burned for air, but he did not relent.

With a growl of frustration, he thrust the sword point into the leaf-covered ground and fell to his knees. Breathing hard, he looked up at the place where he'd imagined Icefire's face. It was completely mangled, a mess of slices and gashes.

Davyn looked down. For a moment, he reveled in the pounding of his heart, the quickness of his breath, the pain in his arms. But as the anger began to flow away, he looked at his hands. He'd forgotten to put on his gloves. Blisters covered his palms, and a smear of blood covered his right hand where he'd broken skin. And yet, despite all his rage toward Captain Icefire, despite all of the uneasy feelings of darkness looming on the horizon, he felt . . . nothing.

A hand touched his shoulder.

With a start, Davyn reached back and grabbed the intruder's arm. Leaping to his feet, he simultaneously twisted around and pulled his other arm back into a fist, prepared to attack. When he saw who it was, he let out a surprised laugh.

"Rina?"

The elf girl held her head high in regal defiance even as his strong fingers crushed her slender wrist. Seeing her here in the middle of the night was surprising enough. But Davyn was once again startled by her pure elven beauty. Golden curls cascaded over her shoulders, which were covered in an armored tunic. Her bright green eyes sparkled in the moonlight. Her full lips were pursed in indignation.

The elf girl raised an eyebrow. "My hand?"

Davyn blinked and let her arm fall. "Rina? How . . . " He shook his head. "Where did you come from?"

Rina smiled and looked like she was trying to contain a laugh.

But the pleasant expression was soon gone, replaced by a sternly set jaw.

"We've had people waiting for you to arrive," she said. "I was . . . alerted that you were coming. We have to talk; it's important. I think your friend Nearra is in trouble."

Regaining his composure, Davyn pulled his sword free from the ground and put it back in its scabbard. Leaning back against the knotted tree, he crossed his arms.

"Well," he said with a shrug, "that's nothing new. Is this about the cleric Kirilin? Do you know if she's on her way here?"

Rina's eyebrows furrowed. "Who?" As she started to walk toward Davyn, she glanced into the trees and nodded, almost imperceptibly. There were others here.

"Guess not," Davyn said. As the girl grew closer, the moonlight shone down along her smooth alabaster neck. Only, it wasn't smooth, not anymore. The flesh was marred with a long scar.

"Rina," he said, as memories of Asvoria's shapeshifter's unrelenting attack against the elf girl during the climactic final battle flooded back. Stepping toward her, he reached out a gentle finger and ran it along the old wound.

Rina took in a stiff breath. Her slender fingers touched his hand, pushing him away.

"Davyn, don't," she whispered. "Please don't make me remember. I . . . I need to tell you something. It's important."

Forgetting his earlier anger, Davyn lifted Rina's chin and looked into her eyes.

She was Elidor's sister. She'd been by his side as he faced the trials of the cursed Viranesh Keep to claim the title of Dragon Knight. She'd helped Jirah and Mudd find his friends, and then she fought side by side with them to defeat Asvoria. She'd been loyal and kind, playful and beautifully dangerous, and very suddenly he missed the feeling of having an actual friend that he could count on. He'd spent too much time with companions he didn't trust, couldn't look at, or downright hated.

"It's good to see you again," he said as she met his gaze. "Why did you leave so suddenly? You didn't even say good-bye. Catriona read your note. She said you needed to go home, but she didn't say why. Is everything all right?"

"Yes," Rina said. "I mean, no, not now. There've been attacks, but . . . At the time, yes, everything here was fine. I just needed to be away from you, and Jirah, and . . . everyone."

"But why?" Davyn asked. "We were companions, if only for a short time. Maybe we could have talked more about your brother. Or you could have come with us on this quest. We certainly have some catching up to do." He smiled.

With a shake of her head, Rina pulled away. "You don't remember, do you?" she whispered. Crossing her arms, she stared into the dark forest. "What you said, what Jirah said to me. All you cared about was Nearra. You didn't need me to help her. You didn't want me there, in your way. So I left."

"What?" Davyn asked, his anger like a sudden earthquake sending tremors through his limbs. "What are you talking about? I was trying to lead my friends without getting us killed! I'm sorry I didn't have more time to make small talk." He narrowed his eyes. "Wait, are you mad at me?" Letting out a disgruntled sigh, he leaned back against the tree and crossed his arms. "Of course you are. Why wouldn't you be? Everyone else is."

Rina didn't turn around. Shoulders trembling, she continued to stare into the trees. Davyn wanted to reach out a comforting hand, to ask her to explain what had happened that had made her leave. But he was weary of his supposed friends turning away from him all the time. If Rina wanted to do the same, then fine. He'd let her.

"Did you want to tell me something?" Davyn asked after a long moment of silence. "Or did you send scouts to wait for me just so you could tell me how much I wronged you six months ago?"

Her hands clenched and her chin high, Rina turned to face him once again. Her face was set with resolve, but there was no mistaking the hurt in her eyes.

"The Messengers," she said. "Ring any bells?"

Davyn thought for a moment, then shook his head. "Why? Should it?"

The elf girl rolled her eyes. Leaves crunched beneath her feet as she began to pace. "When we fought Asvoria, two blond children went and found your friends so that they could come help us fight. They called themselves the Messengers, remember?"

Davyn nodded. "Yes, of course. What about them?"

"They were here in Southern Ergoth. They're not children, Davyn. They're powerful elf mages. Powerful, angry, *vengeful* elf mages. And they're after Nearra and the Trinistyr."

Hunching his shoulders, Davyn snorted. "Of course they are," he muttered. "All right, so we have some new people to look out for. But they helped us with Asvoria. They can't be all bad, can they?"

Rina shook her head. "I don't think you understand," she went on. "The boy, Tylari? He's insane. I saw him at the prison where their father is being held. He took his sister's power. He was talking about becoming a god. Maybe they wanted to help Nearra in the past, but not anymore. Tylari was going to kill me, but I ran away when he was distracted. He'll try the same for anyone else who gets in his way. I heard stories about the Messengers, why they were banished." She shook her head. "They're dangerous, Davyn."

The dread Davyn felt earlier that night once again bubbled up. "Well, now we know about them," he said, trying to maintain his composure. "We can be on the lookout."

"Davyn," Rina said, coming closer and gripping his arm. "It's worse than that. They've been working with Jirah. They told her to kill me."

"What?" Davyn said. "Jirah would never hurt anyone." But even as he said it, he wondered. What about all those times he'd heard her talking to someone, only to enter a room and see no one else there? What about when Rina almost did die by falling off a cliff? She'd claimed she'd been pushed, but of course he couldn't believe anyone he was with would try to hurt another friend. But what if . . .

"By the gods," he whispered. "Jirah."

Ever so slightly, Rina smiled. It was a dark smile, marring her lovely face in a way that made Davyn inwardly shudder.

"That's right," she said. "Now it all makes sense, doesn't it? Everything Jirah's said and done has been an act. And because of her, the Messengers know exactly where you've been and where you're going. The only reason I knew you were on your way here is because Tylari said so, and the only way he could have known is because of *her*."

Davyn shook his head and backed up toward the knotted tree. "They must have misled her," he said. "Used her desperation to get information. She's trying to break the curse, nothing more."

"She's not the only problem, Davyn," Rina said. "Our scouts recognized someone traveling with you, an elf named Icefire. The Messengers weren't always a duo. Icefire used to be the leader of their little group, alongside Tylari's sister, Janeesa. If Jirah's working with them, then I'm willing to bet he is too. And that means that he may not exactly be an ally either."

"Janeesa?" Davyn gasped. He remembered Icefire's tales of lost love, back on the trip south to Icereach. Now he knew where he'd heard that name before, why it had tugged at his memory.

For a moment, Davyn wasn't sure exactly what he felt. The shock of hearing that two of his companions may be working with someone who may be trying to kill them was maddening, a betrayal deeper than he'd ever have expected.

But at the same time, he felt a sick satisfaction he never before knew he was capable of feeling. So, Icefire had been lying to them this whole time? Certainly if Nearra knew about the elf's deceit she wouldn't be so keen to be with him anymore. Certainly if she knew that her beloved Captain Icefire was still cavorting with the dark elf Janeesa, she'd abandon her love for him just like she had for Davyn.

Davyn stood still in the midnight shadows, lost in thought. Only when Rina was at his side did he look up and meet her eyes once more.

"I'm sorry, Davyn," she said. "I know learning this has got to be hard, but you needed to know. I never wanted to meet again like this, but I had to wait until you were alone to tell you. I didn't want Jirah and Icefire to find out that we know about them."

"Thank you," Davyn said, his tone cold. "You've been very helpful. Once our lives are a bit more settled, we'll have to catch up."

Rina opened her mouth as though she was about to say something. Then, after a moment, she looked down. "All right. I have to get back to my village. Seems there are dark quests all around these days."

Davyn nodded curtly, not really listening. His thoughts were too consumed with other things.

Without bothering to say good-bye, he turned and strode back toward the rocky cliff path that would lead him to the cave where his supposed friends dozed. He almost wanted to laugh, knowing now how to get rid of Icefire once and for all. Nearra would be so distraught to learn of Icefire's true nature that she would be able to find comfort only in Davyn's arms, especially if he revealed that Jirah was working with the Messengers too. Then he'd be the only one she could turn to.

"Davyn, wait," Rina called as he walked away. "There's something else. It's . . . it's about Elidor."

Shaken from his thoughts, Davyn stopped and turned to face her. The elf girl stood in a patch of rosy moonlight, her look strangely hopeful.

"What now?" Despite himself, his tone was harsh and clipped. There was too much going on in his head to try and be pleasant. "Elidor is dead, Rina. Just accept it already. He told me about you two—he didn't even think you liked him. Why do you care so much?"

Again Rina's look turned to hurt. She lowered her eyes.

Davyn let out a sigh. "Sorry," he muttered. "I didn't mean . . . " He shook his head. "What about Elidor?"

Silence. After a moment, Rina looked up. "Nothing," she said. "It's nothing at all." With that, she spun on her heels and disappeared into the dark trees.

Davyn shook his head again, then caught sight of the knotted, mangled tree. With a dark grin, he turned and walked back up toward the cave.

"Time to sleep," he whispered to himself. "Big day tomorrow."

CHAPTER

18 THE UNDERTOWER

Bright daylight streamed into the cave, hitting Jirah square in the face. Scrunching her eyes, she yawned and sat up.

Her back ached from the hard stone she'd slept on, and her mouth tasted funny, but other than that she felt fine. Their fire had been relit, and now some skinned animal cooked above it. The hearty herbed smell met Jirah's nose and her stomach growled.

Keene's, Nearra's, and Davyn's cloaks lay empty and disheveled, and Jirah heard their voices carrying in from outside the cave. Only Icefire was there. He leaped up to turn the spit so that the meat wouldn't burn.

Icefire nodded sociably when he saw she was awake. "We thought we'd let you sleep in a bit. Breakfast is almost ready."

She murmured her thanks. Uncapping her water skin, she took a long gulp, then swished the water in her mouth to cleanse it. When she lowered the skin, she found Icefire staring at her with a strange expression on his face.

Wiping her mouth with the back of her sleeve, Jirah gave him a questioning look. "Yes?" she asked. "What is it?"

Icefire leaned back against the stone wall, his arms crossed.

"You need to tell me something," he said, his voice hushed. "And you need to tell me now. What is Janeesa up to?"

Her body tensing, Jirah's eyes flashed to the front of the cave. She saw the others' shadows, but they still talked. They hadn't heard.

"What?" she asked. "I told you before. She's just helping me break the curse. She . . . she's my mentor."

Icefire shook his head. His blue eyes flashed. "Stop lying, Jirah. You need to tell me now so that I can plan. What is Janeesa doing?"

Jirah swallowed. Things were starting to go fine. She was learning magic. She was using the bow. She was actually *helping* on this quest, despite everything.

But she'd known this time would come eventually. No matter how much she felt that she had changed, it didn't erase the fact that the Messengers were out there, waiting to kill them.

With one last look at the front of the cave, Jirah scooted across the floor. Trembling, she looked down.

"Icefire, I'm so sorry," she said. "I was helping them, but they were trying to hurt Keene, and they wanted me to hurt Nearra, and—"

Icefire clutched her shoulder hard and shook her. "Jirah, look at me," he said. "*What is Janeesa up to?*"

Looking into his eyes, Jirah shrugged. "I—I don't know," she admitted. "They just want the magic weapons, and they want the Trinistyr restored. They never told me why. They wouldn't."

Snorting, Icefire looked up at the ceiling. Smoke from the fire wafted above their heads. "Of course," he muttered. "The Trinistyr." Looking down, he met Jirah's gaze. "I read about it in that book you found in the library, Jirah. It said there were four weapons: the three entombed with the wizards, and the Trinistyr itself. Anselm was supposed to use it against the Kingpriest of Istar to heal his mind."

"So?" Jirah whispered. She was still tense, expecting at any moment for the others to come back.

"The Trinistyr was made to heal madness," he went on. "Do you know Janeesa's history? About what happened to her father?"

Jirah shook her head.

"He went crazy. His supposed friends locked him up after their spells did nothing but make it worse. I'd bet anything that Janeesa wants the Trinistyr to heal her father, and probably Tylari too. Then they're going to take those weapons, and they're going to go and attack the Silvanesti wizards."

"Oh no," Jirah gasped.

Icefire shook his head, then leaned past her to rotate the spit. "What did you tell her, Jirah?" he asked. "About the final wizard? You need to tell me, now."

Jirah gulped, racking her brain to remember. "I—I told her we were coming here, to Southern Ergoth. They said they were coming here too."

His eyes raging, Icefire spun on her. "Are you mad?" he asked, his voice dangerously loud. "They're coming here themselves? Do you know how powerful Janeesa and Tylari are?" Rubbing his forehead, he leaned back. "By all the gods, Jirah."

Tears sprung to Jirah's eyes, but she rubbed them away angrily. "Icefire, I broke the mirror," she said. "I haven't spoken to them since. Please, Nearra and Davyn can't know about this. Not now. I've stopped helping Janeesa. I—"

Icefire shook his head. "It doesn't matter. It may be too late."

Footsteps sounded behind them, and Jirah leaped back to sit on her cloak. Icefire calmly leaned forward and lifted the meat from the spit. He carved it with a clean knife, portioning it out.

"That smells wonderful," Nearra said as she drew close. Her face seemed freshly scrubbed, and she smiled. "Jirah, do you want to wash up? There's a stream not too far."

Jirah shook her head.

Davyn and Keene followed. They sat down around the fire, and all bit into their breakfast.

Though her stomach growled, Jirah couldn't eat. She trembled with anxiousness.

"Rina was here last night," Davyn said, his mouth full.

Jirah tensed. Her eyes shot forward to meet Davyn's. He looked at her with a strange gleam in his eye.

"Who?" Keene asked. He bit into his meat, wrenching it back and forth like a wolf.

Davyn swallowed the bite he'd taken and quickly told Rina's story. He explained how she was the sister of a fallen friend who'd helped them fight Asvoria and free Nearra. He left out the part where she had left because of Jirah.

"She ran into some elf mages here," Davyn went on, and Jirah's heart began to pound. "They call themselves the Messengers, and apparently they're after the Trinistyr too."

"The Messengers?" Keene mumbled through a full mouth. "Hey, Icefire, that's what you called—"

Icefire clenched the kender's shoulder—hard. "Don't talk with your mouth full," he scolded.

"Davyn did," Keene muttered.

"The Messengers are here," Davyn said, ignoring Keene. "And they may try to come after us too. Apparently one of them is insane and thinks he's a god, and Rina wanted to warn us."

The ranger looked back and forth, meeting both Icefire's and Jirah's eyes. "Just thought everyone should know," he said. With a shrug, he went back to eating.

Nearra sighed wearily. "Thanks, Davyn," she said. "Icefire, do you think we'll be able to avoid them?"

Jirah's heart pounded so hard and so fast that she felt it would explode in her chest. Icefire would tell them. He'd have to. Janeesa and Tylari were here, and who knows what they would do. And it was all because of Jirah. Guilt latched onto her mind like a parasite, sucking out every thought but one: *it's all my fault.*

But Icefire only shrugged. "Of course we can, Nearra," he said. "We've been developing some strong spells for the bow and the staff. Nothing can stop us. Right, Jirah?"

Jirah ducked her head. "Right," she said.

Nearra smiled, then reached over to squeeze Jirah's hand. Everyone returned to their meal.

Jirah still couldn't eat. She felt nauseated. Trying very hard not to cry, she waited for the others to finish so that they could begin the final leg of their quest.

"It was called the Tower of Amity," Icefire said. "My master told me about it, back when I was studying magic under him. He told the tale to explain the importance of working together."

The companions walked through the forest, as they had been doing since morning. It was midday and the light was cool and comforting beneath the trees. Still, Jirah felt anxious and uneasy. She worried, but now her mind was also racing to think of some way to get out of this. There was no way that she was going to come this far only to let some stupid elf wizards hurt her friends and take away the sister she was only just now getting to know.

Maybe Icefire would keep quiet. Maybe she could *make* him keep quiet. Perhaps if she promised to find the Messengers first and do something to keep them away, Icefire wouldn't tell. Could she even keep them away? Maybe if she tricked them somehow. Maybe . . .

Jirah's mind continued to fill with ideas as they forged a course south from the cave they had spent the night in. She clutched the mystical longbow tightly and followed Icefire, who led the way with Nearra at his side and Keene and Davyn at his heels. They crossed streams and rounded fallen logs, but so far the trip had been easy. There didn't seem to be anyone in this part of the woods, at least no one they could see. Jirah had heard stories of how stealthy Kagonesti elves could be. But if any elves were watching, they weren't bothering them. The most she'd seen was a deer and her young fawn, both of whom watched them warily with their wide brown eyes until the companions passed.

Icefire held aside a tree branch and let Nearra pass. "I've been researching the place to be sure," he went on as he let Davyn take over holding the branch and continued to lead them forward. "But I'm almost positive this is the site of the final wizard's tomb."

"A tower?" Davyn asked, incredulous. He let the tree branch snap back as soon as Jirah passed, then stomped forward. "A *tower*? What sort of hiding place is that? Anyone could just wander in." He crossed his arms. "Let me guess. Your earring told you so."

Icefire looked back over his shoulder and scowled. "Let me finish the story and you'll understand," he said.

Davyn rolled his eyes.

They started up a hill, Jirah's legs straining. Kcene trotted beside her, eagerly awaiting the rest of the story.

"Long before the Cataclysm," Icefire went on, "there was a legendary elf leader named Kith-Kanan. He made a treaty with the dwarves and humans. It was a momentous historic event."

"Never heard of it," Davyn scoffed.

"Davyn, please," Nearra said. Gently touching Icefire's arm, she smiled. "Go on."

"Well, after the treaty, there were plans drawn up in Ergoth for a sort of way post between nations. A tower built to the height of twenty men into the sky, and built to go down just as far below the surface. Kith-Kanan sent someone to oversee the project, as did a representative from each race, and they all brought with them their own team of workers.

"They set about building the Tower of Amity. At first it was all good will and what have you. The dwarves made a good deal of progress on the underground portion, which everyone began to call the Undertower. Elf artists were sent in to decorate the place. But the upper tower wasn't working out. The dwarf leader and the human leader began to clash. Foundation issues, they said. Then the elves got involved and everything went to the Abyss. What had been built of the upper portion of the tower collapsed, and the three nations decided to call the whole thing a wash. Since they didn't want this little incident marring the history of the treaty, it all got swept under the rug." Flashing a grin over his shoulder, he shrugged. "But I'm guessing somehow word must have spread through the ages, and Kirilin chose the Undertower as the perfect place to trap a wizard."

Davyn applauded sarcastically. "Fantastic story. Ever think of giving up the whole wizard captain singer thing and becoming a bard full time?"

Keene leaped ahead to walk at Icefire's side. His tiny feet were a blur as they crunched over fallen branches and leaves.

"So we get to go down in the tower?" he asked. "I wonder if there's been anyone down there in years. Probably lots of interesting stuff to find."

"No exploring," Davyn growled. "No time."

Keene looked up expectantly at Icefire. "Captain?"

The elf shrugged. "We'll see."

They continued up the hill, which grew steeper the higher they went. Jirah clutched at small trees that scraped her hands as she pulled herself up. Rocks loosened beneath her feet, tumbling back down behind her. Everyone ahead of her seemed to have no trouble, especially Nearra, who used her staff to haul herself forward. Maybe she just wasn't concentrating. But how could she?

Finally, they crested the hill. Jirah was the last to reach the top, and so she was the last one to see the tower. Or, at least, what was left of it.

"There it is," Icefire said.

Ahead, the top of the hill flattened out into a plain covered with rustling grass. Piled at its center were dozens and dozens of stone blocks. At first they seemed like some sort of natural formation, perhaps the result of some long-ago avalanche. Grass grew on the stones, and moss draped from their sides. But as they headed forward and Jirah got a closer look, she could tell that the stones were much too perfectly square to have been natural. Time had eroded their edges smooth, and some of the blocks had fallen into halves, but at one time these had been the building blocks of a towering structure.

Icefire ran ahead and leaped onto the stone. Graceful as always, he jumped sideways from block to block until he reached the center of the mound. Kneeling, he peered down.

"This is it!" he called back. "The entrance!"

The others followed, Jirah again at the rear. Keene gave her a hand up onto the blocks, but she still scraped her knees, and mud got under her fingernails. Trying her best not to get her feet caught between the haphazard stones and twist her ankles, she followed Icefire's leaping path.

They all crouched near Icefire and peered down. Between the blocks was a hole in the ground revealing a deep, black chasm. A breeze wafted up from the hole, puffing once, bringing with it the scent of soil. It seemed very much to Jirah like a bottomless well.

Nearra whispered a few mystical words and the orb of her staff flared to life. Holding the staff upside down, she lowered it into the hole. The orange light illuminated the first bit of darkness, revealing ancient stone steps that seemed to be the start of a spiraling staircase.

"This *is* it," Nearra said. "Icefire, you were right."

"Well of course he was," Keene said, dangling precariously far over the edge. "He's the captain."

"Who's going to go first?" Jirah asked. Another breeze puffed up out of the hole as she lowered herself to sit next to Keene. Her heart pounding, she let her legs dangle over the edge of the stone blocks.

"I—" Icefire started to say.

"I will," Nearra said, her voice firm. "I've got the light, after all."

Jirah looked up at Davyn, curious to hear his thoughts. He'd seemed in a strange mood ever since that morning when he told his tale of Rina—almost happy, in his own fashion, at least. But now the ranger crouched down to study the stone blocks at the lip of the wide hole.

"Someone's been here," he muttered. Reaching down, he felt the moss, studying it with knowing eyes. "The plant life around here, it's been disturbed." He looked up and raised an eyebrow. "Could be our good friend Kirilin. Or—"

"—the Messengers," Nearra finished.

Again Jirah began to tremble. Could Janeesa and Tylari have found the Undertower without her telling them? Could they be below, waiting to reveal her betrayal and then kill everyone so that they could have the Trinistyr and the weapons?

She glanced to the side and saw Icefire's cheek twitch. The same thoughts were undoubtedly running through his head as well.

"Kirilin could be down there?" Keene asked. Standing to his full three-and-a-half feet, he grinned dangerously. An unsettling gleam was in his eye. "Then let's go. The sooner we get to that wizard, the sooner Kirilin's destroyed, right?"

Nearra nodded. "Right." Biting her lip in thought, Nearra turned to face Jirah.

"Jirah?"

Swallowing, Jirah scrambled over the mossy stone blocks to her sister's side. Holding the longbow awkwardly, she tried not to let it scrape against the rock. "Yes?" she asked.

Opening her pack, Nearra reached in and pulled out a small wooden box. Then she held it forward to Jirah.

"Nearra?" she whispered. "The Trinistyr? Are you sure?"

Nearra nodded and smiled. Blond hair flowed gently across her lovely face. Her expression seemed proud.

"I'm sure, Jirah," she said. "I've taken off the enchantment so that you can hold it. If Kirilin or the Messengers are truly down there, I don't want to leave the Trinistyr vulnerable should they attack while I'm reliving the last curse. You guarded it for so long, and with all that you've learned lately, I think you're the perfect girl to keep it safe."

Jirah trembled as she reached forward to take it. "Thank you," she whispered. "I . . . I won't let you down."

"I know you won't." Standing, Nearra held her head high and met Icefire's gaze. "Icefire, lower me down."

The elf grinned. "You're the boss."

Jirah watched as Icefire gripped Nearra's wrists and carefully lowered her down to the first step. Another breeze wafted up, hitting Jirah in the face and blowing back her hair. The darkness below suddenly seemed a living, deadly thing, waiting to swallow them whole.

Jirah started to put the box holding the Trinistyr back into her pack, but instead slid open its lid. The small black dragon statue lay snug inside the velvet lining.

She ran her finger over the statue, following its shape from the tip of its tail to its intricately carved snout. So much trouble had been caused by such a small artifact. But so much good could come from it as well.

Nearra can never know, Jirah thought. *She can never know what*

I've done. I *will* find a way to keep the Messengers away.

"Ready, Jirah?" Keene asked her with a tilted head. "This'll be exciting!"

Snapped from her thoughts, Jirah tightened her lips and looked up to meet the kender's wide brown eyes. "I'm ready."

CHAPTER

19   DESCENT

Nearra stepped down gingerly. Her foot met the stone step and, certain it would hold her weight, she lowered her entire self down. Icefire let go of her wrists.

The flaming orb of her staff sent out a radius of light that illuminated the walls around her. Thorny vines covered the wall to her right, bursting through cracks before climbing up toward the opening above. The stone step felt slick with mud and moss, and she noticed tiny clusters of toadstools in the corners.

"It's all clear," she called up above. "I think we can go down fine."

While the others climbed down behind her, Nearra took a tentative step forward. The vine-covered wall seemed to curve out, and in the shadows across from her she could see that they were in a rounded shaft. Peering over the edge of the steps, she saw that the staircase spiraled down alongside the wall below to where there had once been a flat level. But the majority of the floor had crumbled long ago, and now there was nothing but a vast opening Beneath it, there was darkness.

"There's a ledge here," Icefire said from the step above her, "lining the walls. But it's broken. Probably a floor here once."

Nearra nodded and pointed across to the other side of the Undertower, where the steps did not go. "You're right. I can see old doors. This place was probably sectioned into levels and the stairs led to each one." Suddenly nervous, Nearra turned to meet the elf captain's blue eyes. "What if the room we need to be in doesn't connect to the stairs?"

"We'll find a way," Icefire said. "Do you sense the wizard's magic yet?"

Nearra shook her head.

"Me neither."

Behind him, Jirah clung to the wall, her eyes wide with fear. Davyn stood beside her, his arms crossed and waiting. Keene, however, bounded past Icefire to Nearra's side. Kneeling down, he fingered the wall beside her.

"What is it?" she asked.

"There's something on the wall," he said. He craned his head around to beam back at her. "I think it's a picture."

Leaning close with the staff, Nearra saw it too—intricate images of men and elves and dwarves in old-fashioned clothes, clasping hands and appearing all around jolly. It must have once been a tapestry of some sort, but what cloth hadn't been eaten away by bugs was now muddied and worn with time.

"Wow," Nearra whispered. "This place must have been amazing back when it was built."

Davyn cleared his throat. "I know that you and Icefire find all this history fascinating and all, but how about we start heading down? If you don't sense any magic yet, then the last wizard is probably really deep. And I want to get this over with before we run into any other people who want to kill us."

Sighing, Nearra leaned back from the ancient tapestry. Without responding, she raised her staff high, lifted the hem of her dress, and began the perilous journey down the spiral staircase.

The lower she went into the decaying dark, the more Nearra noticed the gusts of wind rising from the seemingly bottomless pit beside them. It blasted up in bursts, catching her blond hair and blowing it off her neck. It was almost as if the earth far below was breathing. She shuddered and tried to forget the thought.

Their footsteps on the mossy stone echoed between the stone walls as the companions followed Nearra down. They reached the next level below and the first of the doors. It was wooden and rounded on top. Its old-fashioned iron handle was fit with an oversized keyhole. As Icefire crouched down to see if he could force the lock, Nearra looked back to see Keene tugging at Jirah's hand.

"Come on," the kender said. "You gotta look down! We're going to be going really deep. Don't you want to see?"

Her eyes still wide with fear, Jirah swallowed and shook her head. "Heights and I are not friends, Keene," she said.

Keene shrugged, then spun around. Jagged peninsulas of stone jutted out from the wall where a floor had once been. Keene crawled on his hands and knees to the edge faster than Nearra could imagine, then peeked down into the darkness. A blast of wind hit him square in the face, sending his auburn topknot fluttering above his head.

"Hmm," he said without looking back. "I think something's down there. Way, way down there."

Biting his lip in concentration, Icefire still tried to pop the lock. "There probably is, Keene," he said. "Bats, maybe, or some other underground animal."

Keene looked back and shook his head. "I don't think that's it." Tilting his pointed ear toward the darkness, he listened, "It's a rumbling," he said after a moment, "like someone's stomach when they're really hungry."

"Oh gods," Jirah said. Gripping at the vines and stone behind her, she sidled along the wall and down the steps to stand next to Davyn.

Nearra smiled in a way she hoped was reassuring. "There's probably some sort of cave below that leads outside," she said. "You see how the wind keeps blowing? It's just the wind making noise."

"You sure?" Jirah asked.

"Definitely."

Swallowing again, Jirah nodded her head. "Just the wind," she muttered. "Just the wind."

Davyn rolled his eyes and shoved past Nearra. "Get out of the way," he told Icefire. Raising one of his strong legs high, Davyn kicked the door. The ancient wood burst inward, splintering and falling to the floor.

Icefire looked up at him from where he still knelt on the floor. "Well, that's one way to do it."

Bored with the darkness below, Keene raced ahead of them and through the door. Nearra followed, urging her staff to glow brighter as she entered the dark room. Immediately a smell of rotting wood and musty air met her.

The room was small and dark. The walls were lined with old shelves, but they were empty and coated with dust. A wooden desk carved with intricate leaf designs sat in the corner, an old high-backed chair behind it. There were overstuffed chairs arranged around a patterned rug, but the cloth on all were worn and marred with ragged holes.

"A study," Icefire guessed, coming up behind her. "Or an office of some kind."

Nearra nodded. Keene raced by her side to climb beneath the desk. He popped up on the other side of it, then sat in the chair. "I bet a lot of very important people sat here," he called. He rubbed his finger across the desk, then studied his fingertip. "It's really dusty in here, though."

"It's so empty," Jirah whispered. Shivering, she came to Nearra's side. Her hands climbed up her arms as she hugged herself. "It's like a tower of ghosts. I keep expecting a wraith to pop out of the shadows or something."

"Comforting," Davyn said. Nearra looked back to see him leaning against the broken doorframe, a scowl on his face. "Obviously there's no cursed wizard here, there's no evil cleric, and there's no crazy elf mage. Let's go."

"Hold on," Nearra said. Something against the back wall caught her eye. Holding her staff high, she walked past Keene, who was still sitting in the chair, dangling his legs beneath the desk.

There was a window there, built into the stone wall just as one would build it in a normal tower. Only the window appeared to be upside down, with its flat side on top and the arching point on the bottom. Leaning close, she saw the faded remnants of a painting. It was an expertly rendered view of a sunny day in a forested area, and it, too, was upside down.

She smiled. Whoever designed this place certainly had a sense of whimsy.

"Nearra," Davyn growled. "Remember the Messengers? We don't have time to explore."

Leaning back, Nearra let out a sigh. The Tower of Amity, this place had once been called. A building signifying the bond between three nations that fell apart because of the personal grudges of three people.

The quest was almost over. They'd come far together. But they were like the tower, Nearra realized. They lacked foundation. They were crumbling as a group, and Nearra felt a deep sense of sadness. Everyone around her had secrets—she could tell. And these secrets were tearing them apart.

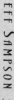

JEFF SAMPSON

She longed to sit them all down and tell them this. The more she traveled, the more she experienced, the stronger she felt. She felt confident for the first time in her life, like maybe this was what she was meant to be. Not just a quiet peasant girl, something *more*.

Even as she realized this, she knew also that each one of her friends brought something valuable to the quest. She was sure of it. It was just like when she traveled with Davyn, Catriona, Sindri, and Elidor so long ago. Except back then, they'd all respected one another. Back then, their triumphs came from being a team.

It felt too late to try and show her new companions now. If she brought it up, it would probably just make things worse. But they had only one trial left. If they could just get through this . . .

"All right," Nearra said after a moment. "Let's keep looking."

There was no door out of the study aside from the one they had come in, so they left and descended farther into the Undertower. They stopped at every level they came to, searching through whatever rooms they had access to. Some had doors that led into hallways, or walls that had fallen down to reveal other rooms. Some had back stairs leading to the next level down, or passages that led deeper. These they didn't explore, hoping that the last wizard would be closer to the main staircase. All the rooms seemed the same, bearing only the most basic of furniture, now old and decayed and covered in dust. They found wooden chests that contained nothing at all and wardrobes holding only a few disintegrating robes. Old bedrooms were equipped with giant beds fit only for kings. But after Keene jumped on a bed, they found them to be full of dirt and bugs.

Insects were everywhere, and in places where the walls had cracked and broken, soil had seeped through. Water dripped down the walls, leaving shiny green stains. Spiderwebs hung from corners.

Jirah was right. The place was so ancient, so decrepit, that it did feel as though it should be haunted. With the only light coming from Nearra's staff, shadows loomed in corners and alcoves, sending shivers down her spine. Their voices echoed much too loudly, and the only other sounds were the constant drip of water and the occasional whoosh of the wind.

The deeper they went, the less finished the rooms were. Some were completely empty and devoid of decoration, and here the stone walls had fallen into heaps on the floor, letting mounds of dirt flow in.

They'd gone down about thirteen stories when Nearra felt the icy cold touch of ancient magic lance through her legs. She let out a gasp and almost dropped her staff as the magic shivered up her spine and jolted her head.

Jirah jumped and clutched her longbow tightly. "What was that?" she asked. "I just felt something."

Icefire's flame blue eyes blazed. "I did too. It's the final wizard. We're close."

Eyes wide, Jirah came to Nearra and Icefire's side. "Th-that was magic? I felt magic?"

"Ooh, really?" Keene cried. Bobbing eagerly, he jumped to Jirah's side. "Jirah, that's so great! It's what you and your father always wanted! What does it feel like? Does it tingle, like when your foot falls asleep? Or is it like when you drink a warm cup of tea on a cold winter day? Or something else altogether? I always wondered, but everyone says kender can't do magic, which, by the way, I think is really unfair."

Jirah shrugged. "It's . . . it's interesting. I'm not sure how I feel."

Davyn shoved past them to a door. Pounding it with his shoulder, he grunted. "You mages think the tomb is close?" Rearing back, he let out a grunt, then pounded the door again. "In here, maybe?" One more pound and the door gave.

"I don't know," Nearra said. "Let's see." Gently she put her hand on his shoulder, and the ranger stepped aside to let her pass. Holding the staff high, she walked into the room.

It was vast, much larger than the rooms above, though much emptier. Here it was only plain stone floor and bricked walls, and the outlines of where the false windows eventually would have been. Rotted wooden boards lay in the corners, as did carts that had carried down supplies.

Waving the staff back and forth, Nearra found that the walls on either side of the room were completely destroyed. It was now almost as if the space was one big room, circling the central column. With a nod to the companions behind her, Nearra turned left and headed farther around.

She could sense the magic grow stronger the farther through the rooms they went. They stepped around fallen beams and climbed over rubble. They avoided clusters of spiderwebs and vines that hung like curtains. Magic pulsed ahead, flowing toward her like a warm summer breeze.

"We're almost there," Icefire whispered. "I can feel it."

Nearra's heart pounded. Despite all the trials they'd faced, despite all the tensions between friends, they were finally here—the final step of their quest. At first she'd taken on the task only for Jirah and her father, but the farther they'd gone along, the more she had become swept up in it all. It wasn't just about getting magic for her family, nothing as vain as that. No, she felt very strongly that they were correcting a wrong that had been brought upon the world very long ago. It wasn't much, it was not like she could go back in time and keep the Cataclysm from ever happening, but at least she could give those brave wizards who tried to stop it some peace. And that was worth something—to her, anyway.

The magic flowed stronger now, and deep inside she felt the

remnants of Asvoria's power flare up, mingling with her own new power into a whirlwind in her gut. Above her, the orb on the end of her staff flashed in bursts.

Icefire's eyes were closed, his head held high in rapture. Suddenly, he began to run.

"Come on!" Nearra hefted up the hem of her skirt and made chase. The magic wasn't affecting her the same as Icefire—no, magic did something *strange* to him—but she sensed something in the power as it flowed past her, a husky male voice crying out in fear. It was Tudyk, the last cursed wizard. She was sure of it. She'd read about him in the book they'd found.

So intent on finding the last wizard to free him of his torture, Nearra almost plunged to her death.

"Nearra!" Davyn shouted. His rough hands pulled at her, hauling her back before she raced over a craggy ledge.

Nearra stopped, gasping for air. Only then did she see the massive opening in the floor. The blocks had given way, falling two stories down. The breeze of magic came from here, she was certain, billowing up from the chamber below.

"Down there," she said, clutching at Icefire's arm. "He's down there."

"Let's go," Icefire said.

Not waiting for Jirah, Keene, and Davyn, the two turned and raced back the way they came. Tudyk's pain was aching, making Nearra tremble with sadness. Though Icefire ran for a different reason, she felt just as consumed.

They ducked beneath the fallen beams and found themselves back at the door they'd come in. The stairs were right outside, ready to take them down to the tomb to fulfill her destiny. Nearra ran to the door—and then stopped in her tracks.

"Dragon," she whispered.

Before her, filling the entire door frame, was the face of a red dragon. Plate-sized black eyes stared forward in fury. Nostrils flared at the end of a long, scarred snout. Sword-sized yellow teeth shimmered in the orange light of her staff.

The giant creature growled deep in its throat, a rumbling sensation that shook Nearra to her core. Fear came over her, freezing her in place. She couldn't move. She couldn't think. All she could feel was the dragonfear that wafted off the beast in putrid waves.

"Human," the dragon hissed.

Then it opened its mouth and let forth a burst of flame.

CHAPTER

20　Mirken

Once upon a time, Mirken had been a dragon. He'd soared between the clouds, blasting the hanging veils of water with balls of flame and watching them evaporate before rising higher into the sky to reform in the cool air. He'd tilted his wings to swoop down to the earth, clutching prey in his claws to take home and feast upon.

He had been an impressive creature: scales as red as blood, eyes as black as night, a roar as loud as exploding thunder. All feared him.

During the war, he'd taken up the cause of the Dark Queen Takhisis, as had his brethren. He'd let men mount him, use him as a steed so that they could sweep over nations. Humans, elves, dwarves—they all fled before him. Their homes burned. Their flesh crackled. Their blood flowed between his claws.

Once upon a time, Mirken had been a dragon. Now? Now, he was nothing. He was a *worm*, a deformed monstrosity hiding in the depths of some long-forgotten tower.

The warriors of the Lance had fought back against Takhisis's forces. But it wasn't the know-it-all knights brandishing their showy dragonlances that had done him in. No, it had been other red dragons.

There had been a battle, and the red dragons had been beaten back. Mirken was the cause, they'd claimed. He'd failed the Dark Queen, and so he was to be punished.

They had leaped upon him when he had his back turned. They'd wrenched the dark soldier off the saddle strapped to Mirken's back and flung him to the ground acres below. That didn't matter to Mirken. The dragonrider had meant nothing to him.

But then the dragons swarmed him. They bit into the joints of his wings, tearing through scale and flesh, muscle and tendon, until the bone snapped and his wings fell free from his body. They let him fall to stone and soil far below, and the fall crushed his back leg. It was useless now, a lump of flesh clogged with fragments of crumbled bone and drifting bits of cartilage.

The other dragons descended to claw out his eyes and slit open his belly. He fought their attacks until they were eventually called back to battle. They left him there, shattered and wingless, his body and face marred with wounds that would soon heal into hideous scars.

Earlier that morning he'd awoken to enter the skies a dragon. He fell asleep that night a mutilated, deformed beast.

He hid. He healed. He traveled far from where he'd been betrayed, and he found a cave. The cave burrowed deep into the earth, above which was a vast column of nothingness. There he taught himself a spell he shouldn't know, a spell that would allow him to climb the walls like a copper dragon, a spell that would allow him to travel up through the emptiness between stone and earth now that flight had been stolen from him.

He claimed the column, the Undertower, as his home. He'd climb all the way to the top, set traps, and wait for an unsuspecting forest animal, monster, or elf to wander by. They would scream or they would fall silent at the sight of his massive head bursting from beneath the rubble of the old tower, his dragonfear overtaking them. Then, he would snap them in his jaws and pull them, as they struggled, deep into the blackness below where they would become his meal.

There were intruders this day, adventurers who dared to enter his home. There were two earlier, and he had sensed their vile magic. Immediately he set out to destroy them, but something spoke to him in the back of his massive head, soothing him into sleep. Later, when he awoke, he sensed even more trespassers. Certainly they were coming for whatever it was deep in the old rooms that sent out the wafting magic.

The voice came again as Mirken noticed the trespassers—a godly voice, a sly voice that spoke of betrayal. The voice gave him visions of what these intruders would do.

They weren't allowed here. No one was. No one was to see him like this and live to tell the tale.

Jirah raced beside Davyn and Keene, following Nearra and Icefire as fast they could. Something had come over the two of them. They heard Nearra mutter something. A moment later, a new voice, a terrifyingly deep voice, responded. Then Nearra screamed, and the rubble-filled room before them exploded into a writhing tornado of orange and yellow flame.

"NO!" Jirah screamed. The force of the blast knocked her backward, the light of it hurting her eyes. Shielding her face, she cowered on the ground. The heat was so intense it dried her skin.

The flames whooshed into the cavern, seemingly endless. Old timber and ancient supply carts burst into bonfires, sending black smoke curling up toward the ceiling. Vines shriveled into husks. Scorch marks marred the stone walls.

Then finally, the flames ended. Tears streaming down her dry cheeks, Jirah leaped to her feet. Her pack thudding against her back

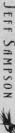

JEFF SAMPSON

and her longbow clattering against her side, she ran forward, not caring for her own safety. She had to see. She had to know. Nearra couldn't be dead, not now when she was only just really getting to know her. Not after they'd come so far.

"Nearra!" Davyn bellowed as he ran beside her. "NEARRA!"

The ranger pushed himself to race ahead of Jirah, Keene at his heels. Then they saw them.

Nearra knelt on the floor, her eyes clenched closed and the staff held high. Icefire lay on the floor behind her, gasping for air.

"Nearra!" Jirah cried. She leaped forward without thinking, skidding on her knees to land at her sister's side. Reaching around her and the staff, she hugged her tight and let the tears fall.

Only then did she feel the tingling dragonfear creeping through her body. Trembling like a leaf caught in a winter storm, slowly she turned her head. A dragon's face loomed outside the small door. Smoke curled from its nostrils. Its scaly red lips were pulled back into a sneer. Its head rose and fell as the creature gasped for air, and its coal-black eyes seemed to bore into her own.

"Trespassers," the dragon hissed. "How dare you invade my home!"

"Hey!" Keene cried. He skidded to a stop right in front of Jirah and Nearra. Pointing, he tilted his head around. "A dragon! See, I told you I heard rumbling."

Rearing back its head, the dragon opened its jaws wide. Orange flames licked up the sides of its throat, building into another full blast.

"Keene!" Davyn cried. "Get behind Nearra NOW!"

With a mock salute, the little sailor leaped forward into a roll. He tumbled behind Nearra just as the flames burst forth from the dragon's maw to envelope them all.

Immediately, the orb on Nearra's staff flared to life, flickering with blue and yellow light. As though an invisible wall had arisen, the flames circled them but did not come forth to sear their flesh. Sparks flew from the ocean of flame, burning holes in Jirah's cloak and nipping at her skin. The heat was unbearable, but they were alive.

Finally, the flames stopped. The dragon clenched its jaws tight, snorting through its nostrils with indignation. Nearra let out a gasp of air. She wouldn't be able to hold the creature's flames at bay should it strike again, and the dragonfear was so ragingly powerful that none of them could move.

None of them except Keene.

"Hey!" he cried. Scowling, he leaped to his feet. "What did we ever do to you?"

"Kender," the dragon snorted. "So idiotically fearless. I can't wait to tear into your tender flesh."

"You'll have to catch me first," Keene crowed. Bounding toward the door, he hefted free his short sword. In one swift move he sliced down against the dragon's snout. It bounced off harmlessly, but it was enough to gain the beast's attention. Without waiting a second, Keene raced up the stairs toward the entrance far above.

Immediately the dragon gave chase. Its head shot up above the doorframe, its scarred belly close behind, followed by its withered leg and long tail.

Jirah, Nearra, Davyn, and Icefire lay among the scorched rubble, gasping for air and trying to regain their senses. They'd faced dragons before, but this one's dragonfear seemed strengthened by a distinct feeling of hatred that left a bitter taste in the back of Jirah's throat.

A roar echoed from high above, followed by the heavy thuds of stone blocks tumbling down the central shaft into the depths of the Undertower.

"Keene," Jirah sobbed. "The dragon will kill him!"

His legs trembling, Icefire climbed to his feet. "He's doing this for you, Jirah," he said. He reached down and offered his hand to help her up. "He knows how much you want the curse broken. So he's helping us to get down below."

Jirah took his hand and let him haul her to her feet. She met his eyes and swallowed. "Idiot kender," she sniffled. "Always believing in me and helping me. He'd better stay alive."

Davyn gripped Nearra around her waist and helped her stand. She wavered as though woozy, then clenched both hands around the staff to help herself stand up straight.

"You all right?" Icefire asked. He was at her side in an instant, caressing her cheek.

"Yes," she whispered. "Let's hurry. The dragon will be back any moment."

"It can never be easy, can it?" Davyn muttered. "Just once I'd like it to be easy."

Clinging to each other, they stumbled toward the door. Keene whooped far above, shouting insults as he leaped from stair to stair. Again the dragon roared, the force of its voice sending stones and dust raining down upon their heads.

Trying to ignore her worry for Keene, Jirah let herself be dragged down the spiraling steps. She almost slipped on slick patches of mud and moss, but she clung to the vines and cracks in the walls, holding herself up. They raced past the level below and its door. She could sense the magic strongly now, wisping past her face. It certainly couldn't be as strong a feeling as what Nearra and Icefire felt, but it was there all the same. And she could feel quite certainly that the wizard's tomb lay one level down.

Finally, they reached the bottom level. Here, the stairs ended quite suddenly. There was the platform beneath the door, then a few steps leading down before crumbling into nothing. Still the shaft continued downward into deep darkness. Still the wind rose in bursts.

Icefire and Davyn leaned back, their muscles taut as they pounded their shoulders against the door. Jirah glanced around nervously and caught sight of a massive wooden door, at least five times the size of the one they were trying to break down. It was set in the wall only a few feet away—and it was certainly big enough for a dragon to fit through.

Wood splintered, and iron hinges bent. The door fell down in a flurry of dust, and everyone bounded through.

White light blazed to their right, and Jirah had to shield her eyes. The magic's pull was stronger here. Both Nearra and Icefire shoved past Jirah and Davyn and raced forward.

Blinking rapidly, Jirah made to follow. Then, Nearra stopped, as did Icefire. Vaguely Jirah could make out a shadowy form in the white light. Her heart began to pound. One of their pursuers had beaten them here.

"Come on," Davyn growled. His strong fingers clutched her forearm so hard that they pinched her skin. She almost tripped on a fallen timber as he hauled her forward.

They came to Nearra's and Icefire's sides, and that was when Jirah realized who the figure was.

Janeesa.

The elf girl stood there, perfectly still. She was just as slender and beautiful as Jirah remembered. Straight golden hair was parted behind her pointed ears, and her wide oval eyes shone like freshly polished steel. Intricately embroidered red wizard's robes covered her, shoulders to feet.

Jirah's breaths came out, rapid and uncontrollable. Her legs felt weak, as though her bones had disintegrated. She wanted to collapse and cower under her arms.

Janeesa was here. Janeesa had come just like she said, and she was going to kill Nearra, and probably her too. Or maybe something even worse.

Holding onto Davyn's shoulder to steady herself, Jirah waited for the inevitable. Still Janeesa did not move. Only then did Jirah notice the tangles and knots in the once well-groomed wizard's hair. Only then did she see the dark circles under her eyes.

Only then did she see the blank, dead look in the girl's gaze.

It wasn't Janeesa that Nearra and Icefire were gawking at. It was something beyond her, something deep within the raging white light.

The room was so filled with the light that Jirah could begin to make it out. Unlike the ones above, it was vast and open, cavernous. Perhaps it had been intended to be a great hall of sorts at one point, especially with the towering doors to her right. But as it was now, it was nothing but walls of stone and piles of rubble.

All except for the tomb.

It stood straight ahead of them, or at least at one point it had. Now the walls lay crumbled. The spectral guardians that guarded it were there, fully formed—but they were frozen, unmoving. Their faces were twin masks of hideous fear. Beyond them, writhing within the raging white light, was Tudyk, the final wizard.

And beside him was Tylari.

The crazed black-robed wizard stood beside the final wizard, his eyes open wide in manic joy. A silver medallion now hung around his neck. Powerful winds pulled his robes taut against his body and tangled his unruly golden hair around his face, but he paid them no mind. His lips moved, muttering arcane phrases Jirah couldn't hear. Red blazed around his hand—a hand that jutted deep within the cursed wizard's chest.

Crimson light flared, and suddenly, the waves of the wizard's magic disappeared. The white light faded away. For a moment, all Jirah could do was blink her eyes to clear her vision.

Tylari stood within the rubble of the tomb, his robes and his hair disheveled. His chest heaving, he grinned a terrifying grin that sent shivers down Jirah's spine. At his feet lay the body of the cursed wizard, his white robes splayed around him, his black hair fallen to cover his face. He seemed very much dead. At either side of the cursed wizard lay a pair of intricate golden gauntlets.

The final weapon.

Tylari bent down, lifting one of the metal gloves to study in the pale torchlight that now lit the room. He tilted the glove back and forth, sending shimmering, reflected light across his face. Holding out his right hand, he placed the gauntlet on. It seemed to shrink and tighten, fitting his hand like it was made for him. Its fingertips were curved to sharp points, like an eagle's talons.

"The weapon," he intoned. "It is mine!"

Everyone stared, unable to comprehend what had just happened. As they watched, Tylari picked up the other gauntlet and shoved it on his other hand. He clenched and unclenched his hands, the clawed tips shimmering dangerously sharp.

"No," Nearra whispered. "How . . . how could he—"

"Nearra," Icefire hissed. "Stay back. It's one of the Messengers. He is crazed."

Tylari continued to cackle in glee, not noticing the four companions standing only a few feet from him.

"Icefire," a tiny voice whispered. "Icefire . . . I know you. I know you."

All eyes turned to Janeesa. There was some flicker of recognition on her pretty face, a flash of comprehension. A slender hand reached forward from beneath the folds of her red robe, its fingers stretching to touch the elf and see if he was real.

"Icefire," she said again. "Tylari hurt me."

"Sister!" Tylari shouted. His eyes blazing, the crazed mage finally looked beyond the tomb and caught sight of the companions. He let out a loud, barking laugh. "Looks like our friends have returned."

Leaping down from the tomb, Tylari sauntered toward them.

He was not the elf mage Jirah had known before. He was taller. His eyes held a sharpness. He was aware—and he was going to tell Nearra and Davyn the truth about his relationship with Jirah.

Not waiting for the elf to reveal her secret, Jirah let out a cry of rage and anguish, and ran forward to kill him.

CHAPTER

21 A New Power

A aargh!"
Jirah's cries echoed in the cavernous ceiling high above. She raced past Icefire, seeming so small in her anger and fear that for a moment she seemed like the fourteen-year-old girl she actually was, and not the adult Icefire always mistook her to be. Awkwardly, she held her longbow high as she ran, her free hand grasping desperately for an arrow from the quiver strapped to her back.

"Jirah," Icefire called, leaping forward to grab her. "No!"

He was too late. Finally pulling an arrow free, she pulled her bowstring taut, ready to fire at Tylari's chest. In a flash the elf mage raised one of the clawed gauntlets. *"Daya belit!"*

With a howl, a whirlwind burst from the gauntlet. It smashed against Jirah's chest, twisting her once as it threw her backward. She landed in a heap at Davyn's side, her pack flying off her shoulders and skidding across the dusty, stone-covered floor. The longbow and the single arrow flew free as well, clattering at Icefire's feet. Blood trickled down Jirah's forehead, and she moaned.

"Now, now, Jirah," Tylari said. "Hasn't anyone ever told you not to try to strike a god?"

224

Beside Icefire, Nearra gulped back her fear. Tears glistened in her eyes, and the elf knew exactly what she was feeling—she'd failed. She'd been chosen to make amends for her ancestor's misdeeds, and after all their work, she'd failed.

"How do you know her name?" Nearra cried. Clenching her staff tight, she took a step forward. "Tell me!"

His gauntleted hands at his side, Tylari tilted his head. "Why wouldn't I know her name?" he asked. "She is Jirah. She is a betrayer."

"Tylari."

Janeesa stood among a pile of rubble, rubbing at her forehead. Worry and confusion creased her features as she stumbled forward, falling at his feet.

Tylari narrowed his eyebrows as he looked down at her. "What is it?" he spat.

Janeesa clutched at her head, shaking it as she rocked back and forth. "Curse . . . I'm remembering," she muttered. "There's vengeance . . . and weapons . . . and the Trinistyr."

Tylari shook his head. "I have the gauntlets," he said. "Hiddukel gave them to me, and we shall have our vengeance. But the Trinistyr shall never be restored, dear sister. Never."

Icefire took in the scene, old emotions coursing through him. The crumbled walls, the ancient tomb, the vast towering door—everything in the cavern seemed to disappear except for the Messengers.

They'd been friends. They'd trained at each other's side. And Janeesa, well, she was his first love. A dangerous love, a terrifyingly dark love, but she had been his, and he had been hers.

He wouldn't give in to her ways. He would not help with her vengeance. But seeing her here, all power and thought torn from her . . . Burning hatred flared within Icefire's gut.

"You did something to Janeesa," Icefire seethed. He stepped

forward, and his boot nudged against the bow lying useless on the cold stone ground. "What have you done to her?"

Tylari looked up and caught Icefire's eyes. Stepping over his sister, he strode closer. Icefire sensed Davyn sidling up behind them.

"She wanted to take away my power, Brother," the elf mage said as he drew close. "She wanted to keep me from becoming a god. But I showed her. I took her power as a donation to my cause. I pulled the cleric's god into my fold, and I killed the cleric. I have been renewed and strengthened. With the final weapon, I am almost ready to ascend." Tilting his head back, he raised the golden gauntlets to the sky. "I am ready for my destiny!"

Looking down, he tilted his head. "Did you like the dragon? Hiddukel riled him up for me."

"Go to the Abyss," Davyn spat. Sword high, he, too, leaped past Icefire. In a flash of gold, Tylari backhanded the ranger, sending him sprawling to the ground. Jirah crawled through the dirt to his side.

"Anyone else want to play?" Tylari asked.

With a thunderous boom, the giant wooden door rattled as something large and angry beat at it from the other side.

"The dragon's here!" Keene cried from behind them as he burst into the room. "I tried to get him to go up, but he made me come back down. I sure hope that curse is broken."

The kender raced from the doorway behind them. Catching sight of Tylari, he skidded to a stop.

"What are *you* doing here?"

Tylari sneered. "I—"

With another resounding boom, the ancient wooden door exploded inward. Wooden shrapnel flew through the room, and Icefire pulled Nearra down, covering her body with his own.

A terrifying roar echoed throughout the cavernous room. Heavy footsteps echoed, interspersed with the sound of sharp claws clinking against stone. Coughing through the dust that had billowed around them, Icefire opened his eyes.

The dragon stood there, between the companions and the defiled tomb, and Icefire got his first good look at the beast. It was the largest dragon the elf had ever seen, a behemoth that could kill them all with a single blow. Its chest rose and fell as the creature heaved in its fury. Its sinewy neck shot back and forth, snakelike, as it scanned the room.

Ragged nubs jutted up on the creature's back where its wings once were, and behind it dragged a useless leg as it stalked forward into the cavernous room. All eyes were on the dragon's bared teeth.

Realizing he could use the distraction, Icefire looked down and saw the bow and arrow still at his feet. In one swift move, Icefire hefted up the longbow and the arrow. Flipping them into position, he nocked the arrow, aimed, and let it fly.

The blue-tipped arrow soared through the air, straight and true. But no magic flared around it. It did not transform into a pillar of water. Clattering against the dragon's scales, it fell to the floor, useless.

"Oh no," Icefire whispered. Only then did he realize that no voice of magic called from the bow, singing for him to use it. Its power had been stolen.

The dragon reared its head back and bellowed. Its massive tail whipped behind him, slamming into a wall and sending it crumbling to the ground. Dust billowed into the room as soil cascaded down.

"Nearra!" Icefire shouted. "Use your staff!"

"It won't work on the dragon," she shouted back. "It's immune to fire!"

"Not on the dragon, the elf!"

Tylari was still distracted by the raging dragon. He'd turned around to stare up at it, a look of awe on his face. Janeesa had crawled across the floor and now clutched at his legs. Her robes were streaked with mud.

Icefire grabbed Nearra's hand and pulled her close. With a nod of her head, she raised the staff high and mumbled magic words.

Nothing happened.

"What—" she said, startled. "Did I say the wrong words? What's wrong?"

"Gods, no," Icefire whispered.

"You shall all pay for your trespass!" the dragon bellowed. Then, rearing back its neck, it prepared to blast another burst of flame.

Davyn was suddenly at their sides, clutching at their arms and hauling them away. His sword smacked against his knees as he dragged Icefire and Nearra around a pile of rubble and threw them down to cower next to Jirah and Keene. Jirah clutched protectively at her pack with all her might.

Icefire spun around, trying to catch sight of the Messengers. Tylari stood still where he'd stopped, his robes rustling gently in an unseen breeze. Her eyes wide and her teeth clenched in fear, Janeesa pawed at his robes as though she were little more than an animal.

The dragon breathed its fire.

"*Daya belit*," Tylari shouted above the roar of the flame. "*Draconis api dalam edar belit!*" He raised his gauntlet-covered hands high.

A tornado burst from his hands. Fire and wind swirled together, faster and faster into a maelstrom of deadly magic. Then Tylari spread his arms wide and the tornado dissipated, blowing the fire out on either side of him.

The dragon crouched down low. Its lips pulled back into a snarl as its front claws clutched at the ground.

"You think you can defeat me?" the dragon bellowed. "You think you can invade my home and harm me?"

Tylari raised his head high. "Of course I do. It was at my command that you attacked. And it is at my command that you shall stand down."

"You do not command me!"

Someone tugged at Icefire's cloak. "Use Jirah's bow!" Keene said. "Water would hurt it, right? Maybe if you shot it down its throat!"

Icefire shook his head. "The weapons don't work."

"What?" Jirah asked. "Why?!"

"I—"

Another roar enveloped the cavern as the dragon sent forth another pillar of flame. Again Tylari raised his gauntlets, and again he dissipated the flame with his wind.

Tylari stamped his foot. "I am to be your god, beast! You dare attack me?"

"I dare," the dragon hissed.

Its head darting forward in a blur, the dragon opened its jaws wide, preparing to grip Tylari around his middle and swallow him whole. For a moment Icefire expected to see the sharp yellow teeth pierce Tylari's flesh, to see Tylari scream in agony as his blood spilled.

But Tylari raised his hands high. Gold shimmered, and another whirlwind arose. It wrenched Janeesa free from her brother's robes, sending her sliding across the floor. Moments before Tylari would have become the dragon's next meal, the magic wind carried him toward the dark stone ceiling.

The dragon's jaws clamped shut, hard, where Tylari had stood only moments before. The thunderous clap echoed around them.

His hands at his side, Tylari tilted back his head and let out a delirious laugh. Before the dragon could react, the elf soared toward its face, his black robes streaming behind him. In one swift swipe, Tylari clawed at one of the beast's ebony eyes.

Roaring in agony, the dragon reared back and lifted its head high into the cavern. It swiped at the air with one of its massive front claws, hitting nothing but air.

Cockily, Tylari spun himself in the air. He scanned the cavern below him, trying to find the companions.

"Jirah," he crowed. "Jirah, you have lost. I know you are down there, cowering behind your sister, the ranger, and the elf. I know you're guarding that unholy statue in your pack."

His hair whipping across his cheeks, his mouth wide in a frightening grin, Tylari lowered himself as he flew toward the back of the cavernous room.

"Give the Trinistyr to me, Jirah," he called. "Give it to me and maybe—"

With a whoosh of air, the dragon's tail whipped around and hit Tylari in his side. With a surprised gasp, the deranged elf mage lost control of the magic wind and flew across the cavern. He reached out with the gauntlet claws only moments before he slammed into a wall of packed soil. Clutching onto the wall, Tylari slowed his descent as he fell into a pile of rubble below.

Trumpeting in rage, the dragon leaped across the cavern, past the tomb where the spectral guardians still floated frozen and the final wizard lay dead. Head down, it aimed to butt Tylari.

Tylari rolled out of the way. Seconds later soil and stone exploded as the dragon barreled into the pile of rubble.

Tylari raced across the floor, his boots hitting the ground in heavy thuds. He almost tripped on his robes, but he caught himself.

Reaching Janeesa's side, who had not risen from where she'd fallen, Tylari looked up toward the pile of rubble behind which cowered the companions.

"I'll be back, Jirah!" he raged. "And I'll bring the fetch with me, you sick, stupid girl!"

Behind him, the dragon shook its head, dazed from the self-inflicted blow. Clutching Janeesa around her shoulders with one arm,

Tylari raised his free hand and muttered more words of magic.

Icefire leaped to his feet. Shoving the useless bow into Jirah's arms, he pulled free his sword. He had to stop Tylari. He couldn't let him get away, not after he took away their ability to break the curse and definitely not with the weapon he stole.

Nearra clutched at his shoulder, pulling him back.

"No," she said. Meeting her eyes, he saw streaks of tears on her cheeks. "The dragon. It'll kill you."

As the five companions watched in despair, wind and dust swirled around the two Messengers. Laughing in manic glee, Tylari let the magic carry him up toward the ceiling. There they saw the craggy hole through which they'd looked down from above, the one the waves of magic had flowed through. Tylari and Janeesa disappeared up through the hole in a whoosh of air.

Enraged, the dragon spun around to follow. It bounded across the cavern, its tail whipping behind it. Bunching its good back leg, it leaped toward the hole. Its front legs scrabbled at the edges of the floor above as it tried to pull itself up. Muffled sounds of bursting flame and angry roars rumbled around them.

"Now," Davyn said, leaping to his feet. "We need to run now!"

"But the wizard," Jirah wailed. "He's still there. The curse—"

"Forget the curse!" Icefire cried. Already he could sense strains of dark forethought racing through his mind. "Go!"

Clutching at each other, the companions raced across the cavern and back toward the small door they'd come through. Jirah screamed, and they all ducked as the dragon's tail flung wildly above their heads. It slammed against a rocky pillar, sending down piles of stone. Still the dragon scrabbled to climb up through the hole, its good lower leg clutching at air.

They burst through the door, skidding on the slick steps. Turning, they leaped forward, trying to get higher. They had made it up one level and were racing up another when a flash of red flew

WIZARD'S BETRAYAL

out of the vast opening below where once the towering wooden doors had been.

The dragon leaped onto the staircase and landed against the opposite wall, sending a shudder through the entire tower. The ground quaked beneath them, but somehow they managed to keep their balance.

Clinging to the curved wall despite its immense size, the dragon reached forward, climbing up much faster than any of them could imagine.

"Keep running!" Icefire yelled. "Get to the next room and run inside. Hurry!"

Ahead of him, Keene, Jirah, and Nearra reached the door leading into the level of the broken walls. Davyn stayed behind, his sword drawn protectively.

"Davyn," Icefire gasped as he strained his long legs to leap forward. "Davyn, we have to form a plan, we—"

Fire flared, blinding him. His boots gave way as they met slick moss and Icefire fell forward. Grasping at the vines uselessly, he gritted his teeth as his shins met the sharp edge of one of the steps.

Then behind him, the steps exploded. Rocks pounded his head as beneath him the stone began to crumble.

"Davyn!" Icefire shouted.

And then he fell into the endless blackness below.

CHAPTER

22   CURSED

Time seemed to slow as Davyn watched Icefire fall. The elf's usual cocky face was contorted with unabashed fear; all semblance of cool collection was gone. He was about to die, and he knew it.

Several thoughts ran through Davyn's mind at once. The first, the loudest, was "good riddance."

He could watch Icefire fall. He could claim there was no time. He could let the elf die and be out of his life forever.

But then came the other thoughts, the ones that told him he could never do that, no matter how much he hated someone. And besides, he hadn't yet gotten his chance to reveal the elf's betrayal to Nearra.

Davyn leaped forward, his sword clattering to the floor. His chest and stomach slammed against the stairs, bruising him, but he paid the pain no mind. Reaching forward in a blur, he gripped Icefire's wrist.

The elf's descent suddenly stopped, and he swung toward the wall. The weight of him dragged Davyn forward, scraping his leather over muddy stone. Scrabbling at the wall with his boots, Icefire managed to find a crack, and he stuck his toe inside to keep them both from falling.

233

"Here!" Davyn cried. "Your other hand. Quick!"

Across the wide-open shaft, the dragon clung to the wall, bellowing in rage. Any moment now he would fire again.

His face tensed in concentration, Icefire grunted and flung his free hand up. Ranger and elf clasped each other's wrists and, tensing his leg muscles, Davyn began to haul the elf up.

"By the gods, you're heavy," Davyn muttered through clenched teeth. Sweat dripped down his face and stung his eyes as his biceps burned from the strain.

Icefire's boots slipped against the stony wall as he tried to find a foothold. "The weight is all muscle," Icefire gasped out.

"I'm sure."

Davyn sensed the dragon's massive head whipping back and forth high above. Glancing out of the corner of his eye, he saw that the one of the dragon's eyes was damaged, sliced through from Tylari's gauntlet. It had paled to a milky blue, and thick, clear liquid oozed down the dragon's cheek like slimy tears.

"YOU SHALL ALL DIE!" the dragon roared. Its voice echoed all around them, and again the stairs beneath them quaked.

"Come on!" Davyn grunted. His back blazing with the strain, Davyn took a breath and hauled Icefire up with all his strength. The elf clutched at the stone and the vines. Finally finding a foothold, he managed to climb back onto the steps.

"Thanks," he gasped.

Davyn sneered. "Anytime." He grabbed his sword from where he dropped it.

As one they raced up the stairs toward the room and, hopefully, shelter. They were four steps away . . . two . . . one . . .

Claws smashed into the wall right in front of them, pounding against the stone so hard that cracks snaked out in all directions. The dragon's mutilated face loomed in front of them and the two froze, dragonfear overwhelming all other senses.

Scalding breath that stunk of the corpses of dead animals washed over them, as did the scent of sulfur. The dragon's one good eye bulged in fury. Opening its jaws wide, it prepared to strike.

Then from the doorway, a small figure appeared—Keene.

Swinging his hoopak staff, he yelled something Davyn couldn't hear over his own labored breathing. Then in one quick move, Keene thrust the staff forward. A jagged piece of stone flew from the sling at its end, flying through the air before embedding deep into the dragon's injured eye.

Shrieking in pain, the dragon fell backward. It caught itself against the walls, its head thrashing back and forth in agony, but it was now out of Davyn and Icefire's way.

"Good job, Keene!" Icefire shouted. Leaping ahead of Davyn, he dived for the door.

Davyn followed. Skidding over the soot that marred the floor where the dragon had breathed its fire earlier, Davyn veered left to follow Icefire. Behind him the dragon's roars echoed, thunderous. It would be after them very soon.

The embers of the burnt carts and timber smoldered in the corners, but their meager glow did nothing to pierce the darkness. Davyn skidded to a stop, looked right, and then left.

There, farther in, he saw a glow of torchlight from the tomb's room a few floors down. It shone through the hole in the floor, lighting the way. Davyn saw Icefire leap over a pile of shadowy rubble, following the light.

Davyn chased after the elf. He ran into stone blocks and banged his head against a beam. Sticky spiderwebs clung to his face as he ran blindly through them. Cursing, Davyn slowed himself. Again the dragon roared. Again it pounded the walls. Davyn stumbled as the ground beneath him shook and dirt cascaded into his hair.

"Davyn!" a voice hissed. "Davyn, here!"

Stopping, Davyn turned to the right to find Icefire cradling Nearra in his arms in an alcove. Jirah was there too, her lip trembling and her features harsh in the deep shadows. Keene sat beside her, tugging at her sleeve.

Davyn dropped to his knees in front of his companions, not caring as jagged stone sliced through his trousers and cut his knee. He was used to the pain now. Dimly he felt that there was a cut on his cheek and his arms, but he ignored the sensation.

The dragon roared again. Jirah clenched her eyes closed, her whole body tense. Nearra let out a gasp and buried her head into Icefire's chest.

"It's all right," Icefire whispered as he petted her blond hair. "We're safe now. We're safe."

"No," Nearra said. "We're not." Pulling away, she looked at Icefire with forlorn eyes. "We lost. Those Messengers, somehow they made it into the tomb. I don't understand. I . . . I just don't understand."

"The weapons," Jirah said, fingering her longbow. She jumped as another rumble echoed around them. "Why don't they work anymore? What's going on?"

"It's the elf mage," Icefire said, shaking his head. "You heard what he said, Jirah. The cleric he killed, it must have been Kirilin."

"Tylari kept me from seeing her die?" Keene asked. He scowled.

Icefire ignored him. "He was saying things about Hiddukel helping him, and he wore that medallion of faith. He did something to the other elf, the girl—stole her power. So now he's twice as strong magically as he would have been before, and with Hiddukel helping him, he was able to enter the tomb, kill the wizard, steal the gauntlets, and take away the power from the staff and the bow."

"How is that possible?" Jirah asked. "How could Tyl—the elf, how could he do that? Why would a god help him?"

Icefire shook his head. "I don't know."

Nearra's eyes wavered with confusion. "The elves," she said. "The Messengers? They . . . they seemed to know you, Icefire." Turning, she nodded at Jirah. "You too. They said your names. They . . . "

Raising his chin, Icefire pulled away from Nearra and leaned back against the rubble. "Nearra—"

"Icefire," Keene said. He leaped to his feet and put his hands on his hip. "You know full well who they were! It was—"

"Keene, please!" Jirah cried. She tugged at his trousers. Tilting his head, the little kender looked down at her.

For a moment, Nearra looked back and forth between Jirah and Icefire, uncertain. Davyn watched her eyes, studied their cast of hurt, and that same strange feeling of satisfaction welled within him.

Now, he thought. Now is the time.

His arms trembling with vindictive anticipation, Davyn rose to his feet. The others fell silent as he stood. All eyes were on his face.

"Rina," he said, his voice hoarse. "When Rina came to me in the woods, Nearra, she told me about the Messengers. She told me their names: Tylari and Janeesa."

Nearra's eyes flared with recognition. Icefire reached to grab her hand, but she pulled it away.

Still no one spoke.

It was all Davyn could do to keep from smiling. "Rina overheard them, Nearra. They were following us, as I told you. They were biding their time and waiting for the curse to break so that they could strike.

"And Jirah and Icefire were helping them all along."

Jirah gasped, and her body went slack. Tears glistened in her eyes as she crumpled in on herself. "No, Davyn," she whispered. "No."

Icefire's jaw clenched and his eyes blazed as he looked into Davyn's own. He didn't say a word.

The words hung there in the air, seeming to echo endlessly. *237*

Davyn's heart beat faster as he waited, the pounding so loud that it drowned out even the dragon that still raged in the central column of the tower.

Then slowly, Nearra stood.

She looked down at first, and her hands were balled into fists. Her blond hair hung in front of her face, shrouding her features.

"Icefire," she said in a low voice. "Is this true?"

Silence. Jirah began to cry, sniffling through her tears as she shook her head and muttered to herself. Keene rubbed her hand reassuringly.

"Icefire," Nearra said, her voice sharp like the edge of a sword's blade.

The elf looked down, his hands clenching the dirt. "Yes. Janeesa sent me to help you on your quest. I didn't know why, but she tricked me into it. And Jirah was helping her, though I don't believe she knew what she was getting into, Nearra. She stopped. She's repentant."

Far to their right, the dragon roared. Orange flame billowed into the room from the distant door, and for a moment Davyn could see Nearra's face very clearly.

Her features were stern, though her lips trembled. Her blue eyes bore into his own. He expected to see hurt, of course, but also thanks. Certainly now that she knew the truth, she'd let him lead her. Certainly, now she would be with him again.

But there was no look of thanks. As Nearra stared into Davyn's eyes, he saw a distinct look of pity and anger—pity and anger toward *him*.

The fire flared out, and once again they were thrust into darkness. A hollow opened deep in Davyn's gut then, and he felt his chin tremble.

"No," he whispered.

"Icefire," Nearra said, her voice devoid of emotion. "We need to

JEFF SAMPSON

get out of here. The elf, Tylari. You know him. He'd kill us?"

Icefire shook his head. "Nearra—"

"Answer me."

"Yes," Icefire muttered. "Yes, Nearra, he would. And from what he said below, he wants the Trinistyr."

"Jirah, do you know why?" Nearra asked.

Her sister sobbed and mumbled something incoherently. Hefting her staff high, Nearra brought it down amid the rubble with a loud thud. "Jirah! We don't have time for this. Tell me. Do you know why Tylari wants the Trinistyr?"

Gulping back tears, Jirah shook her head. "No," she sobbed. "He–he said he–he didn't want it restored. He shouldn't care."

"He's going to come back, you know," Keene piped up. "I never liked him. He was always mumbling and creepy. Something's not right in his head."

Nearra shook her head and paced back and forth in the alcove. More rocks and debris rained down upon them as the dragon resumed pounding the walls. Anytime now it would find a way to burst in, and then it would kill them all.

"We need the weapons restored," Nearra said. "We are going to find a way back below. There's got to be a way. Then we can get out of here and go after Tylari—unless he comes after us first."

Holding her head high, she strode between Icefire and Jirah, who still sat on the floor. Her eyes were on the hazy light shining from the hole up ahead.

Davyn gripped her arm. "Nearra, I'm sorry," he whispered.

She spun on him, her face still stern in her anger. "Don't," she whispered. Then she wrenched free from his grasp.

Gesturing toward the hole with her staff, she looked over her shoulder at the others, still lost in their own emotions. "We're not giving up now," she commanded. "We are friends, and we've come far. We are going to work together to find a way to break the curse, and we are going to get past that dragon and keep the Messengers from doing whatever it is they have planned. Understand?"

Keene leaped to his feet and smiled grimly. "Aye, aye."

"Icefire," she said. "You have your magic?"

The elf clutched at the gold hoop earring dangling from his ear. "I sure do," he said. "Tylari didn't—"

He stopped speaking, and a shocked look came over his face. Nearra didn't notice.

"All right, everybody," Nearra said. She spun around to face them all, her head held high. The golden light behind her lit up the edges of her blond hair. In her fierceness, in her resolve, to Davyn she seemed a goddess.

"We are not giving up," she commanded. "We will find a way to break the curse. Got it?"

Wiping her eyes, Jirah got to her feet. She clutched her pack to her chest. "Y-you don't hate me, do you?" she whispered.

Nearra shook her head. "I don't know."

Swallowing, Jirah bowed her head. "I'm sorry. I'll do anything to help."

"Me too," Keene said as he bounded to her side.

"And me," Davyn whispered.

Nearra looked at him then, and he looked down. He couldn't look her in the eye, though he didn't know why. After all that had happened with Icefire, after all the ways she'd abandoned him, why did he feel so devastated with himself?

"Icefire?" Nearra tilted her head, waiting expectantly.

Another flare of orange flame exploded behind them. This time, Davyn saw a look of fear on the elf's face even more potent than when he was falling into the chasm.

"Nearra," he said. Trembling, he stood. "Nearra, my earring, my foresight It just told me that there's a way. We can still break the curse."

JEFF SAMPSON

Nearra nodded. "Tell me."

"Nearra—"

"Tell me."

Stumbling forward, the usually graceful and confident elf seemed consumed with emotion. "Tylari didn't just kill the entombed wizard," he whispered. "He put a new curse on him. A curse of . . . of death."

"No," Davyn whispered. Jirah let out a sob.

"What?" Nearra asked. "What do you mean 'of death'?"

"I mean," Icefire went on, "that the only way to free the wizard, the only way to restore the Trinistyr and the weapons, and the only way to end the curse on your family is for you or Jirah to relive this new curse, as you did the others."

Icefire stepped forward, his eyes forlorn. He put his hand on Nearra's shoulder and lowered his head.

"Nearra," he whispered. "The only way to end this is if you or Jirah chooses to die."

The story continues in . . .

WIZARD'S RETURN

TRINISTYR TRILOGY, VOLUME THREE
by Dan Willis

Nearra and Jirah have been struggling to thwart a curse that's held their family's magic at bay for more than three hundred years. Just on the eve of victory, the two sisters are forced to make a terrible choice.

To free the final wizard, one of them must make a shocking sacrifice. The decision sends ripples through the group, reigniting the bitterness between Davyn and Icefire. Can the companions find the strength to stand together and fight the final battle for Nearra and Jirah's future? Or will their mission ultimately fail?

Read the story from the beginning in . . .

TEMPLE OF THE DRAGONSLAYER

For a full list of the series, see our site at
dragonlancenewadventures.com

Acknowledgments

Thank you to Shivam Bhatt and Cam Banks, the Dragonlance experts who answered all my questions on Krynn's history and magic. Thanks also to Elsbet Vance, for her constant support and helpful comments on the first draft; and to Dan Willis, for the dinner conversation about our trilogy.

Props to Josh Martin, for the books with the spell components; and to Mom, for not letting me starve.

Finally, and as always, a giant thank you to our amazing editors: Nina Hess, for her guidance, patience, and the last-minute discussion by the mana pool; and Stacy Whitman, for her fresh insight and wonderful notes.

THE NEW ADVENTURES

JOIN A GROUP OF FRIENDS AS THEY UNLOCK MYSTERIES OF THE DRAGONLANCE® WORLD!

TEMPLE OF THE DRAGONSLAYER
Tim Waggoner

Nearra has lost all memory of who she is. With newfound friends, she ventures to an ancient temple where she may uncover her past. Visions of magic haunt her thoughts. And someone is watching.

THE DYING KINGDOM
Stephen D. Sullivan

In a near-forgotten kingdom, an ancient evil lurks. As Nearra's dark visions grow stronger, her friends must fight for their lives.

THE DRAGON WELL
Dan Willis

Battling a group of bandits, the heroes unleash the mystic power of a dragon well. And none of them will ever be the same.

RETURN OF THE SORCERESS
Tim Waggoner

When Nearra and her friends confront the wizard who stole her memory, their faith in each other is put to the ultimate test.

For ages 10 and up

THE NEW ADVENTURES

THE DRAGON QUARTET

The companions continue their quest to save Nearra.

DRAGON SWORD
Ree Soesbee

It's a race against time as the companions seek to prevent
Asvoria from reclaiming her most treacherous weapon.

DRAGON DAY
Stan Brown

As Dragon Day draws near, Catriona and Sindri stand as
enemies, on opposing sides of a feud between the most
powerful wizards and clerics in Solamnia.

DRAGON KNIGHT
Dan Willis

With old friends and new allies by his side, Davyn must
enlist the help of the dreaded Dragon Knight.

DRAGON SPELL
Jeff Sampson

The companions reunite in their final battle with
Asvoria to reclaim Nearra's soul.

**Ask for Dragonlance: the New Adventures
books at your favorite bookstore!**
For ages ten and up.
For more information visit www.mirrorstonebooks.com

Want to know how it all began?

Want to know more about the Dragonlance® world?

Find out in this new boxed set of the first Dragonlance titles!

A Rumor of Dragons
Volume 1

Night of the Dragons
Volume 2

The Nightmare Lands
Volume 3

To the Gates of Palanthas
Volume 4

Hope's Flame
Volume 5

A Dawn of Dragons
Volume 6

Gift Set Available
By Margaret Weis & Tracy Hickman
For ages 10 and up